A LITTLE HELP FROM MY FRIENDS

Compiled by Melissa Hill

POOLBEG

These short stories are entirely a work of fiction. The names,
characters and incidents portrayed in it are the work of the
authors' imagination. Any resemblance to actual persons,
living or dead, events or localities is entirely coincidental.

Published 2007
by Poolbeg Press Ltd
123 Grange Hill, Baldoyle
Dublin 13, Ireland
E-mail: poolbeg@poolbeg.com
www.poolbeg.com

ISBN 978 1 84223 303 0

Typeset by Patricia Hope in Caslon 11/16

Printed by Litografia Rosés, S.A., Spain

Contents

Foreword

Nobody tells you how to feel when you're diagnosed with a serious illness and have no choice but to face your own mortality. Nobody tells your loved ones how to feel either. And while you're trying hard to summon the courage to face the greatest fear of all, the people who love you are trying just as hard to find some way to help.

It's a situation my family faced some years ago when my mother was first diagnosed with cancer. But through some miracle – and with considerable help from the South Tipperary Hospice Foundation – we all managed to come through it.

Other families aren't so lucky.

The Irish Hospice Foundation is a not-for-profit organisation that supports the development of hospice/palliative care. Their vision is that no one should have to face death or bereavement without appropriate care and support.

Most hospice services here are provided not by the state, but by the voluntary sector. Men and women in every county in Ireland – ordinary people from all walks of life – come together to form a group in their local area to fund-raise for a hospice service. Often, they are people who have experienced first-hand the trauma of terminal illness in their families, which makes them uniquely qualified to offer the necessary support that – most of the time – a patient's own family are ill-equipped to do. The IHF receives no on-going government funding, and is therefore hugely dependent on fund-raising to be able to continue the wonderful work they do.

It is for this very reason that *A Little Help from My Friends* came about.

When Poolbeg and I set about compiling a collection in aid of the IHF, we were completely taken aback by the overwhelmingly positive response we received from potential contributors. Almost every one came back with an unequivocal 'Yes' and most had their own account of a loved one who'd experienced the magnificent service and care the Irish Hospice Foundation provides. Something which merely reinforces the fact that almost every family in Ireland has (or will have in the future) the need for such a service.

This book is made up of a diverse selection of stories and true-life pieces from some of our most successful Irish authors and popular media personalities – all of whom are donating a hundred per cent of their royalties to the Irish Hospice Foundation.

A Little Help from My Friends is dedicated to the thousands of hard-working hospice carers and volunteers around the country who dedicate so much time and effort to those who truly need it.

My own contribution is, in addition, dedicated to my mother Nell. The courage and dignity she displayed throughout her illness all those years ago was very much an illustration of the Irish Hospice Foundation's key philosophy, and is no doubt echoed amongst seriously ill patients throughout the country today.

Mam, you're an inspiration, and I hope *A Girl's Best Friend* makes you smile.

Melissa Hill, 2007

Travelling in Style

Mary Bond

Mary Bond

Mary Bond spent her Dublin childhood scribbling in notebooks, often under the school desk. Early motherhood temporarily deferred her writing dreams but in time she dusted off the typewriter and began writing articles, poems and short stories. Mary has had two novels published by Tivoli, *Absolutely Love* and *All Things Perfect,* and she is currently working on her third novel, *If I Can't Have You.*

Travelling
in Style

1977

Through the weave of people streaming under Clery's clock, there's no mistaking Liz's orangey hair. She's obviously had another disastrous run-in with the bottle of false hope and promises. Heedless of her rusty-coloured layers, her head is shaking with laughter at something Audrey is saying. Audrey is even taller again on massive cork-soled platform shoes and she's wearing a drifting midi-dress. She carries a shopping bag boasting the name of a new Grafton Street boutique.

They look so vital and shiny that already I feel tired and dull and outside the loop. Maybe this get-together wasn't such a good idea after all. Not so long ago we shared endless boring days in the back row of the typing pool in Hickey's Insurances. I sat between Liz and Audrey, our monotonous jobs enlivened only by Liz's madcap antics and Audrey's funny jokes. We lived for regular evening booze-ups and coffee breaks full of earth-shattering gossip.

That world seems to have evaporated. I left three months ago and already I feel different, as though I've been catapulted onto a distant planet.

"Maeve! You look terrific!" Liz reaches me first and wraps me in a hug that stops my breath.

"You look smashing!" Audrey's soft brown eyes smile at me.

"Sorry I'm late. I missed the bus," I say.

"We'll let you off this time," Liz says. "You've a good excuse!"

"Right, where to?" Audrey hitches up her shoulder bag. "We're wasting valuable drinking time."

"In that case, the nearest pub." I haven't been out in ages and the words feel strange on my lips.

"You haven't changed!" Audrey laughs.

Haven't I?

"Sounds good to me," Liz winks at me.

"Did you do the hair?" I ask.

She rolls her eyes and links me as we click-clack around the corner. "Talk about a bad hair day. Anyway, Maeve, wait 'til you hear the latest gossip from Hickey's. All hell broke loose in the last couple of weeks. You're so lucky to be away from it all."

Lucky? I don't feel lucky. Right now I feel drained and exhausted. The pub is warm and crowded but we push our way through and find squashy leather seats in the corner. "Well, girls, what are we having?"

"We'll do it in style. No half measures. Pints all round."

We're on our second pint. The beer is cool and easy to drink. Audrey shows off the cheesecloth tops she has bought for her holidays. She's going to Benidorm and has been saving like mad. I've been brought up to date on the goings-on in the office. Mr Hickey has turned into a right slave-driver. He confiscated Liz's

Tippex and got her to type up a proposal five times until it was perfect. The following day it was lashing rain so Liz hid his umbrella and he went mad. There's been a strict clampdown on bad timekeeping and Friday lunch-time boozing. Liz and Audrey shake with laughter. I can't help joining in even though it's a world I can no longer visualise and I'm feeling a little disconnected.

"Danny's asked me to go on holidays to Donegal with him," Liz chats. "The parents won't be happy."

"But you're practically engaged," I point out.

"Yeah, but there's no ring on my finger." Liz looks at her bare ring finger. "Am I right to go off with him, or will he think I'm easy?"

"I'd say it's about time you went off with him," Audrey giggles.

"So long as he doesn't think I'm a pushover."

"You? Never!" I say.

"Make sure it's an expensive hotel," Audrey advises.

"We were thinking of camping . . . under the stars and all that . . ." Liz rolls her eyes.

"Tell your mum it's separate sleeping bags," I suggest and we all rock with laughter.

Liz orders more drinks to celebrate her first holiday with Danny.

"I've split with Brian and I'm finished with men," Audrey announces. "Wait 'til you hear what he did . . ."

Audrey's rollercoaster love life is legendary. I listen, enthralled, and the leather seat in the corner is becoming more comfortable.

"You're better off without him," Liz says loyally. "Let's have more drinks to celebrate your freedom."

"You should have a think about Seán in Sales and Marketing," I tell her.

"Seán?"

"Give him a chance. He's always fancied you, Audrey. You look so confident that he's probably a bit shy," I find myself saying, my distance from the office helping me to see it more clearly.

"Do you think so?"

"Ask him to my twenty-first," Liz suggests. "We're starting at six o'clock for drinks and finishing up in the nightclub. You'd better be there, Maeve. Get Tom to mind the baby and we'll all get sloshed. Mum wants a house party for the family the following night, aunts and uncles – boring stuff. So I'll need to be properly anaesthetised."

"I'll be there, don't worry. Can't miss that," I say.

"How *is* the baby?" Audrey asks. "It seems no length since we visited you in hospital!"

"I have some photos," I tell them, dipping into my bag.

"Great!" Liz pushes up closer on the seat and I pass over snapshots of my baby son, also my whole life and the sum total of existence as I know it.

"He's six weeks now, but he's still keeping me awake at night," I venture. My carefree friends wouldn't have a clue about the way my life has changed, or the exhausting effects of sleepless nights, and anxious days filled with nappies and bottle-feeding.

They admire him as though he's the most precious thing in the world.

"He's absolutely gorgeous," Liz coos.

"God, Maeve, you look so confident holding him," Audrey says. "I'd be a nervous wreck. I wouldn't know how to change a nappy, never mind get him dressed."

I'm surprised at this admission from super-confident Audrey. "I didn't in the beginning," I tell her. "I was in a sweat, especially when it came to dressing him. I didn't know where to put all those arms and legs. I'm still terrified I'll stick the pin into him when I change his nappy."

"My sister was the same," Audrey smiles. "That was on top of the sleepless nights. How do you manage to cope and stay sane?"

"Some days are tough . . ." My words begin to tumble.

Funny how the major anxieties of the last few weeks fade a little when they're shared. And somehow the gap between us has dissolved. The links might have shifted a little but they're still there. I look at Liz and Audrey and think of Tom at home with the baby, and my two worlds mesh and settle comfortably together.

"I can't help feeling jealous," Audrey sighs. "I'd love a nice husband like Tom and a cute baby son. About this Seán guy . . . what do you think . . .?" she invites.

I'm only too glad to offer advice.

The night draws to a close. Twice I've changed my mind about going home and decided to get a later bus. Giggling and laughing, we click-clack out of the pub. Audrey starts to sing "Viva Espana" until Liz and I tell her to shut up. It's just like old times and I feel giddy and yes, a little carefree.

"Can we do this again?" I ask

"Sure we will," Liz promises. "Maybe you've escaped the clutches of old Hickey, but we won't let you get away that easily."

1987

The January breeze is biting as I wait on Eden Quay. I forget who suggested this spot. There's nothing wrong with Clery's clock – after all we've been meeting there regularly for years.

I knew I'd be waiting. Maeve will have missed the bus as usual, and Audrey will be shopping. I tell myself to stop feeling resentful. We're supposed to be out for the evening and enjoying ourselves. Too bad if I'm feeling a bit off. Sure enough Maeve arrives in a warm winter coat with a lovely fur collar, and a face full of apology. Then Audrey comes along in a stylish leather jacket, and of course, a posh carrier bag.

We hug and kiss. I can't help noticing how happy and relaxed Maeve looks, or how glamorous Audrey is, despite the busy husband and little daughter.

Where did I go wrong?

"Where to?" Audrey asks.

"I can't get too pissed," Maeve says. "I've work in the morning."

Nice of Maeve to remind us that she's back in the big wide world, taking executive decisions. *And* affording fashionable coats. My biggest decision these days revolves around choosing the best value breakfast cereal.

"Come on, Liz," Maeve puts her arm through mine. "Let's have a laugh and put the world to rights."

"I like your coat," I say to her, trying not to sound too grudging. It seems a long time since I bought a new coat. Whatever spare cash there is these days is going on the kids.

"My cousin's cast-off," Maeve says, unwittingly cheering me a little. I feel a little better as we clatter up the path and around the corner.

Audrey gets the first round.

"Pints for everyone and hurry," Maeve giggles. "Doing it in style, eh, Liz?"

I can't help smiling. A knot inside me is starting to unravel.

Audrey comes back with two pints and a glass of white lemonade.

"Who's on the dry?"

"I am – I'm pregnant again!" Audrey tells us.

10

"That's wonderful!"

"Congrats. When are you due?"

"Next May. And I know we've spent many a get-together swapping labour ward agonies but not tonight, girls!"

"Don't worry, we won't put you off!"

"Anyway, second time around is always easier than the first," I tell her.

"I hope so! Devlin's almost three now. Look what I bought for her!" Audrey pulls a fluffy pink cardigan out of her carrier bag that we all admire.

"Time flies. Mine are ten and eight now," Maeve says proudly.

"Yours are practically reared," I say, envious of her relative freedom.

"Make the most of it while they're deliciously small and you're still the omnipotent one," Maeve advises me. "You'll never get that time back again."

"At the moment it seems endless," I shake my head and fiddle with my beer mat. "I mean, three kids under six. I love them all to bits, but the work involved is no joke. I feel I've all but disappeared. Except for my tummy. That never disappeared at all."

Maeve smiles. "I know what you're going through. Don't worry, you haven't gone away," she assures me, patting my hand. "You're still the crazy typist who drove Mr Hickey absolutely nuts."

"Old Hickey! Do you remember the day that . . ." Audrey starts off.

In no time we're laughing our heads off and tears are pouring down our cheeks. I take out a tissue and mop my face. It's true what they say about laughter — it is the best medicine.

"I heard he's taken early retirement," Audrey says, when we've calmed ourselves down a little.

"Retired? Never!"

We fall silent. It's sobering to think that the gimlet-eyed manager of the typing pool is out to grass, all his fire and fury redundant.

"Love the hair," Maeve tells me.

I put my hand up to my brassy blond hair. I'm sick of bad hair days and Maeve's only being kind because it feels dry and brittle, but nonetheless, I'm slightly cheered. "The supermarket special offer," I admit. "I can't afford the hairdresser's. Not now."

"Who can, in this recession?" Maeve says staunchly. "We wouldn't survive without my job. I absolutely hate it, but it pays the mortgage. Tom's on a three-day week and he mopes around the house the rest of the time."

"That's tough," Audrey says. "I've the opposite problem. Seán works all the hours God sends to make enough to pay the bills. I hardly ever see him."

"I've a different problem," I tell them, taking a deep breath. "Danny wants to go to Birmingham. To work. It's good money, but I'll be left to manage the kids . . ."

My friends look at me with such concern that it's balm to my soul. Maeve says that the recession won't last. She knows that Danny has been out of work for weeks now and at least it's a job, but tactful to the last, she's not pointing this out. She'll come and visit, she says and we'll arrange a day out with all the kids.

Audrey tells me that even though she's preggers, she's at the end of a phone. Anytime.

At the end of the night we hug goodbye, then I dash over O'Connell Bridge to get the last bus. I'm conscious that I feel free and easy without the kids. I see my reflection in darkened shop windows and I wonder who this woman is, unencumbered with buggies and bags.

She's still there, waiting in the wings. Maeve said to enjoy them while they're young. It'll fly in. And the recession won't last. All of a sudden I see some light at the end of the tunnel.

1997

I'm not one bit in the humour of this get-together. But it's almost six months since we've met and Liz went to a lot of trouble to organise us. That's the only reason why I'm hurrying towards the Central Bank on a breezy Sunday afternoon.

Liz and Maeve are already chatting and laughing. They look like they're all set for a good time. I should really turn and run and not inflict myself on them. When we hug and kiss I decide it's best to stay quiet and get on with the show.

"I've booked a restaurant off Grafton Street," Maeve says. "They do a good Sunday lunch."

"Lunching in style," I force a smile.

A far cry from the boozy catch-ups of yesteryear. Maybe we're beginning to get some sense. Liz's hair is lovely. She has finally come into her own and found a hairstyle and colour to suit her. Maeve's wearing a pair of designer jeans. She has a lovely suntan as she's just back from the Canaries with Tom. Her eldest son is twenty now and he drove her into town. *Twenty!* Already a couple of years older than we were when we first met in Hickey's. God.

We were all at Mr Hickey's funeral last year. I was surprised to see his wife and grown-up children there. I'd never really pictured him having a life outside the office. I was even more surprised to see that his wife looked as though she almost belonged to the same generation as us. I found the whole thing rather unsettling and the only comforting thing was the fact that Maeve and Liz thought exactly the same as me.

13

We give our orders to the waitress and ask for a bottle of the house white.

"No, thanks," Maeve sensibly refuses a third glass. "I need my wits about me for the office tomorrow. *And* I put on a load of weight during the holiday which I need to shift. So no dessert for me either."

"Since when did you have to watch your weight?" asks Liz.

"Since I turned forty." Maeve makes a face.

We were all forty last year. We had a celebratory meal and consoled ourselves with the fact that our lives were only beginning, but I don't think we really believed it. Our only consolation was the fact that we were all in the same boat.

"I'm going easy on the booze also," Liz says. "I can't afford to have the teenagers see me stumbling home. I'd be sending out all the wrong messages. Danny and I don't know which is worse," she laughs, "the sleepless baby nights or sleepless teenagery nights."

"Teenagers or not, you look great. Even your hair . . ."

"I have to look well with my part-time job in the Credit Union. Mind you, I do as much work in three days as some of the young ones do in a week. Honestly! You just can't trust them," Liz says. "I always have to recheck their figures. Especially on Monday mornings after the weekend hangovers. At a guess, some of them would have had only three hours' sleep over the entire weekend."

"And we were never like that!" Maeve chuckles as she takes the words out of my mouth.

"Old Hickey would certainly be proud of you," I can't help saying, feeling gratified when Liz dissolves into laughter.

"Well, some things never change," Maeve grins as she points at my shopping.

There's a lump in my throat and I'd glad we've gone easy on the wine. Otherwise I'd be in floods.

14

"Audrey? Are you okay?"

I can't answer. I feel tears pricking my eyes.

"Are you pregnant again?" Liz asks softly.

In spite of everything, that makes me smile. "God forbid," I say. "I'm forty-one after all and Megan is eleven. No, it's Mum . . . it's terminal, girls. She's going into the Hospice and it's just a matter of time . . . I don't know how I'm going to cope . . ."

Their empathy surrounds me like a warm comfort zone and I bask in the glow. Already I feel a little unburdened. Liz's mum died suddenly a couple of years ago, and Maeve has already been down this sad road so I know they appreciate how I feel.

"The Hospice is special," Maeve says. "It's like a waiting room for Heaven. I can't praise it highly enough. Ring me any time you want to talk. And I promise, Audrey, you'll get strength from somewhere."

"It'll be tough, but you'll come through," Liz assures me, a soft sparkle in her eyes and I know she's remembering her mum.

Seán collects me at the end of the afternoon and Liz and Maeve decide to share a taxi home. I wave at them as we pass the taxi rank, knowing I'll be seeing them again pretty shortly but in different circumstances.

You'll get strength from somewhere. It'll be tough but you'll come through. Like a lifeline, the words resound in my head and lift me up.

2007

Through the weave of pedestrians swarming around under Clery's clock, I catch sight of my friends.

We picked the Clery's clock on purpose. I suppose we were trying to prove that everything is still the same. Liz's hair is blond and cheerfully bright and she's wearing skinny jeans. Audrey's tall

15

figure is perfect in a slimming cream suit. She throws back her head and laughs with Liz. Together they turn to watch me as I hurry towards them.

"Late again!" Audrey jokes.

"Well, girls, where to?" I ask, after our ritual of hugs and kisses. I give Liz an extra tight hug, but I don't know if she notices or not.

"We're *definitely* doing it in style today, we've so much to celebrate," Audrey says.

We get a taxi to the Four Seasons and order the best champagne. Nothing less will do. I forgot my reading glasses so Audrey puts on hers – designery ones, of course, so we tease her to bits. She calls out the selection available before we choose.

"Cheers, Audrey!" I say, lifting my fizzing glass. "How do you like being twenty-five years married?"

"Brilliant. We're off to South Africa for six weeks. So what if we put a dent in the pension funds or spend some of the kids' inheritance? We deserve it."

Liz and I are enthralled as Audrey outlines her travel itinerary. Then we compare pension investments and we roar with laughter when Audrey says we're following in good old Hickey's footsteps.

"Hold on, where's all your shopping?" asks Liz.

"Did it all on-line, girls. The way to go. Hey, wait 'til I tell you about Megan . . ."

Her youngest daughter is twenty-one. She's refusing point blank to have any kind of party, even though Audrey would love to have a house party for the family, like Liz had for her daughter. Instead she's heading off to Italy to celebrate. With her new boyfriend. Of two months.

"Am I mad to be worried, girls?" Audrey asks.

"No. I've been there and I was up the walls."

"Just make sure she packs plenty of condoms."

"Or tell her separate beds."

"Fat lot of help you two are," Audrey shakes her head and laughs.

"Right, what's next to celebrate?"

"To sleepless nights!" I joke.

"Are we ever going to get a decent night's kip?" Liz asks. "First it was babies, then teenagers, now it's the dreaded hot sweats."

We compare horror stories about dripping sheets and duvets, almost as though it's a competition to come up with the most lurid scenario. We can't stop laughing when Liz describes the way her expensive night cream sloughs off her face at two in the morning. She tells us that her pillow is swiftly regenerating itself. Audrey shares some gems of advice gleaned from her older sister.

"Hey, let's cheer ourselves up and get another bottle," Liz suggests.

The next toast is to ourselves. The champagne is flowing. Who cares if we're already a bit tiddly. We more than deserve it. And we've so much to celebrate.

We were all fifty last year, but we didn't manage to get together to party. Tom was ill with heart trouble and had to have emergency surgery. Liz and Audrey dropped everything and sat out the endless hours in the waiting room with me, sharing watery coffee laced with memories.

Then Liz was out of action for months when she found a funny spot on her leg. That lovely blond head of hair she's proudly sporting is a wig. She has three altogether and she switches them around depending on her mood. Her red wig signals danger. She had us all laughing when we went with her to the salon and helped her to choose them. She out-performed Naomi Campbell as she flaunted herself in the mirror. Then she said she was going to save a fortune on the hairdresser's. *And* she'd never have a bad hair day again.

She's finished all her treatment now. Danny and the kids – pardon, twenty-something adults – were fantastic. They pulled out all the stops and fussed over her no end. Payback time, she joked.

"Here's to being older and bolder!" Liz raises her glass.

I look at her laughing across the table as though she hasn't a care in the world and think how brilliant she is.

"Onwards and upwards!" Audrey joins in. My glamorous friend is even more glamorous than ever. She's wearing the platinum jewellery Seán gave her to celebrate her fiftieth, but her kind brown eyes meet mine and smile the way they smiled at me in Hickey's over thirty years ago.

Then Liz turns to me, "Hey, Maeve, we've something else to celebrate, haven't we?"

"Oh, yes," I can't help the grin from spreading across my face. "I brought some photos," I say, dipping my hand into my bag.

Liz and Audrey move closer and admire my new little granddaughter as though she is the most precious thing in the world. The start of the next generation. May she be blessed with friends like mine.

Audrey pours more champagne for a toast and I feel kind of funny and it's not from the drink. I want to thank them for travelling with me in style. But words are superfluous, for as we clink glasses and exchange smiles, I know we all feel the same.

Anyway Audrey would tell me I sound like good old Hickey giving his retirement speech, and Liz would roll her eyes and say that I ain't seen nothing yet.

Final Destination

Colette Caddle

Colette Caddle

Colette Caddle is the author of eight bestsellers: *Too Little, Too Late;*
Shaken & Stirred; A Cut Above; Forever FM; Red Letter Day; Changing
Places; The Betrayal of Grace Mulcahy and – her latest offering – *It's All*
About Him. She lives in North County Dublin with her husband
and two sons.

Final Destination

"What on earth have you got in this bag, Jackie?" Don grumbled as he gave the bag another poke in an effort to squeeze it into the overhead locker.

"Mainly your books," she replied with an apologetic smile at the man who was waiting patiently for them to take their seats.

"You'll have to go in the middle," Don was saying as he squeezed himself past her. "I'm going to be crippled as it is in this cramped little space. Every year it gets worse. I'm warning you now, Jackie, I'm not going charter again."

Jackie hurriedly took her place beside him and then smiled at the tall, good-natured man who was gracefully lowering himself into the aisle seat. "Sorry about that."

"No problem," he said amiably.

"Would you look at that!" Don nodded towards the seats by the emergency exit where two young girls sat. "Why did they go and give two little shrimps like that the seats with the most legroom? I'd like to see one of them try to open the door in an emergency. I don't know what kind of eejits run this airline."

"I don't think they measure people before assigning the seats," Jackie said lightly, wishing Don would shut up.

"They could use a bit of common sense," he argued. "I must be a foot taller than them and yet they expect me to squeeze into this ridiculously tiny space."

Jackie glanced briefly at the jean-clad legs of their neighbour, thinking he must be at least three inches taller than Don. "Why don't you relax and read your book?" she suggested quietly to her partner of five years. Five years! Lord, where had it gone?

Don grunted but obediently opened his thriller as Jackie gazed past him to the tarmac of Palma airport. She was sorry to be going home. It had been a peaceful and relaxing break and she had met some lovely people. And thanks to Don deserting her in favour of the golf course most days, she had been free to do all the things she loved and he hated. Namely sightseeing, poking around the tacky gift shops, hunting down the tiny authentically Spanish restaurants and trying out her schoolgirl Spanish on the friendly waiters who encouraged her lame efforts.

"Excuse me, sir, could you fasten your seatbelt?" A flight attendant smiled politely down at Don.

He smiled back. "I'm sorry but I was wondering if there was any chance of us moving seats. I don't mean to be difficult, but I have a bad back and this," he gestured down at his legs jammed against the seat in front, "isn't going to help."

"Let me see what I can do," the flight attendant said and went to talk to a colleague.

"For God's sake, Don," Jackie hissed, "it's only for a couple of hours and since when did you have a bad back?"

"Since trying to get your bloody bag up into that overhead

locker," he said with a grin. "Ah, Jackie, sure there's no harm in asking. You don't get anywhere in this world if you don't ask."

She didn't respond as the attendant returned, her smile apologetic. "I'm very sorry, sir – I'm afraid there's only one seat available by the emergency exit."

"He'll take it," Jackie said gratefully.

"Are you sure?" Don asked, but he was already standing.

"Sure. I'm probably going to sleep anyway."

"All right then, see you later." Don beamed happily as Jackie and the Aisle Seat Man stood to let him out.

"Sorry about that," she said again to the man as she slid into Don's window seat, "but at least you get a bit more space now. Oh, would you like the window seat? Only I'm not bothered."

"Thanks for the offer but I have work to do," he said, gesturing to the file in his lap.

"That's terrible. The holiday's not quite over yet," she joked.

"Oh, it wasn't a holiday for me," he told her. "I live in Majorca."

"Really?" Her eyes widened.

He chuckled. "Really."

"What a wonderful place to live," she said wistfully. "That scenery, the food and such lovely people."

"It is quite special," he agreed, smiling, "except for the more commercial resorts."

She shuddered. "Yes, I hate them."

He shrugged. "But they play their part. They bring money to the island and give a lot of employment."

"True," she said, "but they've got so rough in recent years. And I can't understand why people who pay to travel to another country then go out of their way to drink in Irish pubs, sing Irish songs and eat Irish and English food!"

He laughed. "To each his own."

"You must think I'm very judgmental," she said, thinking that for all she knew he might work in an Irish pub.

"Not at all." He held out his hand. "I'm Carlos Magee by the way."

"Jackie Kane," she said, taking his hand, her lips twitching. "Carlos?"

"I'm half Spanish," he explained. "I got a terrible slagging at school I can tell you.

"I can imagine," she said. That explained his olive skin and those amazing, dark, hazel eyes. "It must be wonderful to be brought up in a mixed culture family."

He shrugged. "It was the norm for me, I didn't know any different."

"So you speak fluent Spanish?"

He nodded. "Yes, my mother made sure of it. She wasn't able to afford to bring me to Spain that often when I was a child but she made sure I knew everything there was to know about her family and their customs and we spoke both English and Spanish all the time." He laughed. "And then when I started school, she insisted that I teach her Irish!"

"She sounds like a wonderful woman."

"She was," he said with a sad smile. "She died last year."

"I'm sorry," Jackie said gently. "And your dad?"

"Oh, he's still going strong although he misses her terribly," he chuckled, "especially her cooking."

"Did she cook paella?" Jackie asked, in an effort to distract him and chase the sadness from his eyes. Why did she care? She'd only just met the man.

"The best," he assured her. "Sorry, I must be boring the hell out of you."

24

She shook her head vehemently. "Not at all. I adore Spain and I think your story is fascinating."

"Still, enough about me; tell me about you."

"Nothing to tell really. Born in Dublin, grew up in Dublin and still in Dublin. Terribly boring," she said sadly.

"I don't think so. Presumably you've stayed because you're content."

"I suppose," she said doubtfully. Content? That wasn't really a word she would have used to describe herself. "So do you live in Majorca full-time now?" she asked, thinking that it was much more interesting and probably a lot safer to talk about him.

"Yes, but I go back to Dublin for a couple of days every month or so to see my dad. I want him to come and live with me but he isn't keen. You see, he was going to retire to Majorca with my mother and now he just hates the thought of being there without her."

"He must have loved her very much."

"Yes, yes, he did. Anyway, we're supposed to be talking about you," he reminded her. "Is your husband from Dublin too?"

"Oh, he's not my husband," Jackie said hurriedly, glancing to where Don was in animated conversation with the two young blondes. "He's my partner. We've been together five years."

"That's quite an achievement in this day and age. I don't think I've managed to get past eighteen months myself."

"Too busy being a high flyer?" she teased.

He made a face. "On the contrary, I've been so busy trying to get my business up and running that I've made very boring company."

"I find that hard to believe," she murmured. Jackie Kane, what the hell do you think you're doing? You're flirting! She assumed what she hoped was a look of polite but detached interest. "What business are you in?"

"I own a small hotel in Portals Nous. It's one of the smaller resorts –"

"Oh, I know it. It's beautiful!"

He smiled. "Yes, I think so. You must come and stay the next time you visit the island."

She laughed. "Somehow I doubt if I could afford to stay in your hotel." She had been very aware of the expensive restaurants and hotels around the small port, stuffed with huge yachts and stunned at the style and glamour of the clientele when she'd stopped for an espresso in one of the pretty quayside cafes.

"My hotel is one of the smaller ones and quite affordable," he said modestly. "Of course we don't have many facilities – nightly entertainment or pool tables or slot machines. Our target market is the tourist who's looking for some peace and quiet in beautiful surroundings."

"It sounds like heaven to me," Jackie said wistfully.

"What hotel did you stay in?" he asked.

She made a face. "Some huge anonymous place in Alcudia. It was very noisy but it was near the golf course and very central. Don likes to be in the centre of things."

"And what do you like?" he asked, watching her steadily.

"If he's happy, I'm happy," she trilled, realising that it wasn't true.

"Would you like something to eat or drink, madam?"

Jackie looked surprised to see a flight attendant standing over them. Goodness, she hadn't even noticed they'd taken off, never mind that the seatbelts sign had been switched off and food was being served. "Just coffee, please."

The attendant handed Jackie her drink and then turned to Carlos. "Sir?"

"Two bottles of champagne, please," he said, pulling a fifty-euro note out of his jeans pocket.

Jackie sipped her drink and stared out of her window. Champagne! Twelve euros a pop – no pun intended – and he'd bought two; he really was a high flyer.

"I hope you don't mind but you're making this a very enjoyable flight and I just wanted to say thank you."

Jackie turned to find him proffering a glass to her. "Oh, you shouldn't have!"

"Like you said, the holiday isn't over yet."

"But you're not on holiday," she reminded him, smiling. "In fact, shouldn't you be working?"

"I should," he said, his eyes locking with hers, "but I'm not going to. Cheers!"

"What's all this?"

Jackie looked up to see Don looming over them, a frown on his face as he took in the champagne. She shrugged and smiled. "I thought I'd treat myself."

"Very extravagant," he replied, his eyes flickering to Carlos's glass.

Carlos bent his head over the document he'd pulled from his file and sipped his drink.

"Are you more comfortable now?" Jackie asked Don politely.

"Yes, grand, but I feel bad about leaving you."

"That's okay. Don't worry about it."

"You didn't get to sleep yet then," he said, his gaze sliding from her to Carlos.

"No, maybe this will help," she said, raising her glass.

"I'm sure it will," he muttered. "Right, just off to the loo. See you later."

She nodded. "Yeah, see you."

"Sorry about that." Jackie shot Carlos a guilty smile. "I'm not sure he'd have liked it if he knew you'd bought the champagne."

"No problem. So, he's the jealous sort, is he?"

Jackie thought about it. "No, not really, more possessive than jealous."

Carlos nodded thoughtfully. "How do you feel about that?"

"I never really thought about it." But she had. It annoyed her when Don marked his territory, for that's exactly how it seemed to her.

"Do you love him?"

Jackie met his eyes, startled. "That's a bit direct considering we only met an hour ago."

He shrugged. "Sorry but I feel as if I've known you a lot longer."

She smiled. "Yeah, me too."

"So, do you?" he persisted.

"Are you always this pushy?"

He grinned. "Yeah, which probably explains why I'm unattached."

Jackie thought the women of Majorca must be blind and stupid. Carlos was charming, intelligent and incredibly attractive. She bit her lip and then blurted out her answer. "I'm not sure any more."

"Pardon – oh!" His eyes widened as he realised what she was saying. "I see."

She wriggled in her seat and wondered why she was confiding the details of her personal life in a total stranger.

"So what are you going to do about it?"

She looked up. "Do?"

He shook his head. "Forgive me but I'd say you must be close on thirty."

"Close enough," she said with a smirk, wondering if he'd deliberately shaved five years off her age. She wasn't complaining.

"So don't you feel you're wasting your life with someone that you're not even sure you love? Incidentally, you don't."

"I don't?"

"No." He was adamant. "Even *I* know that you either know or you don't. There's no maybe."

"You're an idealist," she said, with a sad smile. "We can't all be swept off our feet and fall madly in love. Anyway, companionship and friendship are much more important."

"Ah, I see. And you have those, do you?"

Jackie thought of her solitary holiday while Don played golf and sighed. "If you're trying to depress me you're doing a very good job."

He shook his head. "I'm sorry. That's not what I intended to do at all."

She raised her eyes to meet his. "So, what exactly are your intentions?"

He hesitated for a moment and then clearing his throat he set down his glass and turned in his seat so that he was facing her. "I suppose I just want to make you see that sometimes you need to take chances. Sometimes you have to dive right in and see what happens. Sometimes, it might be worth taking a risk."

She studied him closely looking for any sign of a smirk or twinkle in the eye but Carlos looked deadly serious. "Why are you saying this?" she asked slowly.

For a moment he looked almost sheepish. "Well, I'm beginning to realise that it's time *I* took a chance. I'm nearly thirty-four, Jackie, and I've spent most of my adult life building up my business. I've achieved some success but that's not going to mean much if I've no one to share it with. My parents had an amazing relationship, a wonderful marriage and I suppose that's what I aspire to." He sighed. "I think it's time I put as much as much effort into my personal life as my professional one."

Jackie nodded silently. So that was it. He was just using her as a sounding board as he worked through his midlife crisis. She was surprised at how much the realisation disappointed her.

"And you think I should too? You know it's a bit presumptuous of you to assume we are in the same situation."

"Maybe but you told me you weren't sure if you loved Don. Don't you think you should try something or someone else before you settle?"

She rolled her eyes and faked a yawn. "Yes, well, much as I appreciate your words of wisdom, I think it's time I caught up on my beauty sleep. Thanks for the champagne." She drained her glass, reclined her seat and shut her eyes.

"Now I've pissed you off," he muttered.

"Not at all. I'm just tired."

"You can't go asleep now." He nudged her elbow. "We've only got about fifty minutes left."

She opened her eyes. "I can't imagine you have anything left to say."

His eyes twinkled. "You'd be surprised. Oh, come on, sit up, talk to me! We're having fun, aren't we? If nothing else, we're making your other half insanely jealous."

Jackie followed his gaze and, right enough, Don was craning his neck so he could see them, a deep crease between his brows. She smiled. "Good."

"That's better. More champagne?"

"Are you trying to get me drunk?"

"It's a thought," he mused. "You might reveal all sorts of interesting things."

"I usually just fall asleep and snore," she confided.

"Okay then, no more champagne. You are not going to sleep, you are going to tell me all about Jackie Kane. What do you do?"

"Guess," she teased.

"Brain surgeon? Teacher? Stripper? Professional thief?"

She laughed. "Close. I'm a bank manager."

"No!"

"No," she agreed. "Actually I'm a chef."

"That's amazing."

"Oh, I don't know, it's not really up there with brain surgery."

"No, you don't understand. It's fate; my chef just quit. When could you start?"

She shook her head, laughing. "I have a job and I live in Dublin, remember?"

"Like I said, maybe it's time for a change."

"Please don't start all that again."

"But you just know you'd love to," he persisted. "You obviously love Spanish food and you love Majorca." His eyes swivelled to the back of Don"s head. "That's two cases of love over one maybe."

"Please stop," she groaned, "or I'm definitely going to sleep."

"Okay, okay, I'll behave myself. Tell me about your family." He sat looking at her expectantly.

Jackie shook her head in resignation. "I have three sisters and two brothers."

He smiled. "Cool. It must be wonderful to be part of such a large family. I'm an only child and I would have loved a brother."

"The grass is always greener," she told him. "I would have given anything to have a bed to myself, never mind a room."

"We're never happy," he agreed. "What about your parents?"

"My father died eight years ago but my mother is still going strong, though, like your dad I suspect there's an element of going through the motions. Is that really what you want for your future?" she added, curiously.

He looked at her astounded. "Haven't you heard the saying *''Tis better to have loved and lost than never have loved at all'*?"

She nodded. "Tennyson."

"And regardless of how sad your mum might be now or how much she misses him, I'll bet she treasures every moment they had together."

Jackie's eyes filled with tears and she nodded again, not trusting herself to speak.

He sighed, "I'm really not handling this very well at all, am I? First I make you angry and now I've made you cry."

"You've made me laugh too," she said with a shaky smile.

"So there's hope?"

"For what?"

"For us, of course."

"Us?" she repeated.

"Us, you and me, as a couple. Going forward into the great unknown or simply back to Majorca if that would do."

"You're kidding, right?"

He shook his head. "No, I'm deadly serious."

She blinked. "Are you saying you want to be with me?"

"Isn't that what I've been saying for the last couple of hours?"

"Is it?"

He shook his head apologetically. "Obviously not very well but then, you'll have to forgive me – I've never fallen in love at first sight before. Don't worry," he added quickly, "I don't expect you to marry me straightaway. All I'm suggesting is that you give it, us, a go."

"Ladies and gentlemen, the captain has switched on the seatbelt sign as we begin our descent into Dublin airport."

"Well?" Carlos took her hand and smiled hopefully into her eyes.

"I don't know a thing about you," she prevaricated. "You could be an axe murderer."

He grinned. "There's only one way to find out. Come back to Majorca with me, live in the safety of your own apartment in the complex and get to know me." He winked. "You might even decide that you like me."

She stared at him. "Or I might not."

His smile faltered. "I suppose that's a possibility too."

"Excuse me?" A flight attendant interrupted them with an apologetic smile and Carlos released Jackie's hands and sat back. "I'm sorry, madam, but your partner wants to know if you'd like him to come back and sit with you for the landing."

Jackie looked past the attendant to where Don was watching expectantly. She turned back to Carlos and smiled. "No, thank you," she said to the girl but not taking her eyes from his. "Please tell him that I'll be just fine without him."

Fortune Cookies

Claudia Carroll

Claudia Carroll

Claudia Carroll was born in Dublin, where she still lives, along with several imaginary boyfriends. She has worked extensively as an actress on the Irish stage, but is probably best known for her role as TV's Nicola Prendergast in the long running RTÉ soap opera, *Fair City*, a character she describes as "the horrible old cow everyone loves to hate".

Her most recent novel *Remind Me Again Why I Need A Man* has been published in the United States by Harper Collins and has also been sold to Twentieth Century Fox as a TV series. Claudia isn't married and the book's title comes from a phrase she finds herself using quite a bit. Similarly, her fourth novel is called, *I Didn't Fancy Him Anyway*, another phrase she often uses, particularly after a really lousy date.

Fortune Cookies

Right then, here goes.

HAPPY, POSITIVE THINGS ABOUT TURNING,
AHEM . . . THIRTY-NINE TODAY.

1. I am finally able to handle my hairdresser.

2. I have learned to say 'NO', simply, clearly, emphatically and without any residue of emotional guilt. Unless it's a fella asking me out, that is, in which case, sorry, but at my age as long as he's straight and has a job, then, hey, he passes the Vicky Test.

3. I now understand the concept of Sky-Plus and am able to work it. Sort of.

4. At long last, I accept each of the following, in no particular order:

   • I will never carry off a pair of skinny jeans and may as well stop forking out for incredibly pricey gym membership, which invariably I only use the week before

I go on holidays and am obliged to shoehorn myself into a bikini. I am kidding no one but myself.

- Nor will I ever become the effortless cook I once dreamed of and hereby vow to stop doing my usual trick of buying ready-made meals from Marks & Spencer, then artfully arranging them in oven-proof dishes, while disposing of the packaging, or hard evidence, if you will, in the outside bin so that none of my more devious friends (Barbara Fox, take a bow) will suspect that I'm a dirty big cheat. This, too, also fools no one but me. Particularly as Barbara does most of her shopping in Marks & Spencer too.

5. I'm now *very* late thirties and still single. The time has come to accept that, unless I go down the Grade-A-Gay-Sperm-and-a-Spatula Route, I will never have a child and will end up one of those sad old ladies in retirement homes who no one ever visits at Christmas, except kids from the local school as part of their detention.

Ouch, ouch, *ouch!* That last one really hurt.

6. Furthermore, just while I'm doling out tough love, I will now stop believing that fortune-tellers, palm readers and psychics hold the key to my future. Every year I go to one, every year I'm promised that my future husband is out there for me and every year he's a no-show.

Honest to God, if I ever do meet the poor eejit I'm destined to spend the rest of my life with, the first thing I'll do is smack him across the face and tell him it serves him right for being so bloody unpunctual.

7. And while we're on the subject of monumental let-downs, the time has come for me to come clean and finally accept that feng shui isn't all it's cracked up to be either.

Embarrassment prevents me from recording on these pages how much I forked out for a self-styled 'lifestyle and home-design guru', (I am *not* making this up) to call out to my house, make me shift the TV out of the relationship corner and then place pictures of lovey-dovey couples in my south-west corner with big lumps of rose quartz beside them.

She then gave me a daily affirmation ('Love does not conform to schedule') and told me that I should really stop panic-dating, tell myself I'm a goddess and fully embrace my alone-ness.

And there was me thinking you had to go to a hairdresser for that kind of deep, psychological insight.

Right, enough's enough. Decision made. At the grand old age of, ahem, thirty-nine, I hereby make this, my solemn vow. No more clairvoyants, psychics, mystics, cosmic ordering, on-line tarot readers or spending ages in the office pretending to be working when in actual fact I'm checking out my astrological compatibility with whatever fella I happen to be daydreaming about at the time. Time to act my age and leave my destiny in the very capable hands of the Universe.

Yes, love it, brilliant plan.

Oh yeah, except that . . . em . . . well, maybe I'll just start tomorrow. Well, the Mind, Body, Spirit, Health and Healing fair is on all day today, and I can't very well miss out on that, now can I?

Birthdays are so fabulous, the one day out of three-hundred and sixty-five when you are allowed full emotional leverage with your best friend to drag her along to anything, against her will, with the promise of a lovely Thai meal afterwards and as many margaritas as she can handle. My best friend, the aforementioned Barbara Fox, is just fabulous. You'd love her. When I grow up, I want to be her. We've been mates ever since primary school, all the way through college and, as Barbara always says, fellas may come and go, blue eyeliner and the bubble perm may come and go, but true friends are like the Manolo sling-back or the Hermes Birkin bag . . . here to stay whether we like it or not. In all our years of friendship, we really have been through thick and thin together (thick mostly) and in short, like I always joke with Barbara, my love for her is a bit like my appendix scar. Ugly and permanent.

So anyway, I drag her off to the exhibition, kicking and screaming. I'm not messing – only my solemn promise that, come her birthday, I'll be her white slave for the day and will even go to one of her beloved Leinster rugby matches with her, should she so decree, shuts her up.

"This is what community service must feel like," she whinges as we head into the packed hall, forking out twenty euro just for admission. "Deliver us from drivel, that's all I ask, and if anyone comes near me with a crystal and threatens to cleanse my chakras, I'm so outta here!"

Barbara, I should point out, is absolutely cynical about anything remotely otherworldly and is probably the only woman I know who doesn't even bother reading her horoscope. Back in college, she was even a member of the Sceptics Society. I, on the other hand, will try anything once and by that, I really do mean anything. I even did a novena to Saint Clare at one point, a few years back now, which according to my mum, has never *ever* been known to fail. Mum, the polar opposite of Barbara, is a daily Mass-goer and so deeply religious that she's still not over the death of Pope John Paul II.

"I can't take to that new German fella, Benedict or whatever he calls himself," she's always saying. "Ah sure, there'll only ever be the one Pope."

Anyway, I was just so knickers in love with this particular emotionally unavailable guy (invariably the usual type I attract) that even if it meant going down on my hands and knees to Heaven for things to work out, then that's what I was prepared to do. The novena itself was straightforward enough. All you had to do was say nine Hail Marys for nine days and it promised to deliver three favours for you: one personal ("Dear Saint Clare, if he's the right man for me, then please let things work out with . . . well, let's just call him Mr X"); one professional ("Please can Barbara get the part she's up for in that movie with yer man who used to be James Bond. She's an actress and hasn't worked in so long that she's actually starting to wonder if the profession is any different now and this would be the big break she really needs. Please, Saint Clare, ah, go on!"); and one impossible ("Finally, please can I be married and pregnant within a year, Saint Clare . . . well, you did specify impossible, didn't you?").

You should have seen me. I was like Aladdin discovering the magic lantern and making my three wishes but, wouldn't you know, the success rate of that particular excursion into Catholicism was zero out of three. Although, to be brutally honest, I didn't really expect it to work anyway, on the principle that life just isn't like that really, is it? Mum had the last word on the subject, wisely pointing out that God is not a bit impressed with people like me who don't attend Mass, don't do anything they're supposed to do and then expect favours to be lavished on them, just because they bothered asking.

Ho hum. Back to the drawing-board.

The exhibition hall is jammers and when we eventually do get inside, we're immediately approached by this hippy-dippy-looking guy wearing open-toed sandals at a stand with a sign in front of it saying: *Cosmic Orders Accepted Here!*

Well, actually it would be more correct to say that he approached Barbara, who's just one of those women who fellas seem to lose their reason over. We all have a Barbara in our lives, you know, lucky, lucky women who men just fall over themselves to go out with, begging them for dates. She, for her part, does absolutely nothing to encourage this, isn't particularly looking for anyone special and effortlessly flits from relationship to relationship leaving a trail of broken hearts behind her. Theirs, never hers.

I don't know what her gift is, but the best way I can describe it is like this lethal, man-eating pheromone which she exudes from her pores that says, "You can ask me out, or not, whatever – frankly I couldn't be arsed. I'd rather stay home and watch my DVD box set collection of *Lost*" . . . and they go *bananas* over her. The irony is that here's me dying for a man I can call my own and they run a mile from me, whereas all Barbara has to do is be her fabulous, non-committal, nonchalant self and they turn into her slobbering lapdogs.

I swear, she was a 'Rules Girl' before they'd even invented the term, but never with marriage as her end goal – she's just having a laugh and casting her dating net, as she calls it, wide, all the while waiting for her big break in showbiz to come along. We often talk about this; I moan about how I'm turning into a human man-repeller and she jokes about how unemployable she feels and how every single casting she now goes to, the parts invariably go to younger, perter, perkier twenty-somethings, so hungry they'd scratch your eyes out just for a walk-on part in something . . . *anything*.

Barbara, fab wing woman that she is, invariably points out that, while I may be single and whingeing, I am doing pretty much my dream job, which I do have to admit is true. I run my own PR company and, yes, I am very, very lucky. It's great craic, loads of lovely invites to launches and more freebies than I or my pals can sometimes handle. And business is booming so much that I've had to take on two extra staff, so no complaints there. So, in other words, while Barbara has a string of fellas practically impaling themselves to ask her out, I may be on my own but at least I do have disposable income.

We're always telling each other, if we could just trade life problems, we'd be grand.

Anyway, back to the exhibition.

"Ladies, would you care to place an order with the Cosmos?" asks Sandal Man and I'm not joking, the combined whiff of garlic, incense and stale BO from him is making my tummy churn a bit. Talk about taking a holiday from hygiene . . .

"*What* did you just ask me?" Barbara practically snarls back at him, reacting as if he'd asked her for the loan of a kidney.

I decide the best thing is to exercise extreme tact and diplomacy here and gently steer her away. "This way, honey. You're not ready for Cosmic Ordering," I say firmly, "but it was worth the admission price alone just to see the look on your face."

"Cosmic *Ordering*? Explain please, in words of one syllable."

"Well, the theory is, instead of asking the Universe for what you want, you order it, with a set delivery date and all, then you relax and forget about it and just wait for it to happen."

"Right. So it's a bit like the way you used to write into *Jim'll Fix It* when you were ten."

"In a way, yeah."

"And has this cosmic Whaddya-call-it ever worked for you?"

"Emm . . . well, you see . . ."

"Yes or no?"

"Okay, not really, no, but then I worried and stressed about things *not* happening fast enough for me and that just delays delivery, apparently. When you order something and let it go, it acts like an express order on the Universe. At least that's what the book says."

"God, you sound like a prescription-pad job. Lucky for you I'm your friend and therefore non-judgemental about the amount of money you waste on this shite!"

"It is *not* shite and what's more, I'm going to prove it to you."

I take a glance around at the aura consultants (no, Barbara would run a mile,) channelers (ditto) and face-readers (let's not even go there) before I hit on something.

"Right, come on then, whether you like it or not, you'are having your tarot cards read. You have no choice, it's my birthday."

"Okay then, but I'm telling you now, you're only allowed use that once today."

There's a fortune-teller sitting behind a very official-looking desk, so I steer Barbara over. She's doesn't look anything like those Mystic Meg types you see in magazines – you know, all dressed in black with beaded headscarves on them, beads hanging out of them and three teeth saying "Cross my palm with silver, lovey".

No, this one almost looks like she might work in the passport office – she's even wearing a suit, which I feel might appeal to Barbara's, ahem, no-nonsense nature. I plonk her down, fork out fifty euro for the reading and tell her I'll be back in ten minutes and that on no account is she to make a bolt for the exit.

Then I spot another fortune-teller just across the hall, ooohh . . . *now* we're talking! This woman looks right up my alley. She has a crystal ball in front of her and a sign that says *SHARON, SPIRITUALIST, SHAMAN & SAGE TO THE STARS*. There's even a photo of her standing beside Cherie Blair so that proves she must *really* be good, mustn't it? I mean, everyone knows Cherie Blair is like this total genius so she'd hardly waste her time with a complete messer/chancer/con-artist, now would she?

All excited, I sit down, hand over another fifty euro, shuffle the tarot cards Sharon the Shaman hands me and then hand her ten, exactly like she asks. There's a long pause as she looks at the layout in front of her, but I'm supremely confident, full-sure that she'll predict that a soul mate will enter my life, whisk me off my feet, and plonk an engagement ring on my finger quicker than you can say "Boodle me, Baby".

Oh yes, and then I'll ask Barbara to be my bridesmaid and my friend Susan to be matron of honour and I'll definitely have to try on a few of those empire-line dresses that you see in all the Jane Austen adaptations and I might even get a wedding planner because I've just waited so bloody long for this that I want it to be bigger, longer and costlier than even Liz Hurley's . . .

"Mmmm, all right then, love," says Sharon the Shaman, in a *Coronation Street* accent, "just by looking at your cards here, I can tell that you're a nurse."

"Em, no."

"A doctor?"

"Nope."

"But you definitely work around hospitals, love."

"Sorry."

"Oh no, now I see it, you're a teacher then. Primary school."

"I'm afraid not."

"But you definitely work with small children. I see you mopping up a lot of wee."

Bloody hell. I wonder if Barbara's getting on a bit better than this.

And if the fifty euro is refundable.

"For the love of God, can we please leave now?" Barbara says when we meet up, precisely ten minutes later. (Considering these people work in an esoteric field, the length of time they dole out to

45

you is incredibly precise.) "I need a margarita and a cigarette, in that order."

"What did your one tell you?"

"Oh please, don't even go there. Apparently, I'm going to be pregnant by next Christmas and give birth to a girl that my great-great-granny's spirit reincarnated. Pathetic. For the love of God, can we go now? This place pushes the parameters of sanity."

Right, that's it, I officially give up. I'm just about to admit defeat and steer her towards the exit then the nearest bar, in that order, when something catches my attention.

"Anything you want in your life is yours, if you just *ask, believe and receive*. It's as simple and as profound as that," a woman with long, red hair and an Aussie accent is saying. You should see her. She looks like an angel and is speaking soft and low, but with such absolute conviction it stops me in my tracks. And Barbara too, I notice.

She's standing on a sort of podium and almost looks like she's giving a seminar, with a microphone in one hand and a sheaf of notes in the other. But there's only one other person in the audience listening to her, a fair-haired girl about my own age.

"But I've been asking for the right man for years now," this girl is saying, almost pleading. "And all I meet are uninterested, unavailable eejits. Now either my emotional sat-navigational system is *waaaaay* off kilter or I'm doing something wrong. And believe me, I will pay any money to be told what that is so I can fix it, move on and who knows? Maybe even find some tiny modicum of happiness in this life."

Red-haired woman puts the microphone down and steps down from the podium to where the girl is standing. It flashes through my mind that this is nice, sensitive thing to do. After all, there are some conversations you don't want anyone overhearing.

46

Barbara and I are hovering close, not wanting to seem rude, but at the same time dying to know what she'll say.

"The law of attraction is available to you at any time. It's working as often as you're thinking. The question you need to ask yourself is, why am I attracting the wrong kinds of men into my life? What is it that I need to learn here? What's the Universe trying to teach me?"

Okay, that's it, I can't contain myself any longer. Fair-haired girl doesn't exactly look impressed with this answer and moves off, so I'm in like Flynn.

"Excuse me," I say in a voice I barely recognise as my own, "but I couldn't help overhearing and, well, I can fully sympathise with that lady's dilemma. I hope you don't mind the interruption."

"That's okay," says red-haired woman, smiling kindly. "That's why I'm here."

"Ask, believe, receive? Is that true? Can you explain to me then how come I've been asking to meet my husband for nearly two decades now and still no sign of him?"

"So, what have you learned?" God, for a total stranger, this one really has that unflinching, direct eye-contact thing down pat.

"That it's probably a bad idea either to calculate your Weight Watchers' points in front of a guy on a first date and that it's generally received wisdom that if you keep asking a fella what he's thinking at regular two-minute intervals, it's a racing certainty that he will eventually crack. There you go, twenty unsuccessful years summarised in two sentences."

I'm aware that I'm making light of it to cover up how defensive I really feel and I'm also aware of Barbara standing close to me and I'm glad of it; I want her to hear this for herself.

"Then I can help you," says red-haired woman, nodding sagely, like she's seen my type a thousand times before. Which let's face it, she probably has. "The law of attraction couldn't be simpler. Your thoughts determine your destiny. It's a well-proven scientific fact that like attracts like. When you talk about dating, all I can hear in your voice is negativity, a woman who is *expecting* to fail. If you expect failure, then that's all the universe is going to deliver. A simple mind-switch is all you need to change your entire life and the choice, my dear, is yours."

Her words hang there and for a minute I can't say anything. I'm too busy thinking, could this total stranger actually be right? Am I so busy focusing on how rubbish my love life is, that all I'm creating is even more of that?

Then Barbara's over, all business-like with her 'you watch me while I put manners on this one' face.

"May I just point out," she thunders, "that my friend here runs a highly successful business so to make out that she attracts negativity all around her –"

"Oh, do you? Tell me a bit about your business," she interrupts, shutting Barbara up.

"Oh, well, yes, it is doing very well," I say, a bit wrong-footed.

"It's doing brilliantly," says Barbara defensively. "Go on, tell her about the contract with the beer company."

"Well, you see, we're up for a huge contract and I won't know for another few weeks whether we have it or not, but I think it's pretty much in the bag."

"You see?" smiles red-haired lady. "Even your tone of voice changes when you're discussing an area of your life where you feel confident. You absolutely believe that success will come to you, so of course it will. How can it not? Your very thoughts are attracting it to you as we speak. That's the thing about the law of attraction, ladies; it's very obedient."

"So how come I'm virtually unemployable as an actress then?"

Barbara demands and I can tell this one is *really* getting to her. "Here I am trying to attract a decent gig for myself and – big, fat *nada*."

"What are you doing to attract the right part to you?"

"Everything. I learn the lines, do my homework, turn up and pray very hard that the two-hundred-odd hot chicks in the casting queue ahead of me all drop dead so the gig will be mine. Simple."

Red-haired woman just looks at her. Doesn't even raise her voice, nothing. "You're attracting failure because clearly that's what you expect. In fact, it sounds to me that you're so busy focusing on what you *don't* want to happen that, in actual fact, all you're doing is attracting jobs for other people."

"Now hang on a minute here. I don't go into auditions trying to fail!"

"So what *do* you think when you're auditioning?"

"That here I am, classically trained and reading for the part of a life-sized cigarette in a Nicorette ad usually, that's what."

"And your negativity is only attracting more negativity into your life, just like a magnet. There must be some aspect of your life where everything's going your way – think about what it is you're doing right there and apply it to your work area."

"She attracts fellas like flies to – em – manure!" I blurt out.

Sorry, I can't help myself. God, I sound like the class swot ratting on my friend to the teacher. I just think she could really be onto something here.

"There you go then," smiles red-haired woman. "It sounds to me like you ladies need to learn from each other. You need to figure what your friend is doing to attract men so easily and you," she says turning to a very pole-axed-looking Barbara, "need to be as confident and self-believing in your work area as you are in romance. If you walk into every casting with the attitude that everyone around you is far more suited to the part than you, what are you attracting? Unemployment, what else? There's a saying I often use to anyone who comes to me looking for help: 'If you want to fly, first of all get the shit off your wings.'"

Hours and hour and *waaaay* too many margaritas later, Barbara and I were still talking about her.

And that's when we make our pact.

Maybe it's drink talking (Barbara always reckons she makes all her best decisions after three stiff cocktails) but here's what we decide. From here on in, for a period of twelve months exactly right up until my birthday next year (a good suitable book-end, you'll agree) she will take control of my love life and more importantly my attitude towards it. She will personally vet all flings, dates, casual Mr Ah-sure-he'll-do types and monitor my behaviour at all times to make sure I'm only expecting and attracting the best, not the worst, like I normally do. I, for my part, hereby agree to take full charge of Barbara's career, and similarly, make full sure that she only attracts wonderful parts for herself which lead onto even bigger breaks and more magical things.

Oooh, I'm already hatching a plan! She and I could set up our own production company and produce a classical play that audiences might actually *want* to see. Shakespeare meets *The Sopranos*, that type of thing. God, she'd make a fabulous Lady Macbeth, wouldn't she?

Why not? What's to lose?

After all, maybe, just maybe, if we can think it, we can do it . . .

THE END . . . ?

My
Fabulous
Friend

Norah Casey

Norah Casey

Norah Casey is the CEO of Harmonia, Ireland's largest consumer magazine publishers, and the Veuve Clicquot Businesswoman of the Year 2007.

My
Fabulous
Friend

I loved him, of course. He was the only boy in town that wasn't related to me so he was most definitely going to be mine. But she had other ideas. Foolish me for insisting she came along for our annual trip to my mother's homeland every summer. There we were, all glammed up for a night of pool-playing and street corners. She with her Dublin glitz out to dazzle the Leitrim boys. Far too pretty to be a best friend. I should have known I was destined to live in her shade. Liam didn't stand a chance. When she turned those big blues on full beam he was mesmerised like all the others. I sulked. For days on end that summer I seethed and simmered plotting my revenge. She never noticed. She stayed infuriatingly frivolous while I grew ugly with bitterness. Then one sunny day as we walked the lanes of Leitrim she linked my arm and squeezed – "Let's be friends for ever". And so we were mended. She was impossible not to love. Who the hell was Liam anyway?

When you're young you get notions about best friends. I went through six or seven before I decided that Ruby was my "bestest friend ever". I was only five at the time though and friends were fickle. But Ruby was the one constant. We played dolls, shared pretend tea parties, beheaded my brother's Action Man and dressed up in flouncy dresses on rainy days. As we entered the twilight zone of those early teen years I can hardly remember the tantrums (my mother said they were spectacular) because Ruby and I were united against the common enemy. We had the worst parents in the world. Every other girl in the school had more understanding and forgiving parents than ours and we constantly reminded them of the hardship we endured at their hands. Not only were they totally uncool, they were seriously lacking in the wealth stakes. In other words they refused to indulge our every whim (mostly designer jeans and shoes to die for!).

I can't recall exactly when it happened – probably around our fourteenth year. We were moping around after school bemoaning our lot in life and the tragedy of homework. A couple of my brother's friends were skulking outside the newsagent's. Red-faced, lanky, smelly boys who suddenly seemed strangely attractive. In the weeks previous we had taken to giggling loudly and throwing our heads back to show off our flowing locks. Ruby would shriek melodramatically at the slightest provocation – a passing dog, a missed step or just for the hell of it. And Oh My God, I discovered something that day. She was so bloody good at all this attention-grabbing stuff I didn't stand a chance. We had been equals up until now – at least I thought we were at the same level in life. It was a revelation. Suddenly I was no longer linking arms with my best friend, I was walking with the enemy. Who was this blond beauty next to me who laughed longer and louder than I did? From then on the competition between us was ferocious but there was never any contest – she always won. The boys whistled and catcalled but they only had eyes for her.

The Leaving Cert, now that was almost our undoing. I slogged into the night, she partied on the town. She still beat me by two honours. The devil was on my shoulder that day I can tell you. As the nuns bustled in the hallways and the girls crowded around the notice-board, I stood stock-still wondering at the cruelty of a God who matched me with a friend who was destined to always shine brighter. And then Ruby turned and laughed and grabbed my hand and we were running down the street shrieking and leaping – we were free, we were together and life was just beginning.

Leitrim wasn't big enough for our gallivanting that summer. In truth it was big enough for me but she had notions of France. Where I would have flustered and over-explained she persuaded and cajoled our respective parents to let us off the leash for a few weeks.

Wild, wonderful weeks where we threw off our American Tan tights and grew brown and beautiful on the Côte d'Azur. We survived on her smiles, disarming the French boys who filled our glasses with wine and fed us romantic dinners. We were inseparable, always two with two. She with the Adonis and I with the plainer friend.

We returned to Dublin more women than girls and spent endless late summer evenings filling out application forms for the paltry jobs on offer. The year was 1986 and most of our classmates were heading for New York or London where the prospects were better – for both jobs and men. University was out of the question – neither of us had the money or the motivation to continue our studies. Ruby, of course, progressed to interviews and soon had her pick of the best. I filed the reject letters and worried silently about what the future might hold. She started in the bank – "a permanent, pensionable job," my father said as he hid his disappointment at my own lack of progress in the employment stakes. I was envious and cross. When she celebrated her first pay-cheque with a night on the town I pretended to be sick. In truth I was sick – sick of her talents, her beauty and her unrelenting sunny disposition. Of course I eventually persuaded some mediocre company to give me a start and I too was in gainful employment. Our friendship healed and my other, and much better, half was back in my life making me whole again.

Life was ours for the taking. Nights were filled with fun and hapless boys desperate to woo my fabulous friend. And I of course followed in her wake, content by now to be the also-ran. It was inevitable Ruby would be snared first. The gorgeous Greg won her heart and promised to mind her for evermore. I was heartbroken, bereft of my friend. My weeks were long and lonely. There was no longer us – there was them and me, the single friend with nowhere to go on Saturday night. And then I found Stephen – my lovely Stephen. Uncomplicated Stephen. For the first time I had a great friend who was my equal.

She and I drifted apart, babies arrived, and houses were bought. Then one day I was walking down Grafton Street with my little Harry and there she was right in front of me with two children in tow. We hugged. A lukewarm embrace. Neither of us knew what to say. We used the children as a go-between, insisting on polite introductions. "Say hello, Lily. Say hello, Thomas!" "This is Harry." She's living in Castleknock, I'm in Stillorgan – miles away from each other. She's given up work and Greg is now a partner in the law firm. Her dad has died and so has mine. We're stilted and unsure, no bonds to tie us now.

Ruby is drawn and pale. God forgive me I feel a touch of triumph that I have improved with age while she looks ten years older. We say goodbye and as I walk away she calls back.

"Could we have a coffee – do you have time?" she asks hesitatingly.

I have to be somewhere but something, and I hope to God it isn't just idle curiosity, makes me say yes. We find a corner table and the kids chatter happily. We're halfway through our large skinny cappuccinos when I sneak a proper look at her. She's distracted by Lily's spilt orange juice so I get to do a full-on assessment.

I could tell there was something troubling my former friend. It wasn't hard. She had all the telltale signs of a troubled soul. Her beautiful blonde hair hung lank and unwashed, there were dark shadows beneath her eyes, and her whole body seemed to sag. My Ruby was vibrant. This Ruby was bowed by some ailment. I had a moment where I contemplated sticking with the banal and getting as far away from this troubled Ruby as I possibly could. And just as I was about to launch into a long diatribe about the weather I caught a look in her eyes, the slightest hint of my old friend hiding there behind the hollows.

"I know I look dreadful so please don't tell me how fantastic I look or how I've never changed," she challenged.

I felt the red *brought-on-by-nerves* blotches rising on my neck because dammit how did she know that was just what I was going to do. "I wouldn't say dreadful . . ." I faltered. "You're right, you look – I don't know – maybe a little tired . . ." I squirmed and winced, wishing I could find some words to bridge this awkwardness.

She laughed – not quite the old Ruby throw-your-head-back laugh but a full-on throaty laugh that reached the eyes.

I started for a moment and found myself smirking and then grinning and before long laughing out loud and clutching my stomach and crossing my legs and doing all of the things we nearly middle-aged women have to do to keep from wetting our knickers. After an unseemly few minutes of guffawing I stopped long enough to notice that her eyes were brimming over with big fat tears. The final cackle lodged in my throat. "What's wrong, Ruby. Tell me. You're upset . . . What's the matter?" I was babbling, concern replacing my previous reserve.

"I have breast cancer," she says quietly.

I am too shocked by this admission, this appalling news to do much but stare.

Ruby laughs, a weary sad laugh. "At least, I did have breast cancer and now it appears I have it in other places. They took both my breasts last year and I thought – I hoped – God, I prayed – that it was gone away and never to return."

The years fall away along with our unease and I reach over for her hand. There's a lump in my throat choking the words that are struggling for air. "I'm sorry. I'm so so sorry . . ." I grip her hand tighter and look into those lovely blue eyes and search in their depths for my beautiful, fabulous, frivolous friend. Words tumble out, inadequate useless words which constrain rather than explain the true depth of my sorrow and heartbreak.

She's stoic and calm. "It's too late," she says, "much too late."

The cancer came back just two short weeks ago and is unrelentingly invading her body. There is an anger building inside me at this terrible injustice. But like always I follow her lead. We don't talk about the C word any more. She talks about the past, recreating scenes and events in vivid detail. We remember together, each filling in bits the other has forgotten. And we laugh – loudly. Our children stare at their two mad mothers every now and then but quickly lose interest in our antics. I don't know how it happened that we moved from laughter to crying but when our tears were spent we held each other tight and promised not to lose one other again.

I kept my promise but Ruby of course did not keep hers. It was not a long goodbye. Two months – eight weeks – 56 days – not long enough to say everything that had to be said. I wanted to say how much I loved her – my amazing, fabulous, wonderful friend. I wanted to be honest with her and admit all of the crazy jealousy and pettiness of my youth. But as those precious days passed I got to know Ruby in a way that I never had before.

I said goodbye to Ruby on a damp autumn day with the wind-whipped trees shedding their dying leaves. And yet again I found myself doing her bidding. This time I was content to follow her lead.

"A party" she declared, "not one maudlin moment, please. This is my day and I want everyone to remember me as I was. Speak for me and make me come alive for just that day."

And so I did. It was no hardship to remember my beautiful Ruby the way she really was – a kind and generous friend who laughed loud and long and lived her brief live to the full. And in remembering I realised that she really was the best friend I had ever had.

Blood Sisters

Tracy Culleton

Tracy Culleton

Tracy Culleton won the 2003 Poolbeg/Open House 'Write A Bestseller' competition, with her debut novel *Looking Good*. She has since had two more novels published by Poolbeg: *Loving Lucy* and *More Than Friends*. Her websites are: **www.tracyculleton.com** and **www.fiction-writers-mentor.com** (for lots of advice and information about writing).

Blood
Sisters

On that hot August day Tara McGoldrick was making her way to work. She had taken the DART into Dublin's city centre, and was now walking from her stop to her office, which was either a fifteen-minute stride or a twenty-minute stroll away. Today she was in stride mode, seeing as she was late. It was gone nine o'clock, and so the pavements were not overcrowded – although there was still a good contingent of late stragglers along with herself.

Ah, there was that woman again – walking just ahead of her. Tara had seen this woman often before. Their respective routes clearly intersected for some of the journey, and their times of travel overlapped relatively frequently.

It wasn't surprising that Tara had noticed the woman, because her tangible *joie-de-vivre* made her stand out from the rest of the dull and leaden commuters (including Tara herself, she had to acknowledge). The woman's tiny frame seemed to almost effervesce with the sheer joy of being alive. Her shoulder-length blonde hair bounced enthusiastically on her red-shirted back, matching the rhythm of her jaunty walk.

Tara couldn't see her face as she was still walking behind her, but based on previous sightings she could guess that the woman's face wore a relaxed and open expression, with a tiny turn-up to the lips as if she was thinking about happy things, and was on the verge of breaking into an exuberant smile, or even uproarious laughter.

Tara often thought how she'd love to have this woman for a friend. They were even about the same age – mid-thirties – so it would be perfect. Tara didn't know why she was so powerfully drawn to the woman. For sure the jaunty walk, the permanent half-smile, and the joyful energy were part of it, but somehow Tara felt (fanciful though she knew it to be) that there was more to it than that, that there was some unknown connection between them.

But to make friends with somebody you have to start by talking to them, and how on earth could Tara possibly manage that? It was much easier for children. They can just walk up to other children and say, "Can I play with you?" or, "Would you like to be friends with me?"

But adults can't do that.

Maybe, Tara often reflected, life would be a lot better if adults *could* do that. Maybe there would be a lot fewer lonely people in the world if they could be so open and honest about asking for friendship. But our culture didn't work like that – she'd be considered mad if she tried that. The person you approached would be nervous and intimidated. There was just no way.

She couldn't even contrive a conversation, not easily. Even manoeuvring it so that she was in step with the woman and passing a pleasantry would be odd, and make the woman feel uncomfortable. You can say hello to strangers on country walks, but not on city streets. Them's the rules.

The best she could hope for was that some time, some way, they'd meet in person. It was very possible. Forget six degrees of separation! In Tara's experience, in Dublin there was only ever one degree of separation. No matter who you met, a few minutes' conversation would find you *somebody* or *something* in common. No doubt the same applied to her and this woman.

If only she knew what it was!

Maybe they had a friend in common, or shared a dentist, or had been to the same school a couple of years apart. Maybe they lived near each other without realising it; maybe their children (if the woman had children) were at the same school. It could be anything, but it was bound to be *something*.

So it was very possible that they would meet. Their mutual friend might invite them both to a party. Or they might meet at a school reunion, or in the dentist's waiting room, or at their children's school's open day. And meeting in outside circumstances – even a circumstance such as a dentist's waiting room – would make it very possible for Tara to lean forward and say, "Excuse me, but don't I know you? Don't you work in the Four Courts area?"

And the woman wouldn't be intimidated by that approach. She'd no doubt answer happily, and they could share notes about where they worked and the qualities of the dentist, and have a great conversation. And then the next time they shared a route to work, *then* they could fall into conversation.

Really, Tara often thought, the rules of society were strange and arbitrary indeed.

But anyway, the point was that it was *possible* that she and this fascinating woman would meet. It was possible, but – she acknowledged ruefully – unlikely. Even if they shared a dentist, the odds were against them sharing an appointment time, for example.

She wondered what the woman would make of *her*, if she

should happen to become aware of her. Not that there was any reason to notice her, Tara thought, being – as she was – so nondescript. Tallish, thinnish, shortish brown hair, sharpish features. Not much to remark upon, really.

Everything would have turned out very differently if Tara hadn't been studying the woman. If Tara – like all the other commuters – had been immersed in her own thoughts then she would never have seen the concrete wall begin to wobble and fall. In that case the wall would have fallen unhindered – and the woman, all unsuspecting, was right in its path. The wall would have fallen directly onto her, crashing into her head on the way down, pinning her under its uncaring weight. The woman would very possibly have died; she certainly would have been very badly injured.

But Tara *was* studying the woman, and Tara *did* see the wall totter and begin its descent.

In an instant a number of thoughts flashed through Tara's head: she couldn't just shout to the woman – it would take too many precious seconds for her to realise someone was shouting at *her* – and even then, she'd most likely just stop and look around, wondering what the problem was . . .

The only solution was . . .

Tara leapt forward, launching herself at the woman, pushing her out of the path of the wall. The woman gave a cry of panic and shock, no doubt thinking she was being attacked, and then a cry of pain as she landed heavily on the pavement, and a *whoomph* as her breath rushed out of her.

Tara landed more or less on top of her. The woman's body broke most of her fall, but she tried to take at least some of her weight, and her arms and wrists took the brunt of it. She gave her own cry of pain.

Then the concrete wall completed its fall.

But Tara hadn't fallen clear – the concrete landed on her left foot and ankle and she screamed in panic and pain.

The events had jerked their fellow commuters out of their stupor, and immediately people were rallying around.

Through her pain Tara could hear the murmurs. "*What happened?*" "*The wall fell, look!*" "*Are they hurt?*" "*I don't know yet.*" There was genuine shock and concern in their voices, but excitement too – a sort of delight at the drama of it all. They'd have *loads* to share with their colleagues!

A fiftyish silver-haired man took charge. "Can somebody ring for an ambulance?" he demanded, "and can you, and you" – he indicated two other men – "help me shift this wall off her? And whoever else – come on!"

There was a silver flashing flurry of mobile phones as people rushed to do his bidding, and the two men he had indicated, and three or four others, moved towards the fallen wall with him, and began to try to shift it.

In the meantime Tara's rescuee had realised what had happened. "Oh my God," she whispered hoarsely into the ground, as she and Tara lay together in an inelegant heap on the grey pavement, "you saved my life. Thank you, thank you!"

But Tara didn't hear her. She had no room for awareness of anything else through the piercing throbbing pain in her ankle, and the rushing swooping fear that she had irrevocably damaged it. How would she go cycling with her children, ever again, if her foot had permanent damage?

Everything seemed blurry and distant to her; the crowd's shocked and excited murmurs were fading, and she was feeling dizzy and nauseous.

"One – two – three – *lift!*" commanded the take-charge man, and with that the concrete was lifted off Tara. "Pull them away," he commanded, a strain in his voice from the weight of the concrete. "We can't hold this for long."

Willing arms gently pulled both women that critical metre away, lifting Tara off the woman she had rescued, and laying her gently on the ground. Somebody even had the foresight to lift Tara's injured foot so it didn't drag on the ground. But still it hurt and she let out another howl of pain. With a *whoomph* of relief, the men lowered the concrete slab to the path.

People began to pull the woman Tara had rescued to her feet. "I'm okay. I'm okay," she kept telling them, dusting herself down. But there was a wobble in her hands and a catch in her voice.

A kind-faced woman hunkered down beside Tara. "You're all right, you're all right," she said, placing her hand on Tara's shoulder. "The ambulance is on its way – in fact, I can hear it now."

Sure enough, through the haze of her pain Tara could hear the distant siren.

Three or four minutes later the ambulance pulled up, followed by a Garda patrol car.

The ambulance men carefully and gently manoeuvred Tara onto a stretcher, and lifted her into the ambulance.

"We'll head off to the hospital in a jiffy, I promise," one of the ambulance men told her, with a sympathetic smile. "We'll just get your friend."

She's not my friend, Tara thought. But it wasn't worth pointing that out to him. And for sure she'd got what she wished for – a chance to meet that woman. But what a way for it to happen! God certainly had a sense of humour, that was for sure! She would appreciate it a lot more if her foot didn't hurt so much.

"Can you give me something for the pain?" she asked, her eyes closed and her expression pinched with pain.

"Not yet, I'm sorry. They'll sort you out in the hospital, and we'll be there soon. I'll just – "

He went back outside and Tara heard him talking to the woman she had rescued.

"Come on and we'll help you into the ambulance, love."

"I don't need to go to hospital at all, I think," she said. "I just fell heavily. I'll be fine."

"Let's just take you to hospital, get you checked out, love. Best to be sure."

"Okay," the woman agreed. "But I don't need the stretcher."

"Fair enough," said the ambulance man, "but come quickly whatever you do – your friend isn't critical, but the sooner we get her checked out the better."

And the sooner they'll give me something to stop this pain, Tara thought. But still, what was this compared to somebody's life?

Tara felt the ambulance shift slightly as the woman and the ambulance man got in. They strapped her in, and then they headed off to the hospital.

She heard the woman leaning over her. "I'm Jennifer, Jennifer Holden."

Funny, Jennifer was Tara's daughter's name too, only they called her Jenny. But Tara didn't have the energy to explain this. She barely managed to whisper her own name.

"Hi, Tara. And listen – words will never *begin* to do justice – but thank you so, so much for what you did back there. You saved my life, you know. Thank you."

"'s okay." Tara couldn't say more.

"Are you in pain?"

Tara gave a short jerk of a nod.

"I'm sorry," Jennifer said.

"'s okay," Tara said again.

Jennifer gave a big, juddering intake of breath. "Do you know, it's only sinking in now – I could have died! It's just hit me. I mean, I really could have been killed! I know I said thanks for saving my life, and I meant it, of course I did. But I don't think I realised just how close it was. Oh my God, oh my God!"

Tara could hear a mixture of emotions in Jennifer's voice, including huge relief that she didn't die, and equally massive shock that she *could* have.

Tara reached out and groped blindly for Jennifer, her hand eventually landing clumsily on her arm.

Jennifer kept talking, the shock of it all causing a deluge of words. "Or I could have been badly injured. I might have had brain damage if that wall had hit my head. I might have been a vegetable for the rest of my life. Or I might have been paralysed from the neck down maybe. Oh God, that doesn't bear thinking about! And you saved me from all that. Thank you, thank you, I'll never be able to thank you enough."

With Jennifer speaking these thoughts over and over, and Tara giving her arm a comforting squeeze now and again, the journey to the hospital passed quickly.

Once there, with soft voices and gentle hands, the ambulance men took Tara off the ambulance and handed her into the care of the hospital staff.

She assumed that Jennifer, in her turn, would be looked after, but she lost sight of her in the hospital bustle.

They took Tara into the hospital, and carefully transferred her to a hospital trolley. Gentle as they were, she moaned with pain at the movement.

"Miss, I just need to take some details from you," said a young woman, who was wielding a clipboard and pen, "and then we'll get you X-rayed."

"Can I have some pain-killers, please? I'm in agony."

"Sorry," the nurse shook her head sympathetically. "Not until you've been checked out. In case there are problems we don't know about."

They took her name and address and so on, and then she just had to wait. While she waited she texted her best friend at work to tell her what had happened, so they wouldn't worry when she didn't turn up. She would contact her husband and children later, when she knew what the situation was. No point worrying them unnecessarily.

After a wait of a couple of hours – a long painful couple of hours – she was wheeled down to the X-ray room. The radiographer took X-rays of her wrists and her ankle, and then the doctor had a look at them.

"Hmm," he said, holding the images up to the light. "Your wrists are fine, just a bit of a sprain. But you've messed your ankle up pretty badly. It's broken here, here, and here – look." He indicated the breaks with a pen.

Tara looked as instructed, but it didn't mean anything to her – she didn't know what the X-ray of a foot should look like, so couldn't see how this X-ray deviated from that standard. She'd take his word for it. Her foot certainly *felt* broken in three places. At least.

The doctor continued, "We'll need to operate on that, put a few pins in. It'll be a long process, but you should make a full recovery."

"Thank God," she breathed.

She had to wait more hours for that operation, but at least they gave her morphine for the pain in the meantime, now that they knew it was safe to do so.

That evening she was lying in the hospital bed. Her foot was still painful, but thanks to the morphine it was easier. It wasn't that the pain was any less, it seemed, but rather that it seemed more distant. It was there, but it wasn't quite belonging to her. It was a strange feeling.

She had contacted her family after the operation, and they had come straight in to see her. There were tears and hugs and expressions of relief that she was okay, and declarations of pride in her that she was such a hero. It all brought a tear to her eye and a tightness of emotion in her chest. Her children, particularly, looked at her differently, shaken out of their teenage indifference to her.

"You risked your life." Jenny realised. "You could have *died*."

"I could have, but I didn't."

But she was glad that her children realised this. For now – for however long it lasted – they appreciated her, acknowledging that they could possibly have lost her. She knew, none better, that you never value anything as highly as when you nearly lose it.

They hadn't left long when Jennifer came in to see her, barely visible behind a huge bouquet of flowers.

"Hi, Jennifer! Oh thanks, they're beautiful." She rested the flowers on her lap, enjoying the sight of them. "I'll ask the nurse to get a vase in a minute. It's good to see you."

"Oh, and it's good to see you too. You're looking a *lot* more cheerful!"

"Well, I'm on drugs now!" She indicated her morphine drip. "It always helps. And they've operated on me, so I feel more cheerful about my foot. It's going to be fine!"

"Oh, I'm so glad!"

"How are you? Did they find any problems?"

"No, I'm fine, thank God. Badly bruised, and stiff. It's going to hurt for a while. But God knows I'm not complaining. When you think how it could have been . . ." she gave a shudder at the thought. "It really makes you appreciate your life, you know, when you've nearly lost it. I mean, I love my life anyway, don't get me wrong. But in a way I took it for granted. I assumed I'd have life for – well, for ages yet. But now I realise how fragile it is and how precious it is. Oh –" she groaned in frustration – "I don't know if I can explain it."

"I know what you mean." Tara smiled at her. "I nearly died once, and was lucky to survive, and it really changed me too. Now I never grumble, little things just don't get me down. It's wonderful."

"So you understand!"

"I surely do. I just wish other people knew what a gift life is. Without having to nearly die, I mean. Because after all, that's a rather high-risk strategy!" Jennifer laughed, and Tara smiled at her before continuing. "Whenever I hear people moaning and complaining, I just want to shake them and tell them how lucky they are! I mean, people complaining about little things, you know the sort of thing. The weather, a husband leaving dirty socks on the floor, a late bus, that sort of thing."

"I think I know what you mean, and I'm certainly going to be a lot more zen about stuff in future. Now, listen, maybe – well, when you're better could I bring you out to dinner? To thank you properly."

"For sure. I'd like that. I'll give you my number."

Jennifer got her phone out and programmed in Tara's number as she dictated it to her. "That's great! You know, I wouldn't have wished for it to happen this way, of course, but I'm glad we've met. I used to see you on the way to work, and you always looked so kind and serene I used to think that I'd love to meet you. But you can't just walk up to people, can you, and start talking to them?"

73

"No, you can't, you're right." Tara decided that she'd tell Jennifer another time about how she, too, had wanted to be friends. They'd have a laugh over it.

"I really am so, so grateful," Jennifer said again. Perhaps she'd never tire of saying that. "I'm so glad that I didn't even get an injury. I've a terror of needing a blood transfusion!"

"Have you a phobia about needles?" Tara asked with a sympathetic grimace.

"No, it's not that. It's that I have a very rare blood type. The rarest in Ireland, actually," she said with a mixture of ruefulness and pride. "AB Negative. I discovered this when I first donated blood. And so, it's hard for them to get the right blood for me, seeing as only 1% of Irish people have it."

"Really?" Tara asked, clearly fascinated. "What a –"

But Jennifer spoke over her. "In fact, once I got a call at work asking me to drop everything and come in to donate blood, that they had another AB Negative person who desperately needed it. A young mother who'd just given birth, seemingly, and who was haemorrhaging badly."

"When was this?" Tara asked, her expression focussed and her voice intent.

"About twelve years ago."

"In June?"

"Well, it could have been." She shrugged. "It was the summer anyway, I remember that. Why, do you – oh . . ."

They stopped and looked at each other.

"I was going to say," said Tara, "what a coincidence! About the blood group, that is. Because I'm AB Negative too. And – this is just *amazing* – twelve years ago in June I gave birth to my daughter. Jenny. And I haemorrhaged so badly that I nearly died. I told you, a minute ago, that I nearly died once – that's what I meant! They told me afterwards that somebody had to come in specially to give me blood — it must have been you!"

Tara and Jennifer stared at each other, eyes bright with excitement as the realisation came to them.

"I wanted to know afterwards who had saved my life. I wanted to contact her — well, you. But they wouldn't tell me. The best they would do, and they weren't even supposed to do that, was to tell me your name so I could call my daughter after you. It was the least I could do. But now I can thank you — thank you, thank you, thank you, thank you! You saved my life."

"And you saved mine!"

"And think — if *you* hadn't saved *my* life all those years ago, I wouldn't have been there to save yours today."

"This is just amazing!" Jennifer said, her facing shining.

She rose and gave Tara a big hug, mindful of the drip. When she sat back into her chair, she said, "And you know, in years to come, when people ask how we met — well, we can tell them that we're blood sisters!"

Playing Happy Families

Martina Devlin

Martina Devlin

Martina Devlin was born in Omagh, Co Tyrone and lives in Dublin. She is the author of five novels and a memoir, *The Hollow Heart*. Her latest book is *Ship of Dreams*. She also writes weekly newspaper columns for the *Irish Independent* and the *Sunday World Magazine*. More information is available on her website:

www.martinadevlin.com

Playing
Happy Families

"There's something you should see." Moira Kelly reached her ex-husband a sheet of notepaper filled with their son's irregular-shaped, exuberant handwriting.

"Can it wait until later? I promised I'd be home by six and the traffic is nose-to-tail." Adam Kelly fiddled with the collar of his rugby shirt, barely glancing at the page. He was anxious to climb back into the car and zoom off, wary of antagonising his beautiful young wife whose mood swings were erratic since the new baby's arrival. She had warned him he was not to be late tonight. No excuses – not if aliens abducted him, not if nuclear war broke out, and especially not if his ex-wife wanted a heart-to-heart. Adam and his second wife were hosting a Christmas drinks party for his work colleagues – specifically the managing director and heads of department. Even in a seesawing hormonal state, Jennifer was ambitious for Adam.

Moira Kelly tried to bite back a barbed remark, but could not help herself. "Is it too much to ask, Adam, that you'd read our son's letter to Santa? He spent all morning composing it." Immediately she regretted her outburst; she and Adam had to stay amicable for Conan's sake. Moderating her tone, she continued, "He wouldn't show it to me, he said the letter was a secret between him and Santa, but I came across it in his bedroom while he was at the ice-rink with you this afternoon. I took a peek, and, well, read it yourself. Go on. Conan's in the sitting room playing a DVD. He won't know. You could have had it read by now."

Adam scanned the page, glanced up uncertainly at Moira, and studied the letter more closely.

Dear Santa
I don't want any Presents this year I have loads of Toys but pleas could you make my Mum and Dad and Jennyfer and Baby daisy and me all be together for Chrismass Just like a proper famly
Love from Conan Kelly, aged 8
xoxoxoxoxoxoxoxoxoxoxoxoxoxoxox
PS We live at 47 Glencam Road in case you forget The house with the green Door

"Poor kid," said Adam. "I hate to disappoint him but the Christmas arrangements are all finalised. There's no way Jennifer will agree to change them. It's Daisy's first Christmas and Jen has invited her parents over for the day. She has nothing against you –"

"Decent of her." Moira's tone was acid.

"– but it's our first year in the new house and she has her heart set on a traditional family Christmas. There's nothing traditional about an ex-wife at Christmas dinner. I wouldn't mind, but Jennifer is sensitive about these things."

"So she has her heart set on a traditional family Christmas. Doesn't our son count as your family too?"

"Of course he does. Jennifer's mad about Conan. He's a lovable little fellow and good as gold with the baby. He'd be more than welcome to spend Christmas Day with us. But I didn't even suggest it because I thought it wouldn't be fair on you. If you're willing to spare him, we'd be glad to have him."

"It would be like cutting off my right arm but I'd part with him like a shot if it would make Conan happy. But that's not what he's asking for – he wants all of us together on Christmas Day, just for an hour or two. Like it or not, we're his family. All of us. Including your Child-Bride. We're what's called a blended family. Even if the only one prepared to do any blending is our son. Come on, Adam, he's even prepared to trade the Xbox he had his heart set on – he told Santa not to bother with presents. How many eight-year-olds do you know who're willing to sacrifice self-interest?"

"Maybe it's just a notion he has. He might forget all about it in a day or two. The plans are fixed; he knows the drill – I'm dropping in to see him for an hour on Christmas Eve before bedtime, and then he's coming on the skiing holiday with us the day after Stephen's Day while you go to your family in Scotland for the New Year. That suits everybody."

"Judging by the Santa letter, it doesn't suit Conan."

"He's eight years old. He can't expect to run the show. I'll make it up to him in Austria – he'll have a whale of a time on the ski slopes."

Moira made a breastplate of her arms, trying to stay reasonable, although her body language told a different story. Don't let yourself get prickly, she cautioned. Moira had spent all afternoon mulling over her son's letter, wondering whether there was any way the grown-ups might be able to set aside their differences for his sake. Adam seemed intent on dismissing it as a whim, but instinct told his mother this was important to Conan. "Listen, I'm not wild about spending part of Christmas Day with your wife and baby daughter, but at least I'd consider it for Conan's sake. Couldn't you persuade the Child-Bride to behave like an adult?"

"She's twenty-three, Moira, hardly a child."

"And you're thirty-eight." Whoops, that spiteful tone was back in her voice. "How about if the three of you drop in to see Conan on Christmas morning? Just for an hour? Half an hour, even?"

Adam sighed. "I'd love to give Conan what he wants as much as you. It goes without saying. But Jennifer's counting on Christmas Day in our new house. There's no way she'll come out here to Glencam Road. Jen's enormously proud of our home and insists we're going to have a perfect Christmas Day in it."

"Bully for her. But what I'm proud of here is Conan – our son. Now, are we prepared to do nothing and let him think Santa can't deliver? Or are we willing to go the extra mile and give him a Christmas to remember? This could be the last year he believes in Santa Claus."

Adam Kelly scuffed his feet against the hall carpet, wishing he didn't have to try and keep everybody happy. Being divorced and remarried meant he had two women to take into account instead of one. He couldn't write off Moira because she was Conan's mother. But she always looked so aggrieved when they met – resentment etched grooves into the freckled face he had fallen in love with all those years ago, when they were both second-year students at UCD. That was a lifetime ago now. His shoulders slumped and he dragged his hand down the side of his face, a livid weal pooling in its wake. "I'm wrecked, Moira. Daisy's a fitful sleeper and I had about two hours' kip last night. I don't remember it being this hard with Conan at the five-month mark.

Tell you what, how about if I talk it over with Jennifer and come back to you?" Perhaps his wife would be in a generous mood when the champagne was flowing at tonight's party.

"I guess so."

He jingled his car keys. "Good. Maybe Jennifer would consider having you and Conan call over to our place on Christmas morning – that might be the best compromise. We could say it's to help Daisy open her presents."

"Whatever. I can't pretend I'm wild about playing happy families on Christmas morning with your new kith and kin, but if it makes Conan happy I can stomach it."

"I'll do my best to find some middle ground here, Moira. Leave it with me. I'll be in touch." He called down the hallway. "Conan, I'm off now! You got a high five for your dad?"

A blond child in a Harry Potter T-shirt cannoned out of the sitting-room and slapped the palm of his hand against his father's. "Thanks for the ice-skating, Dad. It was cool."

"No problem, chief. Be a good boy for your mum, you hear? See you soon."

Jennifer erupted into sobs when Adam mentioned the Santa letter. He laboured the sentimental aspect, repeating Moira's observation about how rare it was for an eight-year-old to show altruism. Conan had volunteered to go without presents, he reminded her. Jennifer only cried all the louder.

It was the following day before they had their conversation – the time had never seemed right at the party. Adam brought Jennifer a pot of Earl Grey tea in bed, waiting until she was on her second cup before broaching the subject.

The tears might have alarmed him once but he was less moved by them now, for Jennifer leaked like a faulty tap since giving birth to Daisy. He passed her a tissue, moved the cup to safety and stroked her hair while she blubbered.

Finally the shudders eased enough for her to speak. "It's only six days to Christmas. How can you spring this on me?"

"Kitten, I had no idea Conan was going to write this letter to Santa. I'm as surprised as you are."

"It's not fair. I was depending on Christmas Day in our own home – it's all arranged. I wanted everything to be perfect for us."

"He's only a little boy, Jen. He's had it tough with his mum and me splitting up. I'd love us to work something out for him."

Another batch of tears welled up in Jennifer's eyes. "What about me and Daisy? Don't we matter?"

"Of course you do, but Daisy's too young to care about Christmas and I was banking on you seeing the big picture."

"I don't want to see the big picture. I just want Christmas Day to be the way I planned it. It's unnatural expecting your two wives to spend it together." She rolled away, buried her face in a pillow and howled.

Adam tugged on the ponce's velour dressing-gown his wife had bought him, having thrown away his cosy old towelling robe without consulting him, and stomped off for a shower. What he really fancied was a cigarette, but the situation was precarious enough – Jennifer would lose the plot entirely if she smelled smoke on his breath. She was virulently anti-smoking. At least Moira hadn't minded so long as he lit up outdoors, he thought, feeling less disloyal than he usually would if he found himself making comparisons.

"And what about my mother and father?" snuffled Jennifer, when he returned from the bathroom.

That was the trouble with women; they continued conversations hours – sometimes days – later as though there had been no break. He rooted through the sock drawer. "I guess they can put up with it if we can."

"You're such a lapdog to that woman. She has you on the end of a lead." Jennifer would have flounced if she hadn't been lying down. Instead she sat bolt upright, face flushed.

Adam buttoned up a pair of jeans and ignored the jibe. "I'd better go and collect Daisy from your parents. What time did you say we'd fetch her?"

"Oh, so you're worried about Daisy now? I thought Conan was your priority."

"Jennifer, you're being silly. What kind of a father would I be if I forgot about Conan just because Daisy came along? I love both of them equally."

"Equally's not good enough."

"It has to be." Adam's mouth thinned.

Jennifer hesitated. Adam was hardly ever angry. She reconsidered the wail she had been about to vent, instead looking at him with her most appealing expression.

Adam's annoyance faded. "You're overwrought, kitten. You beavered away making sure last night's party was a triumph. I'll go for Daisy while you have a lie-in. Why don't you run yourself a bubble bath by and by? You're always telling me you have no time for baths any more." Adam dropped a kiss on his wife's forehead and closed the door behind him.

By Christmas Eve Jennifer's position still hadn't softened. She had nothing against Conan, but she was jiggered if she was going to exude seasonal bonhomie towards an ex-wife whose pert little nose always looked pinched, as though it smelled something rancid, when they met. Nothing would blemish her Christmas: it had to be idyllic. It just had to be. If it was simply a case of inviting Conan she wouldn't object, but there was no way an ex-wife could be allowed to clutter up her Christmas Day. Jennifer knew Adam was disappointed in her, but she was confident she'd be able to wheedle him into submission – especially when he saw the flimsy confection in ivory lace she'd bought for their holiday. As for Conan, she'd fuss over him extravagantly in Austria. She hummed as she put the finishing touches to her hand-made crackers, while Adam set off to visit his son on Christmas Eve, as arranged.

Moira made a final assault on her ex-husband during a whispered conversation in the kitchen. "He's only eight years old," she pleaded. "Come on, we owe it to him. God knows, we've cheated him enough on the family front."

"It's not down to me – it's down to Jennifer and she won't budge. I can't force her. There's no law that says she has to put our son's interests above her own. Besides, she's a bit nervous of you."

"I make every effort to be civil to your Child-Bride, nobody can accuse me of being impolite towards her. I've nothing against her. It's not as if she was involved in our split – she was too busy making her First Communion at the time."

"Moira, you know perfectly well Jennifer is twenty-three, not thirteen."

"So what do I tell Conan tomorrow morning when he bounces out of bed thinking Santa has laid on the Christmas he's expecting?"

Adam pretended Conan was calling him and walked away.

Moira rang him on his mobile as he was about to turn his key in the ignition.

"I'm still waiting for your answer. What do I tell our son when he asks where his daddy and baby sister are on Christmas Day?"

"You tell him he'll see them in two days' time, when they're all going on holiday together."

"It's not the same, Adam, and you know it."

He held the mobile phone away from his ear and looked at it bleakly.

"Adam?" it crackled. "Are you still there?"

He leaned it against the side of his face again. "I'm still here. Look, all I can promise is to have another crack at Jennifer. I'll ring you if I get any joy, OK?"

"Suppose it has to be."

Conan was puzzled by the Xbox under the Christmas tree. "But I told Santa I didn't need any presents except the one I wrote to him about."

"Maybe he thought you were such a good boy you should have another present anyway." Moira ruffled her son's hair, but he wriggled off her lap and raced to the window.

"I hear a car!"

"It's visitors for next door. Come on, Conan, aren't you going to open your Xbox?"

He regarded it doubtfully. "No, I better not. I'm still waiting for my real present. Santa might have left the Xbox by mistake."

Moira sat looking at him play with the contents of his Christmas stocking, wondering how to spare her son the disappointment she realised was inevitable. "Santa might not have had a chance to read that letter you sent him," she began cautiously. "He gets lots of post in December, you know – millions and millions of Dear Santa letters."

"He'll have read it. Santa can make time to do everything. He's magic that way."

Moira turned aside to hide her expression. "OK, big guy, let's get you dressed and the chocolate wiped off your face, then we'll ring Granny and Grandad in Scotland. They should be back from church by now."

For the rest of the morning Moira kept her ear cocked for the phone, but there was no word from Adam. Conan continued to ignore his Xbox – superstitiously afraid that if he played with it, his Christmas wish might be derailed. Moira watched his eager little face flush with anticipation every time a footfall sounded near their door. By 5 p.m. she could bear the suspense no longer.

"Come on, Conan, coat on – I have a special surprise for you."

"You do?" He fidgeted as she buttoned up his duffel coat, wrapping a scarf around his neck because he was prone to colds.

"Yes, we're going for a drive."

"But what if Dad calls when we're out? We wouldn't want to miss him."

"Little worry-wart." She kissed the tip of his nose.

After two false turns, Moira found the address she was searching for in a cul-de-sac of six houses. She took Conan's hand inside its woollen mitten and led him to the door. "Want me to lift you up so you can ring the bell?"

Sensing something amiss, he shook his head.

Moira pressed her finger against the bell, noticing the tasteful icicle wreath tied to the knocker, and the white fairy lights girdling a palm tree in the garden. Maybe trespassing on someone else's Christmas wasn't such a clever idea, she thought, and an adrenalin jag urged flight.

Just then the door opened. A stranger wearing a taste-bypass tie stood on the floor-mat.

"Hallo," he said.

Moira was dumbstruck. She had expected Adam or Jennifer –

this must be Jennifer's father. She was about to retreat when Conan piped up.

"My name's Conan. What's yours? Is that Rudolph the Red-nosed Reindeer on your tie?"

"It is. If you squeeze his nose he plays 'Jingle Bells'. Would you like a go?"

Conan extended a mitten to the tie, fumbled with it, and as the tune tinkled the silver-haired man observed, "You must be Daisy's brother. I suppose that makes me your grandad too, in a kind of a way. My name is Eddie."

Conan tilted his head to the side, considering. "I have a grandad already, he lives in Scotland. My other grandad's dead."

"Who's at the door, Dad?" Jennifer appeared, carrying a baby.

"Daisy!" Conan broke away from his mother and crossed the threshold, charging towards his sister. He pulled off his mittens and slid a forefinger into her dimpled fist. "What did Santa bring you, Daisy? Did you get lots of presents? I got an Xbox but I might have to give it back."

Daisy burbled at him, drooling.

"Why is everybody standing out here in the cold?" Eddie mimed an exaggerated shiver. "Daisy's granny is inside and I bet she'd like to meet Conan." He raised his eyebrows at his daughter, waiting for her to confirm the invitation.

Jennifer looked cross. Her eyes locked with Moira's; yes, the first wife's nostrils were flaring as if they detected a nasty smell.

Moira cleared her throat. "Merry Christmas, Jennifer. Is this your daughter? She's gorgeous – the image of you."

"Do you think so? Everyone says she takes after Adam."

"Nonsense, she's her mother's daughter. Look at those pianist's fingers."

Jennifer pressed her cheek against Daisy's downy scalp. "She does have long fingers. Nobody except me ever notices."

"It's freezing in here with the door open," said Eddie pointedly.

Jennifer repositioned Daisy in her arms as she attempted a kamikaze dive into Conan's. "Would the two of you like to come in? We've already eaten dinner but I could heat up some mince pies to warm us all up."

"We'd love to, wouldn't we, Conan?"

"We were just about to pull the crackers." Eddie caught Conan by the hand and walked down the hall with him. "Jennifer made her own this year. She has nimble fingers, our girl. Come on, lad, I'll find you a cracker."

"I only made enough crackers for one each," protested Jennifer.

"That's all right. He can have mine. Want to pull it with me, Conan?"

He bustled into the dining-room where Adam and his mother-in-law were clearing the dishes.

"I'm pulling a cracker with Eddie," Conan told his father. "He says if he's Daisy's grandad he's mine too."

"Good for you, chief." Relief, pleasure and a slipstream of guilt crossed Adam's features.

The cracker popped a cigar and a paper motto at Conan's feet.

"I made that cracker especially for Mum and Dad to pull with each other." Jennifer was pettish again.

"Swap you a box of toffees for a cigar, Conan?" offered Eddie.

"Deal. Mum, I can't read all the words. Can you help me?"

Moira read the motto aloud. "*Both of you being here makes this the perfect family Christmas.*"

A gap-toothed grin sliced Conan's face in two.

Holiday Fever

Clare Dowling

Clare Dowling

Clare Dowling has written stageplays, children's fiction, film scripts and five novels. She is currently a scriptwriter for *Fair City* and her latest novel is *No Strings Attached*. She lives in Dublin.

Holiday Fever

Siobhan had just broken up with Gerry. She had caught him on the computer webcam, flirting with some hussy in Tampa and wearing only his boxer shorts. It was unclear what the hussy was wearing, if anything.

"He was always bone-lazy," Siobhan wept. "He couldn't even be bothered to get off his arse and have a proper affair. How am I going to explain this one to the kids?"

In the end they blamed it on "irreconcilable differences" and he left the house quietly that weekend and moved into a flat in town. She made him leave the computer behind.

They had been married fifteen years in March.

Everybody agreed how well she coped. You would hardly know there was a thing wrong if you met her at the school gates. Occasionally the children would find pegs and car keys in their lunch boxes instead of sandwiches but apart from that she was doing very well.

In fact the only people really who guessed how broken she was were her old school friends, Mary and Chris. They had known each other since the days when the nuns used to beat the legs off them all for sneaking a puff of a Major cigarette behind the bike shed with the lads from the Christian Brothers. They were bridesmaids at each other's weddings, and godmothers to each other's children. When Chris got a lump in her breast Mary and Siobhan were there to hold her hand, and run her business for her those days when she just hadn't the energy. When Mary had her annus horribilis – a tax problem, four deaths in the family, the onset of varicose veins, oh she could go on – the girls were there, making big pots of tea, or else gin and tonics, depending on the mood. Whoever said blood was thicker than water had obviously never been in the pub with these three when a crisis reared its head.

It was Mary who first declared that Siobhan needed a holiday.

"Look at you. You're skin and bone – you wagon – and with those circles under your eyes you'll never get a new man."

Siobhan was appalled. "I'm not looking for a new man."

"I was joking."

But Siobhan was very clear on that point. "From now on, it's just me and the kids."

"Still, a bit of sunshine would do you the world of good," Chris cajoled. "It'd boost your Vitamin D apart from anything else." She was doing a night course in nutrition and had them all plagued with what they should and shouldn't be eating. You couldn't even get a decent cup of tea around her place – everything was decaffeinated or else green.

"I can't leave the kids," Siobhan said stubbornly.

But then didn't it transpire that Gerry had splashed out on tickets to EuroDisney for the kids. He would take them to Paris for a whole week and they would stay in a fancy hotel. He didn't consult with Siobhan, he said, because he had wanted it to be a surprise.

"It's pathetic," she said to Mary and Chris venomously. "Talk about trying to buy them off! They're too old for EuroDisney, anyway. They won't even want to go."

They did. They were dying to go. It was "Daddy this" and "Daddy that" and Siobhan's teeth were ground down to stubs by the end of the week.

"It's a perfect time for you to go away too," Chris told her. "There's no sense rattling around an empty house while they're off having a great time." She obviously didn't want to rub it in so she quickly amended this to, "A goodish time."

"I can't go on my own," Siobhan wailed.

Mary and Chris looked at her in amazement. "As if we would let you."

The local travel agent assumed that, at their mature age, they would want a nice quiet resort, with no loud music and a bit of scenery to look at.

"Jesus, it looks like an old folks' home," Mary said when they saw the hotel brochure. "Come on, girls. I'm after making a pact with the devil to get the week off work – can we not go somewhere a bit more exciting?"

"I just want to relax," Siobhan said. She had five books lined up that she had been saving. "I'm not going out there to get hammered every night of the week."

"I'm not either," Chris said swiftly. She was planning on bringing her acupuncture mat.

Mary rolled her eyes. "Well, this is a great start, isn't it?"

In the end they decided on a week in a resort in Spain. There then followed a round of delicate negotiations. In exchange for her freedom Mary had to promise her husband Finn that he could go on that golfing trip with the lads in November. Chris had to leave Dean a detailed list of meals for the week, because amongst her children she had a coeliac, a vegetarian, a wheat-intolerant, and one who was just bloody-minded.

Siobhan had no negotiations to do. The children were so excited about EuroDisney that they barely registered that she was going away too. In fact, she had done such a good job of cushioning their pain over the break-up that her own pain wasn't real to them at all. Still, they were only children. She couldn't go around bawling and keening in front of them. It wouldn't be fair.

The night Gerry came to collect them they piled into the car with their rucksacks and passports with indecent haste.

She forced herself to look at him, because the children were watching. "Don't forget to put sunscreen on them."

He didn't even have the decency to look embarrassed any more. "Yes, yes."

Fusspot. That's what he thought, what they all thought. They drove off at speed, leaving her looking after them like a lemon.

Then the phone rang. It was Chris. "I'm just ringing to say don't forget to pack mosquito spray."

And Siobhan felt a bit less lonely as she went upstairs to finish up.

The plane journey was an adventure. Mary had goaded Chris into having two vodkas in the airport lounge before take-off – "Go on, you're no fun any more!" – but she had never told either of them about her acute fear of flying and the alcohol nearly sent her over the edge altogether. They ended up saying novenas with her at thirty thousand feet. Then didn't Mary recognise somebody from work, a man, a good-looking man to boot, and nothing would do her but to accost him on his way to the toilet and force an introduction between him and Siobhan.

"I'm not interested," Siobhan hissed, once the poor man had finally been released and let on his way.

"Maybe not right now," Mary said confidently. "You never know how you'll feel by the middle of the week."

"What?"

"We're meeting him for dinner on Tuesday."

"*Mary.*"

"You don't have to hop into bed with him or anything. And don't look at me like that. He's lovely."

And he was. He took them to a little place off the beaten track – an authentic experience, he said. Siobhan went to the effort of putting on a nice skirt because she felt she should, and she laughed at all his little jokes. Mary and Chris kept giving her delighted little glances, and Paul – she had difficulty remembering his name – smiled back at her over the scented candles.

"You're doing great," Mary whispered to her.

Inside she felt lost, dead. Her children were in Paris, she was barely on speaking terms with her estranged husband, and her best friends in the world thought she could be fixed with a few drinks and a flirt with a mildly handsome man.

That night she woke in the small hours with a terrible pain in her stomach. For a minute she thought it was grief, because she had been like that in the first days after Gerry had gone.

But this was different; it was a churning, searing pain that had her heart pounding in her chest. She thought she was going to die. She stumbled to the bathroom, heaving, only to find Mary had got there before her and was bent double over the toilet bowl.

"The fish," Mary whispered weakly.

They'd both had it as a main course, after Mary said it was a local delicacy. Chris and Paul had stuck to lamb.

To be honest, Siobhan thought it served Mary right. But what had she ever done to bring this awful thing upon herself, except put up with a creep for all these years? "Shove over there," she said.

Chris slept through the whole thing. It must have been that herbal tea she had brought with her. When she finally awoke, it was to find her room-mates splayed out on their beds, and an alarming green colour.

"I think we got it all up," Siobhan said weakly. "We'll be grand by lunch-time."

By lunch-time Siobhan's face felt tingly and swollen and an ambulance had been summoned to take them to the hospital.

"I don't believe this," Mary kept moaning. She'd got a full spray-on tan and everything in Dublin before flying out. And now Finn was going to get his golfing trip for nothing.

Siobhan just kept thinking of the children. Supposing something happened to her? They had Gerry, she told herself, brain fuzzy. He took them on exciting trips and let them watch all kinds of questionable programmes on his new plasma TV. They probably wouldn't miss her at all.

"Too much to drink last night, ladies?" the ambulance guy enquired as he strapped them in.

Chris had been outraged, but afterwards Mary maintained that it was quite flattering that he had thought they were three wild girls-about-town.

Unfortunately there was a language barrier between the medical staff and the new arrivals in the emergency ward. Chris did her best to convey what was wrong without using any words. It was like a bizarre game of charades, while Mary and Siobhan retched in the background.

Within minutes they found themselves sharing beds in a room on the fourth floor, hooked up to drips and monitors and having their blood pressure taken.

Then the nurse asked, "Do you want us to contact your families back home?"

"We're not going to die or anything, are we?" Mary asked, alarmed.

She was assured that they were not. But they would be very unwell for a day or two. They were dehydrated, and their blood pressure was either sky high or extremely low – they couldn't deduce which. And Mary kept complaining that her teeth felt loose in her mouth. The nurse explained that this was a normal symptom of this kind of poisoning, and that she might expect some temporary blindness too.

"Better give Finn a buzz so," Mary said grimly.

Siobhan thought of her own house in Glasnevin. There was no one to ring, no one who might be concerned about her. They were all in Paris together.

She burst into tears.

"Oh, Siobhan!" Chris, the healthy one, ran to the side of the bed.

The nurse diplomatically left the room.

"Wait till that drip kicks in; you'll be as good as new," Mary consoled her.

Something in Siobhan snapped. Even though she was as weak as a kitten, she managed to sit up in the bed. "If you hadn't organised that stupid dinner, we wouldn't even be here! How could you possibly think I'd be interested in a man, four months after breaking up with my husband? Do you think I'm such an airhead that I could move on that fast? I didn't even want the fucking fish last night. I wanted the lamb, but you talked me into it!"

Mary looked stricken, and even greener than before.

"Siobhan –" Chris began.

Siobhan didn't spare her either. "No, I'm sick of you two thinking that you know what's best for me! Tell me, since when did we start doing that to each other?" She lurched over and grabbed the dividing curtain. "Now if you don't mind, I'd like to be left in peace." She pulled the curtain across, blocking out their faces. Then she lay down on the pillow and cried her eyes out.

She must have fallen asleep at some point because when she woke up it was dark. She felt cooler, less nauseous. The worst seemed to be over.

She could hear Mary stirring behind the curtain, and she lay very still. She didn't want to face her. She was ashamed of her outburst. They were only trying to support her and help her, and she had thrown it back at them.

Then she heard the sound of Mary being violently sick.

She got out of bed and whipped the curtain back.

"Mary?"

Mary was bent double over a bowl, puking her guts up. She looked awful.

"Will I get a nurse?"

"No," Mary managed. "I'll be all right in a minute." She wiped her mouth, while Siobhan got her a glass of water.

"Look, I'm sorry about Paul," Mary said. "It wasn't meant as a date, just a bit of fun, that's all."

"Oh, stop!" Siobhan was mortified. "I'm the one who should be sorry. Giving out to you and Chris like that –"

"But you were right. We were steamrollering you –"

"You weren't. You were just being kind –"

Then a head popped up on a pull-out bed over by the wall. It was Chris, her hair a fright. "Why don't we just have a group hug and be done with it?"

It transpired that she hadn't wanted to leave the two of them, and the nurses had fixed her up with a blanket and even a toothbrush. Chris had earnestly told them at length that they were streets ahead of Irish hospitals, and that she would be writing into the *Irish Times* immediately upon her arrival home to highlight the differences. They didn't understand a word she was saying.

"I was a right cow last night," Siobhan said.

"Yes, but you were entitled," Chris said magnanimously.

"We won't hold it against you," Mary said, before promptly being sick again.

Mary and Siobhan were kept in for three more days. Chris never left during that time, except to go back to the apartment to get a shower and a change of clothes. And while the nurses were lovely, you wouldn't give the food to a dog, and Chris would ferry them in pizza and paninis and Coke from the local shops. She even smuggled in a bottle of wine one night, and they sat cross-legged on Siobhan's bed ostensibly playing cards, but mostly talking. The more Siobhan talked, the better she felt. She told them all about Gerry's nasty bathroom habits, and his poor performances in bed. She even told them for the first time about the night she'd found him in front of the computer in his undies, the "good pair" that he usually only wore on special occasions, and which he'd obviously put on especially for the Tampa Tart, as Mary had christened her. They were a size too small for him too, so it had been quite a spectacle.

Chris, who'd had a glass and half of wine, was squealing with laughter. "Sorry," she managed. "This is probably very painful for you." And she collapsed in a helpless heap again.

Siobhan was laughing too. It was Gerry who was the big sad eejit in all this, not her. She wouldn't take him back in a million years. Not that he had asked or anything. But she wouldn't anyway, if he got down on all fours and begged.

"Let's go to bed," she said. She felt exhausted, but in a nice kind of a way.

The nurses gave out yards to them the next morning when they discovered the empty wine bottle. Chris tried to pretend that she didn't understand them but they weren't having any of it. They gave her a load of papers to sign and began to strip Mary and Chris's beds.

"I think they're kicking us out," Mary said.

They were in fact discharging them. They gave Chris a list of instructions to give to their GPs at home.

"If you feel up to it, we could be packed and to the airport to catch our original flight home," Chris told them as they got a taxi outside.

Was it Saturday already? Siobhan felt disorientated after her four days in hospital.

Mary looked at her. "I think we want to go home, don't we?"

They made the flight just in time. Siobhan felt weak and clammy from the effort as she strapped herself in. Even Mary was quiet, and dozed off as soon as they were airborne.

Siobhan couldn't wait for her own house, her own bed. Hopefully, by the time the kids arrived home from Paris tomorrow, she would be in some shape to face them.

Finn was there to meet them at the other end as they staggered into Arrivals, drunkenly propping each other up.

"If I didn't know better, I'd say ye had a whale of a time," he said. He had a trolley for their bags. "We're giving you a lift home," he told Siobhan. "No arguments about taking taxis."

Actually, she wasn't going to argue. She felt rotten.

Then there was a bit of a commotion to her left.

"Mum! Mum!"

Chris nudged her and pointed. "Look!"

She saw Gerry first. Then the kids bringing up the rear. They were all hurrying towards her and waving. They looked sick with worry.

"What are you doing here?" she asked rather stupidly. Well, they weren't due back till tomorrow.

The kids all spoke at once.

"Chris rang us. We came home early."

"Mam, are you all right? You look awful."

To crown it all, her big, tough-as-nails teenaged son stepped forward to relieve her of her big pink flowery handbag, and slung it manfully over his own shoulder.

Gerry stepped forward. He looked like he'd had a bit of a fright. He'd probably been worried that he'd be landed with the kids if she popped her clogs.

"They were very concerned about you," he told her. "We all were."

Even though it killed her she managed a smile and said, "Thanks."

It was probably the first civil exchange they'd had since he left. It probably wouldn't last, but anyhow.

Chris and Mary waved, and gave her the thumbs up. "See you for coffee as usual on Tuesday, if we're still alive," Mary called.

Then Gerry picked up her bag and led the way to the carpark.

Siobhan followed with the kids. They walked very close to her, arms linking hers.

"How was EuroDisney?" she said.

The kids exchanged a glance, and made sure that Gerry was too far ahead to hear. They wrinkled their noses. "We were too old for it."

And Siobhan felt better and better.

Jet Set

Anne Dunlop

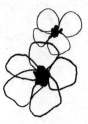

Anne Dunlop

Anne Dunlop has lived in the Middle East where she worked as an airstewardess, mixed with the jet-set and suffered from jet-lag. Anne wears orange lipstick and believes in love at first sight; and she has a passion for Italian cooking. Anne insists that all characters and events in her story are entirely fictitious.

Jet Set

Elaine Darling painted on a flaming orange smile and attached the rest of the armour. Dagger-high heels, parachute-harness brassiere, bullet-proof support tights. Sharpened her flaming orange talons, inhaled her poison-gas perfume.

Thin Lizzy's "Jail Break" blared in the background. Elaine always played "Jail Break" to psyche herself up for work.

Her high heels were polished until her flaming orange smile was reflected in them. Her matching underwear was bleached snow-white, her support tights had no ladders. She checked her tidy handbag. Passport, flying licence, ID. Check. Hairspray, perfume, lipstick. Check.

One last squirt of deodorant. One last quick glance in the mirror. To check. She did not look beautiful but she looked like an airstewardess.

Vanessa Smyth Jones perspired politely in the baking heat of the transport bus taking A Crew to the airport. It was only nine o'clock in the morning but the Middle East is a sauna in the summertime and Vanessa's armpits had begun to seep. It was so humid her sunglasses had steamed up. Already her French Plait was escaping from its staff-issue scrunchie. And her tummy wouldn't stop wriggling with nerves.

She'd been in bed since ten o'clock the night before, tossing and turning, counting sheep, counting aircraft, counting the hours, minutes and seconds remaining until lights, camera, action stations – she had to get up, put on her uniform and her make-up and brave another cabin full of terrifying passengers with their fingers glued to the call bell.

Airstewardessing had seemed like such a good idea at the time – a rite-of-passage in the freedom years between private school and a respectable marriage – her mother had been an airstewardess . . .

"Join an airline and see the world for free!" Mummy said and there'd been endless gin-soaked reminiscences such that Vanessa had truly believed that every passenger she'd meet would wear a floor-length real fur coat and carry real jewels in her hand luggage . . .

Jackie Diamond was the Cabin Crew manager of Ex-Pat Air, the small private airline which ferried ex-pats in and out of the Middle East – her office was at Bahrain International Airport. Through a shuttered window with mirrored glass she monitored all Ex-Pat aircrews as they went on duty and as they came off duty. She missed nothing. Bleached hair, creased uniforms, chipped nail polish, lipstick on teeth, hairy calves poking through support tights. Nothing.

Jackie was waiting for A Crew.

First Elaine. Chin up, shoulders back, chest out, tummy in. Airstewardesses rarely make heads turn but people pointed and stared when Elaine strode through Bahrain Departures. A sea of suitcases parted, hippie traveller types stood to attention and children ran away screaming.

But for the impudent wiggle of her buttocks she could have been in the army.

Jackie rarely smiled, and never in front of the airstewardesses but she allowed herself a tiny pat on the back, a modest flutter of pride, when she saw Elaine.

Elaine, she was confident, had the experience and the panache to fasten *anyone's* seatbelt with aplomb. What a pity there were not more Ex-Pat airstewardesses like her.

"Where is Vanessa Smyth-Jones?"

Jackie looked down the polished marble Departures Hall, past the hippies and the veiled ladies and the children and the suitcases and the briefcases and the rucksacks. No Vanessa.

"Halt!" Jackie commanded, and the airstewardesses halted. "Where's Vanessa?"

Vanessa appeared through the masses. Her posture was perfect of course. She was the only girl never to drop a book balanced on her head in Ex-Pat Air deportment lessons, she oozed education, breeding and manners, but her face was an unbecoming green beneath her make-up and her veil was shining with sick.

"I'm so sorry," said Vanessa poshly, dabbing her crusty veil with a handkerchief. "When we arrived at the airport I began to feel decidedly unwell, then I suddenly realised I had to vomit. I could actually feel my breakfast rising from my stomach. I had just reached the public lavatory when it was propelled out with an inhuman retching noise. I'm afraid passengers may have heard. My eyes were running and all the muscles in my chest and stomach are aching with such convulsive heaving."

Elaine sniggered. She and Vanessa had been best friends since meeting at an Ex-Pat Air selection day in Belfast. They'd shared a hotel bedroom during the six-week training course. They'd shared a flat since becoming fully fledged airstewardesses. There was *nothing* they did not know about each other.

"Poor Posh Paws!" said Elaine. "Did you swallow a dictionary for breakfast? Is that why you're puking?"

"Stage fright," said Vanessa quietly. "Very boring. Very Sorry."

"Come into my office, Miss Smyth Jones," said Jackie in a ghastly voice. "I'd like to have a little word with you . . ."

Jackie Diamond's office had four square, white-mirrored walls and harsh overhead lights. There was one desk, one chair, filing cabinets, in-trays and out-trays and a set of bathroom scales. Ex-Pat airstewardesses stood to attention in Jackie's office. They answered "Yes, Jackie" or "No, Jackie" or "Three bags full, Jackie" when spoken to and they never answered back. If Jackie said "Jump" the airstewardess asked "How high, Jackie?"

Jackie thrust a Letter of Complaint under Vanessa's nose.

"What does this mean? Does this mean you *refused* to give a First Class child a Pepsi?"

"No." Vanessa shook her head, or perhaps her head shook with the rest of her body because she was trembling. "I didn't *refuse* to give the child a Pepsi. The child snapped its fingers at me and said 'Give me Pepsi' and I said, 'What's the magic word?'"

"The magic word?" said Jackie heavily.

"The magic word is 'please'," Vanessa explained.

"This passenger," Jackie enunciated her words clearly, "this *First Class* passenger says you were discriminating –"

"I was not discriminating against that cheeky brat." Vanessa was horrified. She was a nicely brought up young lady – well educated, well bred and well mannered. She'd been programmed from birth to always say the right thing. "I don't discriminate against people. I dislike anyone who has no manners."

"It's not your job to teach our passengers manners," said Jackie and she placed a black mark beside Vanessa's name on the office file. "One more letter of complaint," she threatened, "and you're out!"

Ex-Pat Air flight EX101 was packed with noisy excited families hopping home to Cairo for the summer holidays. After take-off Elaine buzzed up and down the cabin, reading minds and anticipating wishes – she was a natural-born airstewardess and the passengers loved her; ding ding ding went the call bells and she was repeatedly requested to pose for photographs and autographs.

Meanwhile Vanessa was politely checking each passenger's boarding card and serving lunch.

"I'm really sorry, madam. You can't sit here. This is a First Class seat and you have a Second Class ticket."

"You're discriminating against me," said madam, "because I'm a woman travelling without a husband."

When she was moved she said, "Get me milk and diapers for my baby."

And it didn't stop there.

"Do you have a laundry on board?" she asked. "I want my jacket pressed."

"I don't want curried lentils for lunch," she said. "I want a McDonalds."

All in a day's airstewardessing.

Until she said, "Get me a glass of water."

Vanessa flashed an enormous smile. "What did you say?" and the hysterical lady made her fatal mistake.

She said, "You are my servant. Get me a glass of water."

In deadly silence Vanessa lifted a bottle of water from the meal cart and poured it over her head.

When Elaine got home from the airport she showered away the smells of Breakfast, Brunch, Lunch, Afternoon Tea, Dinner and Supper. She poured herself into a shoulder-baring red dress which emphasised her cleavage and hugged her bum. She put Frizz Ease on her hair and Fire Engine Red on her mouth.

Then she opened her *How to Make 200 Cocktails* book.

Two highball glasses had been chilling in the fridge since morning. She carefully measured 60ml of Smirnoff Silver Label and 120ml of freshly squeezed orange juice into each of them. Stirred with a swizzle stick. Opened the bottle of Galliano bought in Bahrain Arrivals Duty Free and floated 20ml on top. Placed the Harvey Wallbangers on a tray robbed from 'Cocktail' in New York and carried them into the living room to where Vanessa lay prostrate, dribbling into her veil.

"Thanks for squeezing the oranges," said Elaine. "I should really, I suppose, have sliced one to garnish the edge of the glass."

"You're welcome, my darling."

But Vanessa had other things on her mind.

"Do you think Jackie Diamond will get a letter of complaint from the rude woman I poured water over? Do you think the next day we go to work she's going to be waiting for me at her office door with a letter of compulsory resignation in her hand?"

Elaine dug into her handbag and pulled out a passenger In Flight survey form. She handed it to Vanessa.

"I forgot to give this to you when we disembarked – here's your letter of complaint. Once the rude woman had finished writing it I offered to take it into the office for her . . ."

Oh, the relief! Vanessa grinned at her friend. "Thanks, Elaine! I owe you!"

Elaine lit a cigarette and offered Vanessa one.

"What are you doing tonight, Vanessa? Do you fancy coming out for an hour? Just an hour. We can come home then if we feel like it."

"I'd love to," said Vanessa, "but I have my Italian cookery class tonight – Alessandro is teaching us to make *tiramisu*. And such a tiresome afternoon I had yesterday scouring Bahrain for *savoiardi*. Up and down the biscuit rows of every supermarket on the island. In the end I had to ask a member of staff and do you know what he told me? '*Savioardi* not in season, madam!' How can a sponge finger not be in season?"

Elaine tossed back her Harvey Wallbanger.

"You'd better be careful, Vanessa," she warned, "or you're going to wake up some morning and discover you're the girl who can't get up because you're depressed because you don't have a boyfriend."

Elaine didn't have a boyfriend either but she was an optimist. Her motto was: "Tonight might be the night. I might meet *The One*, and I won't meet him by staying in."

So every night she went to Slappers, and during Happy Hour got slightly wasted on cheap wine. Then she'd scan the night's talent by walking slowly round and round the nightclub, traversing hidden corners, inspecting every male minutely, giving him time to inspect her.

Last night she'd met two men – Craig, a sailor who was dead funny and had tattoos, though admittedly one did sport the legend *Mum*. And John Jacques, a muscle-bound Adonis from Brittany. Oh la la, he'd ravished her the French way and she still hadn't got over it.

"Well, *I* think you're trying too hard," said Vanessa firmly.

"Waiting for love is like waiting for a kettle to boil – the more you watch it, the longer it takes. Some day, when you're least expecting it, when you're not dressed for it, the thunderbolt of love will strike."

"How would you know? By your own admission, you've only ever slept with a teddy bear!"

By one thirty Elaine had become restless at Slappers. Her jolly, naughty, 'don't care if I do, don't care if I don't, girls just want to have fun' mood was fading. In its place a flutter of insecurity. Tonight wasn't going to be the night. Slappers closed at two. Soon it would be time for 'New York, New York'. Unless it was love at first sight she wasn't going to meet *The One*.

Last night there'd been a scuffle when John Jacques muscled in on Craig. Craig had told him "keep off my patch," and John Jacques had flexed his muscles and suggested they go outside to duel. Elaine had quelled the riot by getting in the middle and looking worried – but feeling marvellous and suppressing joyous laughter at the same time. No thunderbolts, but it was fun while it lasted.

A couple appeared from the sofas at the far side of Slappers and began to dance, the vertical expression of their horizontal desire. Elaine's heart shot into her throat, then dropped like a stone. The man's face was lost in the woman's cleavage but his buttocks in faded Levis were unforgettable. It was John Jacques who had promised her "*le soleil, la lune et les étoiles*" only the night before.

Oh la la, thought Elaine stoically, all's fair in love and war and there *was* the language barrier to consider. "*Oh la la!*" was the only French Elaine knew. John Jacques could have been promising her anything last night and she still would have slept with him.

Elaine decided to have another Harvey Wallbanger when she got back into her flat. She didn't bother measuring the Smirnoff

Silver Label into the highball glass and as there was no freshly squeezed orange juice left she dolloped Vanessa's tiramisu into the vodka instead. She forgot about Galliano.

Elaine allowed a few tears of self-pity to seep through. She took them home, no names, no pack drill and they didn't call her. She played hard to get and they didn't call her. She compromised and snogged them on the sofas in Slappers and they didn't call her. What was she doing wrong?

This time she splashed the Smirnoff Silver Label into the bowl of tiramisu and remembered to add Galliano.

Vanessa heard her in the kitchen and, full of concern, with a slight touch of irritation got up to investigate.

Not again. Elaine was vomiting into her Italian masterpiece.

"It's not very nice, Vanessa. I think the sponge fingers aren't in season."

Carefully Vanessa helped Elaine to undress. She put a bucket beside her bed, a glass of water on the bedside table, a cool wet tea towel on her forehead. She sat with her till she fell asleep.

There were no recriminations. Usually she saved those for morning when Elaine would wake up so hung over she didn't know what day of the week it was, and would pull the sheet over her head and try to die of shame.

Then she'd stand at the end of Elaine's bed and say:

"You vomited down the front of your dress last night again, Elaine. I've soaked it in soda water. It's in the kitchen sink."

Then she'd say what she always said:

"You really should try to learn from your mistakes, Elaine. They don't call you because in that red dress they think you're a prostitute. So they just ship in, shoot their load and ship out again. You should either start charging or stay single. *I* think you should stay single for six months."

And Elaine would promise to change and would genuinely think she could. Vanessa might even make her breakfast in bed. And Elaine would convalesce all afternoon, feeling fragile and thinking long.

By six o'clock she would be feeling better.

"What are you doing tonight, Vanessa? Do you fancy going out for an hour? Just an hour, we can come home then if we feel like it."

And thus the vicious circle would repeat itself.

But this morning was different.

As usual Elaine woke so hung over that she didn't know what day of the week it was; she pulled the sheet over her head and tried to die of shame.

But instead of coming into her bedroom to scold her, Vanessa came in and said:

"I'm taking a picnic lunch to Sheik's Beach. Would you like to come?"

(Sheik's Beach was where the Amir of Bahrain had his summer palace – it was the only place on the island where western ex-pats had an open invitation to wear bikinis, frolic in the pleasure gardens and swim in the Arabian Gulf without offending local sensibilities.)

Elaine lifted her thumping head a fraction from the pillow.

"I don't think so, Vanessa . . ."

"Oh come on! Just an hour. We can come home then if we feel like it . . ."

Reluctantly Elaine heaved herself out of bed and into the shower.

She showered away the smells of Harvey Wallbanger, cheap white wine, tiramisu and tears. She threw a loose cotton dress over her bikini and shook out the thick ropes of her curly blonde hair. A large sunhat, a pair of plastic flip-flops, a bottle of water and a couple of happy-ever-after novels in her beach bag. She was good to go.

Elaine dozed on the tufted grass in the pleasure gardens at Sheik's Beach; her happy-ever-after novels propped up her head. The warm sun kissed the tanned naked skin of her belly, a gentle breeze ruffled her blonde highlights. Already she was feeling well enough to idly scan the sunburnt groups of ex-pat talent playing beach volleyball on the hot sand in front of her.

What a pleasant way to spend a day off! Why hadn't she thought of it before?

Vanessa, singing softly in a caftan, was preparing their lunch – smoked salmon, cream cheese, crusty bread, a fastidious smattering of black pepper, a little squeeze of lemon juice. A bottle of champagne chilled in an ice bucket.

"You've gone to a lot of trouble . . ." said Elaine.

"I'm expecting a friend."

"What friend?"

"Just somebody from my Italian cookery classes – I *had* planned to bring the tiramisu . . ."

Elaine was stretching her best assets in the direction of the beach-volley-ball-playing talent when a man strode out of the hot salty Gulf. He was young and handsome, broad at the shoulders, his biceps bulged, dark chest hair sprouted, and he was squeezed into miniscule swimming trunks that left nothing to the imagination.

"Taxi!" said Elaine – a taxi was the special gold-plated type of talent, so good-looking and attractive that no questions were needed. On the rare occasion that she caught one at Slappers she

117

gratefully leapt into a taxi with him and took him home, no names, no pack drill . . .

The man shook silver water droplets from his black hair and started to walk towards Elaine. Their eyes met.

"I think I can hear a violin playing," said Elaine and she experienced a sudden severe crushing pain in the centre of her chest which spread to her arms and throat and back. Frightened and in pain, her body went into shock. Sheik's Beach blurred and swam hazily in front of her eyes; her body temperature dropped and she began to shiver. Panicking, she forgot to breathe.

It was the thunderbolt of love . . .

"Vanessa," she whispered, "he's *The One!*"

Vanessa waved to *The One*.

"Yes, he's the one we're waiting for – Alessandro, from my Italian cookery class . . ."

The Man
from
Princes' Island
and
Other Friends

A M Forrest

A M Forrest

Anne Marie Forrest is the author of the bestselling novels: *Who Will Love Polly Odlum?, Dancing Days, Something Sensational* and *The Love Detective*. After many years living in Australia and in Dublin, Anne Marie now lives in Cork with her husband and two young daughters.

The Man
from
Princes' Island
and
Other Friends

Chances are, but for Bríd, I'd have gone through life without ever having smeared my face with blackberries. At a guess, I'd say we were aged seven and on our way home from school, dawdling most probably, when we noticed it – a bush thick with juicy berries. Presented with such an opportunity, most kids would have filled their bellies to bursting. We didn't. We took one look at the bush and decided that, of course, we'd rub them all over our faces. What else! No, I don't know what we were thinking either, though it must have seemed like a great idea at the time.

Bríd was my first best friend. We became friends the day I started school. Being a whole year plus a day older than me, she took me under her wing. Until the age of nine, we walked to school and back each day together, hand in hand. Then, one day, a thought occurred to us – weren't we a little too old to be still holding hands? Once that realisation struck, once it was voiced – that was it. There was no going back; we could never do it again. We walked to and from school for many more years, just not holding hands.

I don't remember what we used to talk about in those days but what I do know is that without her friendship I wouldn't be exactly the person I am today. Together, we sounded out ideas and tried to figure out what life was all about. We shared our thoughts and experiences, and had new ones together. Who knows how much of me rubbed off on her, or her on me, through our almost daily contact but I'm guessing traces are still there to this day. Though our lives went separate ways, our childhood friendship helped form our grown-up selves.

And isn't that the way with all friendships? Don't they all leave something behind? But for other friends made later, I might never have developed a liking for singer Jonathon Richmond. Or Neil Young. Or Jeff Buckley. Or Lou Reed. I might never have read *Wuthering Heights* and now count it amongst my all-time favourites. Left to my own devices, there's no way I'd ever have joined a basketball team and neither would I have discovered the joys of a sausage-and-ploughman's-pickle sandwich on a Saturday morning after a late night out.

Without friends I'd almost definitely have got this far through life with fewer visits to A & E. If, at age eight, I hadn't gone for that cycle with friends, I wouldn't have fallen off my brand-new bicycle and smashed my brand-new teeth. If, at eighteen, I hadn't gone camping with friends to Cape Clear I'd never have got so sunburnt that little children scattered in my wake. If, at twenty-eight, friends hadn't convinced me that at a visit to the ice rink was a good idea, I'd never have found myself crashing to the ground and breaking my cheekbone.

But for Bríd, I'd probably never have gone inter-railing at seventeen. But for my friend Marie, I'd probably never have found myself in the south of France a few years later with no money and no way home. But for Gráinne, I wouldn't have gone to London to work that summer. Each of those trips was an adventure, each had a story, or stories rather – too long to recount here, but, to this day, these trips, these stories, these friendships have a place in my memory.

Some poll, somewhere, has worked out (don't asked me how) that on average we make 396 friends in a lifetime. The bad news is that we lose most of them along the way. Out of the group of six of us who went camping on Cape Clear, I haven't seen five of them in as many years. The various friends who introduced me to Jeff Buckley, sausage-and-ploughman-pickle sandwiches, *Wuthering Heights* and basketball are scattered far and wide. Yes, one of the greatest joys of life is making friends. One of the greatest regrets is that we end up losing so many of them.

Wouldn't it be great if we could round up every friend we ever made, take them all off on holiday and spend a week enjoying their company? Or maybe not. Some would have changed. Some would find that we've changed.

It's a little like real life, isn't it? We change. Our circumstances change. I think back to friendships I once had that were such a part of my everyday life. Some friendships ran their natural course and fizzled out, but sometimes circumstances changed, one or other person moved away (as life turned out, most often me) and the friendship gradually became less and less of an important part of daily life, no matter how much one might have wished it to be otherwise.

I've moved around a lot, and made a lot of friendships. Kevin in Dublin, Rosary in Dundalk, Caroline in Wicklow, Deirdre in

Australia and many more besides. Some friends I still see, others not. Once-daily calls give way to weekly calls, and then dwindle to monthly, and, finally, the only contact is a postcard at Christmas. But that doesn't mean these friends are forgotten. Every friend I've ever made has enriched my life in some way. Some in small ways, some in big, but they all leave something behind. I still remember Deirdre's kindness, Rosary's wildness, Caroline's sense of fun. Yesterday, driving along in the car, I found myself turning the radio up when I heard Jeff Buckley coming on to play and memories came flooding back. The other day, someone happened to ask me what my favourite book was. I told them *Wuthering Heights* and remembered the time my friend gave it to me as a present. This morning, I had one of those fat-laden sausage-and-pickle sandwiches and thought of my first introduction to them

Some friends stay with us for years and years, a lifetime if we're lucky, but not all have to be lifelong friends to be a lifelong influence.

When my husband and I were both young and foolish, we decided to go to Turkey on holiday. Before we left, Rob, my husband (then boyfriend), mentioned our holiday plans to a work colleague whose father-in-law, as it happened, lived on one of the Princes' Islands, near Istanbul. He gave Rob this man's number and told him to be sure to look him up.

Soon after, we headed off on our holiday. We took a charter flight to Izmir, hightailed it out of there quickly and set off to explore the country. For a week we travelled around until, finally, we found ourselves in Istanbul. One night, Rob took out the scrap of paper and made a call.

On the end of the line came a worried voice: "Where are you? Didn't you fly in last week? We thought something had happened to you."

Rob assured him we were fine, and then accepted his gracious invitation to come stay with him. It turned out that this man and his wife lived in the grandest house I'd never seen: high ceilings decorated with frescos, huge windows looking out onto a yacht-strewn sea. Every day for a week, our new friend travelled into Istanbul on the ferry with us and brought us to all the sights. If he didn't feel up to traipsing around a particular attraction (he was quite elderly) he simply stayed outside and waited. Each lunch time he took us to some terribly grand restaurant, treating us to an array of meals just one of which would have blown our entire budget. Each evening his wife cooked us dinner and, over a fine bottle of wine, we listened to stories of their fascinating lives.

On the final day, we insisted we take him for lunch for a change and reluctantly he gave in. Rightly guessing our pockets weren't as deep as his, he chose a nice, simple and so, so much cheaper restaurant. Finally it was time to move on. We said our goodbyes and promised to send him postcards. To my greatest shame, we never did.

But you know, I think that man wouldn't have held it against us, he was that kind. He was old and wise enough to understand how careless the young can be. I only met him that one time but few people have made such a lasting impression. He took us as we were. He looked out for us. He looked after us. He enjoyed us. He delighted in our delighting in all the wonders of his city. He didn't want anything in return, apart from our company. More than anything, at age seventy, he was alive, eager, still open to the idea of making new friends. We were lucky to have him as our friend, if just for a week.

I'd like to think I'm a little better for knowing that man on Princes' Island. I'd like to think that, one day, when I'm an elderly woman and I get a phone call out of the blue from two foreign teenagers, friends of friends, I'll find myself insisting that they come and stay; that like him I'll know that strangers are just friends waiting to happen.

One of life's great pleasures is making friends; one of life's regrets is losing them but how much poorer our lives would be without them. Every friendship – whether it lasts for decades, or just a week – leaves something behind. A love of Jeff Buckley, or a new experience, or a new way of looking at things. We are who we are because of the friends we've made throughout our lives.

I'll end by quoting two French writers, François Mauriac and Anaïs Nin: *"No love, no friendship,"* Mauriac knew, *"can cross the path of our destiny without leaving some mark on it forever."* *"Each friend,"* Nin understood, *"represents a world in us, a world possibly not born until they arrive, and it is only by this meeting that a new world is born."*

I'm lucky to have known those many who've left their mark and I look forward to the new worlds, the new friendships, yet to be born.

A Special Breed

Suzanne Higgins

Suzanne Higgins

Suzanne Higgins previously worked in the media industry as a radio broadcaster. She is now a full-time novelist and mum of four. Her previous novels include *The Power of A Woman*, *The Woman He Loves* and *The Will to Win*. She is currently writing her fourth novel.

A Special Breed

Miriam Zietek loved her new job in Madden's On The Corner. They sold the daily papers, sweets and more recently they had started a card section because Mr Madden decided that there "might be a bit of a profit in it". He didn't like all the glitter on some of the cards, however. Nor did he like the smutty ones and there seemed to be a lot of them. For this reason Miriam was put in charge of the cards section. She had to keep stock levels high and liaise with Joe, the (cute) card rep. She liked the responsibility and hoped that maybe, just maybe, old Mr Madden would let her run the entire shop at some stage in the future. After all, he was leaving the place entirely in her care most mornings now.

It was Valentine's morning and Miriam was expecting a bit of a rush on the cards during the day as people started to panic-buy promises of their unending love. Early in the morning an old man, much like Mr Madden himself, came into the shop and began to peruse the stock of romantic cards.

Miriam saw him come in and watched him as he looked through the shelves but she didn't get involved until he glanced around as if looking for assistance.

"Hello," she smiled. "Can I help?"

He nodded back at her. "Yes, please, I'm looking for a Valentine's card," he said, stating the obvious.

The man must have been in his eighties, she decided. He wore a long grey coat that might well have been older than her. His flat cap sat on top of very thin hair and he looked slightly frail.

Good for him, she thought. It was wonderful that a man of his vintage was still trying to keep romance in his life.

"There are a few different kinds," Miriam explained. "There are some really nice romantic ones." She gestured towards the cards that were covered with roses and other nondescript flowers in soft focus. Her customer pulled one out.

He tilted his head slightly as he tried to read the particularly ornate writing. "*My love is like a red red rose . . .*" he started and then he read the inside. "Oh no, no, this will never do. It's far too maudlin. God, I wouldn't have sent her that even in our youth. Who sends these drippy cards? They'd put you to sleep!" He looked at Miriam incredulously.

She smiled patiently. "There are as many different types of cards as there are people," she explained.

He seemed to find this acceptable. With that another customer entered the shop. Both the old man and Miriam turned around.

"You go ahead, child. I'll keep looking here," he said.

She nodded by way of acknowledgement and returned to her spot behind the till. As was always the case when one customer entered the shop, a flock followed. It seemed to be either a feast or a famine in the newsagent's but she had long ago given up finding the logic behind that. It was some twenty minutes later before the place was empty again. Empty, with the exception of her Valentine's card man.

Miriam decided to approach him once more.

"Any luck?" she enquired lightly but he shook his head.

"How can there be so many and I can't find a single suitable one?"

"I don't think you like the over-romanticised ones?" she offered, noticing how thin his hands were. He was running his finger along the tops of the cards as if this would help him decide.

"Definitely not. Me and my gal, we still have a laugh together. I'd like to get her a funny one but so many of these are just blunt and rude," he huffed. "Nothing left to the imagination any more, that's the problem these days. Where's the fun in that?"

"You have a point," she agreed, wincing as she remembered putting in the order.

"Arrah, don't worry," he winked at her. "I'm sure the young bucks will buy them. I'm just an old fella and I like the more traditional methods – but not those," he scoffed, pointing at the rose cards.

Miriam was charmed by him. He really was a character and it was refreshing to see one so mature still full of beans and still courting his woman. She tried to guide him away from the really rude ones to the slightly milder one-liners.

"Do you get her a card every year, then?" she ventured.

The old man beamed back. "I haven't missed a Valentine's Day in seventy-one years. She's the love of my life and I'd get her a card every week of the year if she would let me, only she'd tell me to cotton on to myself."

Miriam laughed. "Oh, that there were more men around like you!"

He looked surprised.

"It's true," she went on. "There are no romantics around any more."

"Ah," he nodded with understanding, "we're *a special breed*, you see. The ones who know how to romance a woman properly." He winked at her and then continued. "You have to treat *every* woman like she's the *only* woman and more than that, you must treat her like a lady. It's that simple, you know. You have to buy her flowers but they don't have to be big and expensive because it's just the thought. All ladies like chocolates too – again, not necessarily a big box – because then they'll only get upset about putting on the weight. You can't beat a wee box of Roses on a Monday night though," he added sagely as he reached over and squeezed Miriam's upper arm. "Gives a woman a lift, you know – chocolate. It's the chemicals."

Miriam had to stop herself from laughing as he continued.

"We romantics know when to tell her she looks pretty even if she's a bit off colour. We say the food is wonderful even if it's gruel. Is that what you mean?"

Miriam clapped. "Exactly! Where has all that romance gone?" He shrugged. "Dunno." He picked out another card with a cartoon of a man and a woman on a bicycle.

"Funny thing is, when we were young we had none of the stuff you have today. No TV, no computers. We didn't even have a car. We made our own fun. In fact, if you had a bike," he held up the card, "you were considered well off."

"Is that what it is, do you think? Do we have too much of everything and now we're just spoilt?"

He rubbed his soft chin speculatively and nodded. "Ah, that might be it." He looked around the shop and spotted Miriam's stool in the corner.

She understood. "Would you like to sit down?"

He gave a tiny nod but it was enough for her to comprehend and so she rushed over to get the seat for him. She was loving their conversation and the shop was quiet, so why not enjoy his company? After all, as he said himself, he was *a special breed*.

The old man looked at Miriam properly for the first time. "I'm Tom," he said, stretching out his right hand to shake hers. "What's your name?"

She took his hand to shake it. "My name is Miriam but most people call me Mim – pleased to meet you."

In a fluid movement he brought her hand to his lips and brushed them with a very soft kiss. "Enchanted, Lady Mim. Now, you . . ." he said, eyes twinkling, "we never had your kind here when I was a lad, by God, we didn't!" He admired her long sheath of platinum blonde hair. "Those eyes, well, surely they're driving some young fella around these parts wild. They're sapphire blue. You're gorgeous, you are."

She giggled skittishly. "I am from Poland but since I got here, and indeed back at home also, I must say there are no men I know as romantic as you."

"What? Are you telling me you have no boyfriend? Are they all blind, the young lads today? This can't be right."

She shrugged. It was sad but true. There was a huge Polish community and although she did socialise with Irish guys too, she didn't seem to meet anybody particularly special.

"It's not just me," she said sadly. "It's all my friends – Polish and Irish. Some of them have boyfriends and, yes, some of them are romantic but not like the way you're describing."

The old man took off his hat and scratched his nearly bald head. "I don't know, at all." He studied Miriam's face for a moment as if trying to weigh up the situation and then he nodded, as he appeared to arrive at some sort of mental decision.

He reached inside his ancient coat and took out his wallet. With a slight shake in his hand he opened it and eased out an old worn black-and-white photograph.

"This," he said studying the photo himself, "this is the woman who stole my heart seventy-one years ago. I tell you she was some honey." He clicked and winked at the picture.

With great care Miriam took the precious photograph. It was obviously very delicate. The corners were frayed and she was scared of damaging it.

Tom sighed. "I met her when I was fifteen years old and it was love at first sight I can tell you."

"Was it the same for her – love at first sight, I mean?" The young girl was enthralled.

He laughed. "Not at all! She didn't even like me. I had to work hard and buy a lot of chocolates but eventually I wore her down. We courted for three years and that's a picture of her on her eighteenth birthday. We got engaged that day," he added proudly.

Miriam studied the lucky young girl in the ancient photograph. She wasn't at all glamorous in a calf-length pleated skirt and a short-sleeved blouse. She stood in the middle of a nondescript small garden and there was a mongrel sniffing the grass behind her. But her smile was still – even across the decades – a one-thousand-kilowatt smile.

"She looks very happy," Miriam said. "Even if she didn't love you at first sight it certainly looks like she came to love you deeply if this photo is anything to go by."

Tom nodded with satisfaction. "Ah yes, that's my Nelly. We had a good life and four lovely children. We've been very lucky."

"Four? Big family by today's standards." She handed the photo back with the reverence it merited.

Tom was deep in thought. "You know, I'm just thinking about

what you're saying – that there's no nice fellas around these days."

"None with your sense of romance. That's for sure."

"Well, Nelly was having none of me in the beginning either, you know. I think what I'm trying to say is you have to give a lad a chance. I only cottoned onto this courtship lark as I went along."

Miriam looked at him but she wasn't convinced so Tom persevered.

"You see, you can't tell a book by its cover so don't jump to conclusions. If a nice boy asks you out but you don't think he's the one, well, go on the date anyway and sure maybe you'll be happily surprised."

She smiled at him. There was some logic in what he said and giving out about the absence of great romantics certainly didn't seem to be working.

"Having met you, I'll certainly think about it," she agreed.

"Now," he said as he gently put the photograph back in his wallet, "I think I'll take that one." He pointed to the card with the old couple on the bicycle.

Miriam knew that it was some joke about recycling and it would probably suit him perfectly.

He rose from the stool and headed over to the counter to pay for his purchase as Miriam headed back behind the counter.

"Oh, and I'll take these two," he added.

She looked up to see him holding two of the ones he had called "maudlin". She couldn't believe it. Was it possible that he had a couple of women on the side? Surely not. He couldn't – not after all he had said about Nelly.

Tom saw the confusion on her face. "They're for my daughters," he grinned. "What did I just say to you about jumping to conclusions?" He chuckled at her expense as Joe, the (cute) card rep walked in.

"Hi, Mim," Joe mouthed over the old man's head.

"Hi," she grinned back.

But Tom saw the teeny tiny spark. The fashions might change and life might move on but the spark was still the spark and he knew it when he saw it.

"Tell me now, son," the old man addressed Joe, "do you have a girlfriend?"

Joe looked surprised but not too put out as he shook his head.

"Great. That's a good start because this lovely young woman here is Miriam but her friends call her Mim and she's single too. She's a fine-looking woman, I think you'll agree."

Joe couldn't believe what he was hearing but found it amusing at the same time. "Ah, yes, I'd definitely agree with you there, sir."

Miriam on the other hand was mortified.

"I'm too old for her and anyway I'm spoken for but you're not. Will you ask her out and show her the sights of Dublin?"

Joe burst out laughing.

"And, son," Tom whispered, "buy her chocolates."

The old man didn't wait for a reply because he knew that his work was done. He took his three cards and bade his goodbyes. The young ones would find their own way just as he and Nelly had done. When he came out of the shop he looked up at the sky and winked at the clouds.

"I'm still doing it, darlin', just as you asked. Every Valentine's Day I'm playing Cupid. Keep an eye on those two, would you?"

He grinned at the heavens and then he slowly headed for home.

A Girl's
Best Friend

Melissa Hill

Melissa Hill

Melissa Hill lives with her husband and dog in Monkstown, Co Dublin. She is the author of five previous novels, *Something You Should*, *Not What You Think*, *Never Say Never*, *Wishful Thinking* and *All Because of You* — all of which have been bestsellers and widely translated. Her new book *The Last to Know* published by Poolbeg is out now. Visit her website **www.melissahill.info**

A Girl's
Best Friend

"I'm thinking of inviting Greg over here for dinner this Sunday – what do you think?" Melanie announced to her parents one weekday morning over breakfast.

Ben nearly spat out his toast. Over my dead body! he growled to himself, looking sideways at Melanie's mother and hoping that she would dismiss out of hand the very notion of having that – that *poser* here for dinner.

OK, so Ben was prepared to admit he could be slightly overprotective of his girls at times, but Melanie's latest boyfriend was a different kettle of fish altogether!

Blond, over six foot tall and very well built, he'd towered imposingly over Ben the first time Melanie brought him home for a visit, and while the others might have been taken in by his posh voice, fancy clothes and uppity car-salesman job, Ben knew better. He could sniff out a fraud a mile off!

Not to mention that Sunday was one of the few days of the week the entire family spent together, and the last thing he wanted was some outsider coming in and upsetting their routine. After stuffing themselves with dinner and dessert, and having a lively chat at the dinner table, the Griffins usually went for a long walk in the nearby park to work off the day's excesses, before spending the remainder of the evening relaxing with the Sunday papers in front of the TV.

And Ben also knew that if Greg were invited, Molly would spend the entire day worrying about whether her cooking was good or fancy enough for the visitor, and wouldn't be able to relax for a millisecond. Ben hated it when Molly got fretful; despite his best efforts she was impossible to soothe, but of course he couldn't confess his feelings out loud.

"Well?" Unnerved by her parents' lack of response to her announcement, Melanie looked at her father for affirmation. "What do you think?"

He squirmed uncomfortably in his seat. "Well, I'm not sure, love – you haven't been seeing this Greg fellow for very long, have you? I mean, none of us really know him all that well and –"

"I knew it!" Melanie glared at him, her huge brown eyes glittering with annoyance. "I *knew* you didn't like him, Dad! That first time I brought him home, you barely spoke two words to him!"

"Ah now, pet, come on – I was watching the football, and you know how stuck into that I can get sometimes."

It was true. When there was a game on TV, everything else faded into the background for him. The house could be falling down around him and he wouldn't notice.

"That's no excuse and you know it!" Melanie huffed. "It was *so* embarrassing, especially as Greg made so much of an effort with you."

So much of an effort! Ben wanted to retort. Well, if making an effort was spending the entire visit lounging around on the sofa, and expecting to be waited on hand and foot . . . then I just don't know . . .

And Ben really *didn't* know. He didn't know what on earth his lovely Melanie saw in that slimy Greg, or how a fake like him had managed to pique her interest in the first place – particularly when a single sniff of his expensive aftershave had told Ben *everything* he needed to know about the guy. How could Melanie be so gullible?

"Look, it's not that, love," Melanie's mother intervened then, much to Ben's relief – he *hated* arguments and loud voices. Molly spoke softly. "I think what your dad means is that –"

"He means that Greg isn't welcome here!" Melanie wouldn't be placated. She moved her chair back from the table and petulantly folded her arms, regarding her parents through angry eyes.

"Now, now, there's no need for that kind of carry-on. All your mother and I are saying is that we don't know this fella very well, that's all."

"Oh, but it's OK for Karen to have James here for Sunday dinner nearly ever second week, isn't it? Whereas I never have anybody!"

Yes, but your sister's fiancé is a decent young fellow with a good set of manners on him, Ben thought with a scowl – not like that pompous prat *you've* taken up with.

Besides the man himself (whom Ben didn't trust an iota), what was getting to him the most was the way in which Greg had inveigled himself into Melanie's life in the last few weeks. It meant that these days she had precious little interest in spending time with him or anyone else in the family. He couldn't remember the last time the two of them had spent a decent amount of time together – just him and Melanie, sitting idly together in the back garden, or going for lazy walks in the park – the way it used to be.

Since Greg's arrival on the scene they'd barely spent any time together at all, and this lack of closeness saddened him. At the same time, he supposed it was inevitable that as the girls grew older their relationship with him would change, and the closeness he'd taken for granted for all these years would eventually start to diminish. Although in fairness, Karen's James was a nice enough fellow, very friendly and not at all threatening; Ben was quite taken with him actually, had been since day one. Why couldn't Melanie find herself a nice, upstanding boyfriend like that?

"Well?" Melanie fixed her parents with another look, and Ben wished with all his heart that her mother would just come out and put an end to the notion once and for all. Make up some excuse about her not having enough time to prepare or something. It was Thursday after all, and she might not have got enough food in to go around.

But by the resigned look on Molly's face, he realised that the battle had already been lost.

Greg would be coming for dinner this Sunday – whether Ben liked it or not.

On Sunday morning, Greg stared at his reflection in the bathroom mirror and sighed. He was looking forward to dinner at the Griffins almost as much as they were looking forward to having him.

They were a nice enough family, he supposed, although a little on the weird side, especially the way they all seemed so close and so bloody *nice* to one another.

Melanie was twenty-five and *still* living at home, whereas Greg had got out of his gaff well before that age – he couldn't get out of there fast enough!

But the idea of spending all day around Ben in particular made him really uncomfortable, especially after that first time he'd visited. While Greg had tried his utmost to be friendly, Ben had been extremely guarded towards him.

"He's just protective of us – me in particular because I'm the youngest, I suppose," Melanie had reassured him afterwards.

Greg wasn't so sure. He didn't like the suspicious looks Ben had been throwing his way throughout; they made him extremely uneasy. Forget protective – *possessive* was probably a better way to describe it.

Well, Greg wasn't going to waste time worrying about that just now. He'd come round in time. Anyway, in the car-sales business, he was well used to sweet-talking the customers, so really, getting Ben onside should be no problem at all to a guy like him!

He ran a hand through his tousled blond hair before checking his watch. In truth, he could do with a shower, but there wasn't much time; he was due at the Griffins' house at noon.

"Greg?" A female voice called out from the other room, interrupting his thoughts.

"Yes . . . um?" Dammit, what was her name again? Greg grimaced and racked his brains trying to remember. Diana, was it? No, no, *Donna* . . . that was it! "Yes, Donna?" he replied.

And just in time too.

"Hey, baby," she said, coming up behind him and snaking her arms around his bare torso, in much the same way as she'd done the previous night – with her smooth, bronzed and oh-so-sexy legs. "Leaving so soon?"

"Duty calls, I'm afraid!" He turned and flashed her a boyish grin, one that never failed to melt every girl's heart. "Promised my mother I'd be home for Sunday dinner." Another thing that never failed, Greg thought smiling inwardly. All the girls *loved* a guy who loved his mum.

"Oh, that's a shame," Donna purred, "especially when we were having so much fun too."

"Some other time maybe," Greg said, extricating himself from her embrace with considerable regret. In truth, he wouldn't have minded a rerun of last night's action, but unfortunately there just wasn't time.

He splashed some cold water onto his face (a poor substitute for a cold shower but at least it was *something*) before gathering the remainder of his clothes and leaving the lovely Donna's flat.

He'd better cop onto himself though, he thought, hailing a nearby cab – if Melanie got wind of his playing around she'd dump him in a heartbeat!

Then again, what she didn't know wouldn't hurt her, would it? he thought, recalling with a thrill Donna's antics the night before. And anyway, if she ever *did* find out, she could blame nobody but herself. Any woman with half a brain in her head would know better than to let a good-looking fellow like himself out on the town on his own. It was Mel's own tough luck that she'd arranged something else with the girls, leaving him to his own devices on a Saturday night. At the end of the day, what else was a red-blooded guy supposed to do?

But he'd better be on his best behaviour today at least, he thought, as the taxi pulled up outside the Griffin household; he and Mel had a good thing going at the moment and he didn't want to mess it up. Having paid the driver, he got out and rang the doorbell.

Melanie's mother Molly answered the door almost immediately. "Greg, hello again, and welcome!" she said, greeting him with a warm and, Greg thought, rather appreciative smile. It was probably the stubble; all women *loved* the stubble.

"Thanks for having me, Mrs Griffin." He flashed Molly his best megawatt smile in return, thinking that for an old bird Mel's mother wasn't half bad-looking herself. Not only that but she seemed like the kind of woman who could do with a bit of a fun – a bit of diversion. Probably your typical middle-aged bored housewife, he deduced; Greg came across plenty of those in his line of work.

But then again, who'd blame Molly Griffin for soliciting the attentions of an attractive guy like him, when she was married to a bloke like Melanie's father – with his balding head, whiskey nose and a beer belly that would make Homer Simpson proud!

"Come on in," Molly said, directing Greg into the kitchen, where the rest of the Griffin family were waiting for dinner to be served.

Amongst them was an older brunette whom Greg didn't recognise, but who he deduced must be Melanie's older sister Karen. Like the rest of the Griffin women she was a bit of all right too, with her dark, oval eyes and shiny hair – although she was perhaps a bit too much on the chunky side for his liking.

"Hey there," Melanie said, kissing him lightly on the cheek, before introducing him to Karen, who said hi and smiled politely as she gave him the once-over. Greg had no doubts that he'd pass muster; where women were concerned he always did. But as he shook hands with Karen, he became once again keenly aware of Ben regarding him intently from the other end of the room.

"What's in the bag?" his girlfriend asked, glancing at the brown-paper bag Greg was carrying.

Greg shrugged nonchalantly. "Oh – it's just a couple of small things to thank you guys for having me," he said. He'd got the taxi to stop off at a service station on the way over, where he'd picked up a couple of treats – wine, chocolates, biscuits and such-like.

"Oh, how sweet!"

"That's very nice of you, Greg, but there was really no need – we're delighted to have you in any case," Molly said, although Greg could tell that this had scored a *major* point in his favour – with the women at least.

Soon after, they took their seats at the dining-room table, where to his dismay, Greg ended up seated nearest to Ben, who despite

Greg's thoughtfulness, still didn't seem the slightest bit impressed with him, and had just about stopped short of turning his nose up at his gifts!

Still, regardless of the slight tension between him and Ben, dinner was a lively enough affair, and to Greg's delight the Griffins were no slouches when it came to sharing the booze. After a few glasses of red wine, he began to relax considerably.

"That was a gorgeous bit of lamb, Mrs Griffin," he complimented, rubbing his stomach appreciatively. "It's been a long time since I've had a meal that nice – in fact, it's been a very long time since I've had a home-cooked meal full stop."

"Thank you very much," Molly said smiling at him. "I can wrap up some for you to take home if you like – there's still quite a bit left on the bone. Ben usually has it for his tea, but I'm sure he wouldn't mind sharing it this once – sure you wouldn't?"

"Oh no, there's no need," Greg said quickly. "I've had more than enough today, honestly." He was now sorry he'd said anything, and especially sorry he'd set himself up to potentially deprive Ben of his grub!

"It's no problem," insisted Melanie's father gruffly. "Take some leftovers home if you'd like."

"Really, I'm fine – thanks anyway."

Melanie nudged him playfully. "I keep telling him to take the time to prepare proper meals, don't I?"

Nagging me more like, Greg thought inwardly. Mel was cute, but she could be an awful pain in the arse sometimes, and he hated it when she got all mumsy. Still, he supposed he'd better humour her – today at least.

"You certainly do," he grinned back, as the family made inroads into Molly's sherry trifle. "I don't know what I'd do without you."

Melanie flushed with pleasure and, glancing around the table,

Greg knew he'd scored even more brownie points with the girls, although her father looked uncomfortable about the exchange. Poor sod – he obviously hadn't a clue how to handle women.

"OK, time for our walk I suppose," Melanie piped up, when dessert was eaten and the table cleared.

Greg's eyes widened. Walk? What walk? In his world, Sunday afternoons were for relaxing on the sofa, watching the telly – certainly *not* for taking bloody walks!

Molly must have seen most of this written on his face. "Maybe Greg would prefer to just relax for a while here for the moment?" she suggested.

Too bloody right, he thought satisfied. And preferably with another couple of drinks.

"Oh, OK then," Melanie said, looking apologetically at Ben, who didn't seem the least bit impressed. "Maybe later, OK?"

While the girls did the washing-up, the men retired to the lounge; Greg having gratefully accepted another glass of wine from Melanie's mother before making himself comfortable on the sofa.

"Any football on today?" he asked.

"Don't think so."

"Right."

Melanie's father was obviously a man of few words.

A few minutes later, Melanie joined them and they all sat in a rather strained silence, until eventually her dad got and up and left the room.

"He hates my guts," Greg hissed, referring to Ben.

Melanie sighed. "He doesn't hate you – he's just a little unsure of you, that's all. Give him a little bit of time to get used to you."

Then, the rest of the family came in and the conversation swiftly came to end. But as the evening wore on, Greg grew more and more uncomfortable around Ben. It was really freaky the way the bastard kept *staring* at him at like that, especially every time he said yes to another drink!

So when at one stage Ben went to sit alongside Melanie on the sofa, Greg decided to seize the opportunity to show him exactly who was boss. Buoyed up by the few glasses of wine he'd consumed, he reached across and pointed a finger at his nemesis. "Listen here –" he began, his voice slurring slightly.

Melanie's father looked at him. "I wouldn't do that if I were you, son," he warned.

"Hey, what the hell are you doing down there . . . *Oww!*" White-faced with shock, Greg shot up off the sofa and grabbed his arm. "Ow!" he squealed again, staring at Ben in disbelief. "I don't believe it – he bit me. The little rat *bit* me!"

"Ben hates people pointing at him," Mr Griffin said, and with a shake of his head went over to the sofa and picked up the little black-and-tan Yorkshire terrier. "And I suspect he's also a bit put out that he didn't get his walk this afternoon, aren't you, Ben?"

Greg was still shell-shocked. "But he *bit* me!" he repeated, waving his wounded arm in front of Melanie, as Ben continued to growl threateningly at him. "*And* he nearly took a lump out of my trousers first!"

But to Greg's immense dismay, his girlfriend and indeed her family didn't seem at all concerned about his injury. In fact something else entirely seemed to have caught their attention.

"Greg," Melanie began, enunciating the words slowly, "what's that?"

"What's what?" Greg followed her gaze down to where Ben, before eventually taking a lump out of him, had been tugging at his trousers. Something was sticking out of his pocket.

Something bright pink and lacy.

Oh shit.

"Are those . . . ?" Karen began, the rest of her sentence trailing off.

"Women's knickers?" said her sister, her tone steely. "They seem to be, but they're certainly not mine."

Greg wanted to die. That little bastard! *Now* he knew why the bloody dog had kept sniffing around him at the dinner table earlier! Ben must have smelt Donna's perfume, must have known something of hers was in his pocket, and had grabbed at it while biting him. But how the hell had her underwear got in there in the first place? Suddenly Greg had a flashback of Donna's hands snaking around his waist that morning. Oh God, how was he going to explain this?

"Look Mel, I really don't know –"

"Funny, neither do I," his girlfriend snapped. "I don't know why I put up with you for so long when it was clear from day one that Ben couldn't stand you."

"What?" Greg stared at her in disbelief.

Melanie took the little terrier out of her father's arms and held him close. "I'm sorry, Ben," she said, stroking his soft downy coat. "I should have taken notice of you all along."

"But he bit me!" Greg cried. What was Mel *doing* - fawning all over that mutt, instead of apologising profusely like any normal – any decent person would do! "That bloody dog should be put down!"

Melanie glared at him. "That bloody dog has been in this family for nearly twelve years. He's my best friend and obviously a *much* better judge of character than I am!" She cast another disgusted glance at Donna's underwear. "Get out, Greg – before I set Ben on you properly."

At this, again Ben growled and bared his teeth, and Greg quickly turned on his heels and raced for the door.

Molly shook her head when they heard the front door close behind him. "I can't believe it – he seemed so nice," she said.

Melanie nodded sadly. "I know, Mum – I know."

"I thought he was a grand lad myself to be honest, if a little showy," her dad said. "Although, at the same time, I knew it wasn't like Ben to turn up his nose at a biscuit," he added, referring to the dog biscuits Greg had brought as a peace offering. "It's a good thing that at least one of us could sniff out his true colours all the same."

"Yeah!" Melanie reached down and ruffled Ben behind the ears. "Thanks again, buddy – I don't know what I'd do without you."

Ben wagged his stubby tail and – satisfied that his latest rival for Melanie's affections had been satisfactorily dispatched – settled down for a relaxing Sunday evening with his precious family.

The
Angel
Gabrielle

Cathy Kelly

Cathy Kelly

Cathy Kelly is the author of ten novels, including *Past Secrets, Always and Forever,* and *Best of Friends.* She lives in Wicklow with her partner and their twin sons and is currently working on her eleventh novel. In 2005, Cathy became a Global Parenting Ambassador for UNICEF Ireland, helping to raise funds and awareness for children orphaned by AIDS.

The
Angel
Gabrielle

As Claire shut the front door behind her, the warmth of 7 Rose Villas embraced her in a giant hug. It was an icy December night and three hours earlier she certainly hadn't felt like heading off to her evening class when the rest of the family were sitting down in front of a cosy fire.

But tonight had been the last computer class before Christmas and, with a determination Claire had thought she'd lost a long time ago, she was determined not to miss a single lesson.

By the time she was finished, the teacher had said confidently, Claire would be able to organise folders, blithely send emails off into the ether and use Power Point. Quite what she was going to need Power Point for was another matter. There wasn't much call for it at home as Lorraine, Claire's nineteen-year-old daughter, had merrily pointed out.

"Will you be printing off the shopping list on Excel Notes, Mum?" she teased.

Charlie, who was two years older, joined in: "No, Mum's going to start flirting with strangers over the Internet now she knows how to use it!"

Even Steven, her husband, seemed to find it all very funny.

"You shouldn't tease your mother," he told the kids, although he was smiling. "When she's running the some big computer industry, you'll be sorry. Next stop, chairmanship of Microsoft, eh, Claire?" he joked.

She managed to smile back at them but still felt strangely wounded.

After twenty years raising a family, she'd decided to change her life. And they all thought it was funny.

Nobody at home seemed to realise what it had cost her to enrol on the course in the first place. It had been twenty-one years since she'd been a student of any kind. She was two months into a management training scheme with the hotel company when she'd become pregnant with Charlie. Instantly it had been bye-bye books, hello nappies.

"We don't need the money, you know," Steven had said in September when Claire had broached the subject of doing an evening course and explained how having a new skill could help her rejoin the workforce. "But if you want a job now the kids are seen to . . ."

Steven's mother said she didn't see the point of all that computer nonsense.

"It's for young people," Mavis had sniffed. "You're nearly fifty, dear. You can't turn the clock back."

Claire, who was forty-nine and a half, thank you very much, held her tongue. Mavis lived in the street behind them and spent a lot of time in Claire's house. "I don't like interfering," was her mantra.

Claire often wondered if mantra was the correct description

for a phrase someone used a lot but didn't adhere to in any practical way.

Now, she hung up her coat, hung the canvas bag that contained all her coursework on the stair-post and went into the living room. Her family, mother-in-law included, were watching the television with mugs of tea and a packet of chocolate biscuits on the small table in front of the couch.

"Bet you're glad that blinking course is over," Steven murmured. "I'm sick of seeing your head in a book. Now you can relax and enjoy Christmas. I'm really looking forward to tucking into your special Christmas pudding, love."

"Oh yes, Mum," Lorraine grinned, "did you make two puddings this year? You said you would because I hate currants and if we could have one with currants and one without, it would be brilliant."

Four eager faces turned towards Claire and she had a sudden flash of reality: she was no longer a person to any of them. She had morphed into Robot Mother, who cooked, cleaned, took orders for festive meals and had no needs of her own. This Christmas would not be any different from all the others.

Claire shut her eyes and wished it was January.

Shelley found that the trouble with lying was keeping track of all the lies.

The first lie was telling Mum and Dad that she wasn't going home to the farm for Christmas because she was spending the holiday with her friend, Fiona, in Greece.

She'd decided to phone them with the news because she was actually a hopeless liar face to face. Over the phone, lying was much easier.

"It's a week-long yoga thing and it just came up. It's impossible to get places on it but someone pulled out and Fiona and I thought it would be just what we need," she'd bluffed and she couldn't help thinking that God, if *He* was listening, would burn her to a cinder for such fibs. And fibs about Christmas weren't the half of it.

As if a week doing yoga could possibly hold any attractions for her. She could be going to Greece, in fact. Fiona had asked her along. But even twenty-four hours away would be torture unless she was away with Jack. And that wasn't going to happen anytime soon. The lie was necessary because she couldn't possibly tell her parents she was going to stay on her own in her flat in Dublin just in case Jack managed to sneak over to see her during the holidays.

The next lie was to Fiona.

Fiona and Shelley worked together in marketing and Fiona made no pretence of her dislike for Jack, who was one of the directors of the large estate agency where they'd both worked for three years. Fiona was much shrewder than Shelley's parents and lying to her was undoubtedly trickier. So Shelley gritted her teeth, tried to look blasé, and told Fiona she was going home to her parents as usual.

"You're sure you're not staying in Dublin because that lying scumbag wants you on tap in case he gets away from his wife for five minutes?" Fiona had asked suspiciously.

"Course not. I'm not stupid, you know." Shelley smiled.

"Good," said Fiona. "I'm glad you're finally listening to me. He's using you."

Fiona had spent hours the previous week telling Shelley what she called The Facts Of Life.

"He won't leave his wife, Shell: get used to it. Dump him. You're just a soft touch and he's taking advantage of that fact."

Fiona just didn't understand, Shelley thought. Love didn't

always work out in traditional ways. Jack loved her. He wanted to be with her whenever he could manage it and he'd already worked out how they could sneak some precious hours together over Christmas.

Shelley thought about the last conversation she had with Jack as they lay in her bed, cosy after making love.

"Maura and her sister are sales mad. They'll be in town waiting for the shops to open on Boxing Day. I'll have plenty of opportunity to slip away," Jack had assured her.

Maura was Jack's wife, a source of huge guilt and sadness in Shelley's life. If only Maura wasn't so emotionally fragile that she'd fall apart if Jack left. If only there weren't two innocent children involved, then it would all be so much easier.

But still Shelley felt the wrongness of the affair like a weight on her soul.

There were so many lies, Shelley thought sadly. A person shouldn't have to lie about Christmas . . . should they?

Mavis had an early Christmas present for her daughter-in-law: an hour-by-hour guide to cooking Christmas dinner which she'd clipped from a magazine.

"It says keep a lipstick handy in the kitchen so you don't end up looking a wreck just because you're standing over a hot oven all day," she explained kindly as she gave the clipping to Claire.

Claire stopped herself from asking why *she'd* been chosen to receive the guide. There were three other adults in the house. Why was cooking Christmas dinner solely her prerogative?

Since the night she'd come home from her last computer lesson, Claire had been having lots of similarly strange thoughts. She felt the buzz of pride from the hard work she'd put into learning about software and email. The rest of them seemed to think it was nothing more than a blip that kept her from more important duties: looking after all of them.

At lunch-time on their second-last day at work before the holidays, Shelley went with Fiona to buy both last-minute presents and yoga gear for Fiona's Greek idyll. Fiona was flying off to Athens early on Christmas Eve. Shelley was supposed to be spending the same morning driving a hundred miles to her parents' small dairy farm. In fact, she and Jack were going to spend as much time as possible in her flat, enjoying their Christmas dinner a day early.

Shelley had already bought a tiny turkey crown from M&S, a miniature cake and splurged on champagne for the occasion. She'd spent all week imagining their wonderful day together: making love; talking about future holidays when they'd be together.

"Why are all sports bras ugly?" Fiona demanded, holding up a solid-looking white thing with disgust and prodding at the straps, so big they looked as if they might possibly be used to bind up some big rugby player's legs. "My boobs are too big to do yoga in a vest."

"Probably to keep the lust out of yoga," Shelley said absently, eyeing up a very sexy peach lingerie set. She was getting her hair done that evening just round the corner, so she'd be able to pop back later and buy it.

"Spose," Fiona agreed. "Yoga isn't supposed to be sexy, is it? Neither will I be in this thing. Hope there's no gorgeous sinewy yoga fellas on this trip because they'll ignore me once I've got this mammoth bra on. Probably think I'm an Olympic shot-putter.'

At six that evening, Claire sat in a chair in Gabrielle's Hair Salon and stared at herself in the mirror. She'd been shopping for groceries and presents all day. She was exhausted and she'd just received a text from Steven: *forgot Mum's gift. Cud u get something? What perfume u like from me & kids?*

The face in the mirror looked older than forty-nine-and-a-half and her plan to look different for Christmas suddenly seemed futile. After twenty-five years of marriage, her husband still had to ask what perfume she liked and she still had to buy every single present for everyone. Tiredness washed over her along with a tidal wave of feeling unappreciated.

"What are you thinking of having done?" the stylist smiled.

Claire burst into tears.

Shelley almost didn't notice the woman crying in the chair beside her. She was still in shock, trying to make sense of what she'd overheard at the office drinks party. It had started at four: drinks and nibbles in the boardroom and traditionally it all went crazy at six when all the partners went home, and the real fun began.

That's what Fiona said, anyway, but for Shelley the real fun was a social occasion where she could be near her darling Jack. Not together, of course. Nobody should know about them, he'd said. He didn't want people talking. It wouldn't be fair to her.

But that afternoon, Shelley had felt the magnetic pull of Jack's presence. She couldn't stop herself from trying to stand near him, although not exactly in his company, and she'd been near enough to overhear him talking to one of the other directors about what they were giving their respective spouses.

"You always give Maura great gifts, you jammy git," the other man was saying to Jack. "What's it this year? The Hope Diamond?"

"A week's skiing in Courcheval . . ."

Shelley could hear the smile in Jack's voice.

"We love skiing and Maura's a real daredevil at it. She did a black run last time. I'll tell you, she frightened the life out of me!"

A daredevil? Surely that couldn't be the same Maura who'd fall apart if Jack left her? And wasn't a week spent skiing a very intimate, coupley present – the sort of holiday you'd share with a lover and not with a woman for whom you had "brotherly" feelings?

Shelley had kept it together enough to put down her glass and not drop it onto the grey office carpet, then she'd rushed out of the boardroom.

In the hairdresser's, with her hair stuck wetly to her scalp and a glass of office wine rattling round inside her, Shelley felt emptier than she'd ever thought possible. And then, the sound of crying filtered in through her own misery and, like seeing someone else yawn when you're tired, the tears started to pour down her face.

Across the salon, Gabrielle – or Peggy to her friends – saw the two women sobbing. Christmas, she thought, shaking her head. It got to the best of them.

Installed in Peggy's office above the salon with two cups of hot, sweet tea and a pile of mince pies in front of them, Claire and Shelley began to feel better. It was impossible not to cheer up in Peggy's comforting presence. In the salon and as Gabrielle, she was a stately sixty-something blonde with a fat gold and diamond Cartier watch and a slightly imperious manner. In her office and as Peggy – "Peggy O'Brien's doesn't have the same ring to it as Gabrielle's," she'd said wisely when she'd started the salon many years ago – she was kind and warm.

"You don't have to tell me, girls," she said gently. "It's just the Christmas blues. If all's not rosy in your world, you can be sure Christmas will get to you."

The two women nodded.

"I'm fine," said Claire, finishing her tea. She felt terribly embarrassed about letting herself down in the salon. What had come over her?

"Thank you," Shelley added, taking Claire's lead. How awful to break down like that? What was wrong with her?

Peggy watched both women put on their emotional armour again and pretend everything was all right. She knew the drill: she'd done if often enough herself until she'd stopped hiding her feelings. What a liberation *that* had turned out to be.

"I have a party every Christmas in my house," Peggy said, handing them each a pale pink card with her address on it. "It's for all my friends who feel like spending a bit of time without family or loved ones. They drop in, have something to eat and chat, and somehow it's all very relaxing. Everyone comes on their own, so nobody feels like the odd one out. You're both welcome."

"I've a family Christmas lined up," smiled Claire, back in control.

"Me too," said Shelley, "but thank you so much for the invitation."

"If you change your mind," Peggy said, "the offer stands."

On Christmas Day, Claire's cooking was timed with military precision. Everyone had loved their presents and after Mass the Christmas spirit went into overdrive as they sat back to enjoy the day while Claire headed back into the steamy kitchen with her bottle of Chanel No 5 (from Steve and the kids – although she'd originally said she'd love a bottle of Allure) and a furry hot water-bottle cover with a bunny face (from Mavis). The scent of No 5 hung about her. She hated No 5, always had. Hated it. How come nobody knew that?

This time, Claire didn't cry. Instead, she thought.

The problem wasn't about presents: it was about respect and

about people taking heed of her and her opinions. Perfume she disliked and no help in the kitchen to cook a meal they'd all eat was part and parcel of this.

Shelley couldn't help herself. She phoned Jack on his mobile to wish him Merry Christmas.

"For heaven's sake!" he hissed down the phone at her. "You know I'm at home, Shelley. Do you want us to get found out?"

Shelley hung up. Surely if they were going to be together – as discussed the day before from the luxury of her bed – then getting found out was a given? Or perhaps not.

Claire and Shelley arrived at Peggy's front door at exactly the same time.

"Don't ask," said Claire, who was wondering how she'd found the courage to walk out on her family, leaving the Christmas puddings simmering away and the oven fit to burst with turkey and all the trimmings. They probably wouldn't miss her for hours.

"As long as you don't ask me," grinned Shelley, who felt remarkably happier now that she wasn't going to be on her ownsome at home waiting for the phone to ring.

"I'm so glad you both came!" Peggy flung the door open.

Behind her, the lovely house was full of laughing, chattering people, clearly having a ball. There were no rows or moods floating around: just music and enjoyment.

"My husband gave me the idea," Peggy said, filling crystal flutes with champagne for her two new guests. "He left me just before Christmas twenty years ago. Said I was a boring old bag, he couldn't bear to stay married to me a moment longer and he was off. He didn't leave me much, either. He was a bit of a gambler, you see. The day after he went, I found out that the house was going to be repossessed. It was a terrible Christmas, that first one. I was alone in a house with no TV and very little furniture – the bailiffs had been and taken nearly everything. And then I thought that it couldn't just be me, there must be other people on their own at Christmas, staring at the wall and feeling sad, and we couldn't all be total rejects, so I came up with this idea: the Old Bag's Christmas Party. Welcome, girls! Just be sure to leave your baggage at the door."

"Is that burning?" Lorraine smelled it first.

The water under the two Christmas puddings needed to be topped up constantly and without Claire to do it, both saucepans had dried out.

Steven, Charlie and Mavis glanced up from the television.

"No, surely not," said Steven with a satisfied smile. "Your mother will have it all under control." And they all swivelled their eyes back to the TV.

Jack dialled Shelley's mobile. He was puzzled to hear party noises in the background.

"Sorry, Jack," Shelley said, sounding merry. "Can't talk. See you in the New Year, I imagine."

She hung up.

She couldn't mean what he thought she meant, Jack pondered. Surely not. His wife was off to the sales the next day, as he'd known she would be. He was tired of the house and the kids yelling at each other. A little bit of pampering from Shelley would be lovely in the sanctuary of her little flat where she'd fuss over him and tell him he was wonderful. He'd phone in the morning.

As Peggy moved through the room refilling glasses, she smiled contentedly at her guests: it had taken her a long time to get to this place but she felt she could truly say that there was no better way to spend the holiday than by adding a little sparkle to other people's lives. After all, wasn't Christmas supposed to be about giving?

Drowning Kittens

Doodle Kennelly

Doodle Kennelly

Doodle Kennelly was born in Dublin and spent her early years there. As a teenager, she moved to the United States, to Massachusetts, where she completed her secondary education. Later she returned to Ireland and attended the Gaiety School of Acting. In addition to her regular newspaper column, she has published autobiographical essays relating to the subject of female identity and body image. She has also appeared on national television. She is currently engaged in completing a memoir and is the proud mother of three daughters, Meg, Hannah and Grace Murphy.

Drowning
Kittens

I was as surprised by his appearance as he must have been by mine. I studied him as he walked in a straight line towards my mother and me. He looked out-of-the-ordinary, special, and appeared as if he were moving in a different atmosphere from the rest of the world. The crowds of happy, hassled travellers parted to let him through, then blurred into insignificance around him. There was a determination to his movements, but they were no longer the practised actions of a functioning alcoholic. In fact, had I not already known he was sober I would have been able to tell just by the set of his face. He was scared but clear-headed, and he had flown three thousand miles to be my father.

"She is a very sick young lady. If she doesn't start eating within three weeks we may be looking at an in-patient situation. I suggest you call her father and tell him he needs to get over here as he is the only person she appears willing to respond to."

I was sitting beside my mother in El Shrinko's office. As usual I was doing my best to ignore him as he spoke. He was a creep, but the word on the liberal streets of our New England town was that he had a certain genius when it came to dealing with problem kids like myself. And because my mother was so angry at my refusal to go to school, worried about my escalating, omnipresent depression, and terrified by my dramatic weight loss, she would have entrusted me to just about anyone if they promised her a possible cure. I didn't tell her how over the course of an entire year, with weekly visits, El Shrinko had never once mentioned the fact that I had lost over 100 lbs. Until today the subject had been a white-elephant skeleton, rattling away in the corner of his modern office. But to appease her I attended every appointment and either sulked on the expensive sofa while El Shrinko smiled at me as if he knew and indeed was above it all, or I played with the strange toys he used to get his younger patients to "open up". I was particularly intrigued with a large plasma lamp he kept on the coffee table that sat between us. When I put my hand on its surface and the electrical beams shot out to meet my skin it was like an incarcerated lover placing his palm against the glass that divided us. It was reassuring that there was still some vital force alive inside me that could attract other energies. I wanted the plasma ball more than anything, El Shrinko knew it, and he cut a deal.

"If you achieve a couple of the smaller goals your mom has set for you, I'll give you the plasma ball – it'll be all yours, to take home."

Even if I hadn't been aware of the most basic rules psychologists were meant to adhere to, I would have smelt something rotten, and known that for once it wasn't the acrid stench of my own hungry breath. But I didn't care; I did what he asked. Within three weeks I had taken the high school graduation equivalency exam, experiencing an unfamiliar sense of pride when I came away with all A and B grades. Then I went ahead and obtained my driver's permit – not that I had any intention of ever taking the full driving test – I just wanted that plasma ball.

I showed up in his office with my two certificates, prouder than I had ever been in my life.

He refused to hand over the magical sphere.

"Why do you think you deserve it? You only went and achieved those small tasks out of greed. I would be remiss as your psychologist to reward such behaviour, but I'll pay you twenty dollars if you baby-sit my kids next weekend."

I hated him, but there was nothing I could do.

Sitting there with my mother I tried to will myself the strength to stand up, interrupt the stream of drivel coming from his smug mouth, and tell her exactly how incompetent and corrupt the man actually was. But instead I stared at the biffle bats in the corner. They were massive dense-foam baseball bats, the kind the tall circus clown would hit the midget circus clown with just before the midget tripped the big guy up to roars of applause. The point was that you could pretend you were beating the shit out of someone you "had issues with" without actually injuring them. I pictured myself pounding my mother and El Shrinko over the heads, knocking them out, then standing victorious on top of them like a spindly, fishnet-clad hunter girl. The thought brought me back to reality.

I looked at my mother and knew I didn't want to hurt her any more. All she wanted to hear was that I was going to be all right, that everything wrong with me was fixable, bacterial, and fleeting. She wanted me to wake up one morning and bound downstairs like a healthy Walton child, rosy-cheeked from a life lived playing in streams and doing chores, I would be the right weight for my height, with a metabolism that never quit, leaving me always hungry for more home cooking to burn in my perfect, supple young furnace of a body. But in her eyes I saw the glazed look of paralysed fear born of the knowledge that she could do nothing. Were I to be privy to her thoughts I knew I would hear a frantic mantra-like non-believer's prayer for a return to the time when she could pacify me with food. She was thinking about when all she had to do was hand me platefuls of pasta, bowlfuls of chocolate mousse, and huge glassfuls of freshly squeezed orange juice, to make my depression lift. She dreamed that I would turn suddenly away from my mission of self-destruction as I caught the scent of food on the air like a dog catching the smell of his missing owner. I knew she thought that if only I would eat I would be everything she imagined her daughter would be. I would go to college, excel in the arts, and stop sleeping with junkies and petty criminals. Instead I would date an exceptionally bright member of the high school baseball team, perhaps even letting him feel my small, perfectly formed breasts on the porch every Saturday night after we returned from seeing a movie she had recommended we see. Or maybe that was everything I wished for . . . either way it wasn't reality. The meals she tried to tempt me with lay rotting in the cat's dish, dumped there after I had ruined them by prodding at them with fingers cracked and bloodied because my dehydrated skin cracked every time I made an anxious fist. On the rare occasions when we were both in the house at the same time I would lock myself in my bedroom and spend hours naked in front of the mirror trying to figure out why it was that no matter how much weight I lost, no matter how long I starved myself for, or how many hours I exercised for, I was still covered in folds of wrinkly skin. I knew every inch of my body even though it disgusted me to look at myself. I imagined that the hundreds of silvery stretch marks on my arms, legs and chest were scars caused by demons that clawed at me with their talons as I slept, determined to punish me for being slovenly and disgusting. The only parts of my body that I could stand to look at were my hands, feet and face, but I hated those too. I dug at the soles of my feet with nail-clippers until I could no longer walk without a limp, chewed at the sides of my fingers, and gnawed at my dry lips until it appeared that great chunks of them were missing. Yet vanity and self-obsession commandeered my life. When I wasn't experimenting with make-up and clothes to try and disguise what I considered to be massive flaw upon massive flaw, I spent hours on the exercise bike that stood in front of my bedroom window. I imagined its mechanics being lubricated by the sweat and fat dripping off my disappearing body as I cycled frantically towards an ever-looming personal oblivion.

Every day I slept until long after the functioning world's lunch-time in my parents' hand-me-down marital bed, rising only when I knew she had left to teach the focused children she wished I were more like. Wearing one of the XXX-L sized T-shirts that had once been tight on me and a pair of heavy woollen socks to protect my cold and bloodied feet, I went straight to the freezer to choose my one and only meal for the day – Lean Cuisine. My excitement would grow as I watched it pirouette for twenty minutes in the low-powered microwave, its beige cardboard casing slowly warping and dimpling as its contents shrank and charred. I liked it overcooked and chewy at one end, even if chewing too hard did make my gums bleed. It reminded me of steak, pizza crusts and toffee. I would carry my precious meal on a tray to the other end of the scary house in the woods, turn on the television, and return briefly to what used to be my constant escape. I ate.

Five minutes later, and the brief tranquillity had gone the way of my daily three hundred calories, consumed and digested by my greedy body. I would sit back on the sofa still starving, and stare at the black ring of burnt food stuck to the inside of the container. Every day I felt the same frustration that no matter how hard I dug and scraped at it, I couldn't get it off. It was then that I started thinking obsessively about the next day's meal and of how I could fend off the hunger pangs until then.

The only way was to focus totally on my appearance. My mission was to change all I was born to be: my mother was blonde, so I would be blonder. I hated that I was unable to reprogram my genetic makeup. I worshipped my father, but I wanted to look like my mother. I wished that at the flick of a light switch I could suddenly be possessed of her Scandinavian flaxen hair and long swimmer's legs, but looking in the mirror I saw a dark, squat, Kerry footballer staring back. There was nothing I could do about the length of my legs, so once a week I bleached my hair. My natural colour was so stubborn it required several applications. I was allergic to peroxide and developed weeping sores all over my scalp each time I used it. Yet still, after I washed out the first batch, I would mix together another bowlful of the toxic baby-blue solution, and tenderly reapply it to my raw and blistering head. It took a few minutes for the burning to begin; it was a white, searing agony and, as it grew, so did my physical panic. My heart pounded so hard that my chest jumped as if I were hiccupping, my legs bucked in angry reaction to the pain, making it impossible to sit, so I ran up and down the landing of the house, clawing at the rough plaster on the walls until my fingernails splintered and my fingertips hurt more than my head. I counted each step out loud until I reached one thousand. Then I started again. Finally, it was time to rinse. I crouched over the side of the bath, my head hanging as if in shame that I was relieving myself from the distress caused by the bleach. The pure fresh water soothed my scalded scalp and briefly took me away from the chaos of my life. Water brought me peace as eating once had. I wished I could allow myself to go swimming, but I couldn't expose my body in public. So instead, I took four showers a day. As the water beat down on my bony shoulders and withered breasts, my mind was still.

Back again in front of the huge antique mirror that leaned against the wall beside my bed, sometimes I caught a glimpse of how skinny I really was. I would briefly see the outline of my ribs showing through the areolas on what had once been my breasts. The area of belly over my redundant and withholding womb was concave. I hadn't had a period in months. Standing there, my bleached hair soaking wet and spiky, my dark eyes huge and troubled, I was reminded of a small white kitten my friends and I had rescued from drowning in the canal back home in Dublin. When I was the fat girl with a pretty face. Back when I was strong, and brave enough to rescue a kitten.

The kids at school loved my Dad. On Wednesday and Sunday afternoons I would meet him in his favourite pub in town, but occasionally he would surprise me and pick me up from school. He would be waiting at the gates, all huge grin, deep dimples and twinkly eyes. Most days I would walk home alone, but when Dad showed up a group of children would follow us all the way down the long affluent avenue that led from school to what used to be our family home. We passed the places that made up the pictures of my childhood, the doctor's surgery where Dad called our GP "a fuckin' vet!" when he had to get a tetanus shot in his behind; the supermarket where we shopped together every Saturday for strange foods like artichokes which my mother had written on a list; the off-licence where on his birthday I had bought him a bottle of whiskey – he looked sad when I gave it to him, but I didn't understand why. Then, when we reached the Village Green he would stop, turn, and grin at us.

"Who wants a cream cake?"

Half a dozen children's hands would shoot straight up towards the sky in greedy excitement.

He led us into the tiny shop that sold everything from china dog figurines to geometry sets, walked bandy-legged shoot-out style towards the counter and stood squat in front of the smiling shopkeeper.

"Me and my amigos here will take every cream cake you've got in the joint," he said in his best John Wayne voice.

We all whooped and hollered around him, firing imaginary guns into the air.

The shopkeeper was in on the act; he faked panic, and hurriedly went about filling paper bags full of cakes, pushing them towards us as if he were handing over the week's takings of gold in moneybags with dollar signs on them.

Dad winked and slipped him a fiver, and we all trooped out again, stuffing our sweet faces as we went.

The choices were clear: Either I could stay in Ireland and go to boarding school, a thought that terrified me, or I could move to America with my mother. Everyone hoped that my dad was going to book himself into the hospital to stop drinking – his brothers and sisters frequently made the long drive up from Kerry to try and talk him into it. I didn't see why he should: I never felt unsafe with him, I rarely fought with him, and as far as I could tell, the whole world loved him. I heard whispers of livers and blackouts, responsibilities and God-given talents, but all I cared about was that he was my dad, and I wanted to stay close to him. I was sure I could convince him to come and live in the house again. Mom could go to America. Dad and me were the same, we looked the same, we talked the same and we laughed the same, which meant we would be fine. When he needed to write I could sit by his desk, like I had played under it as a three-year-old. I would learn to cook and we would look after each other. All I had to do was suggest it to him – how silly that no one had thought of it.

"But I'm not well, Doods."

"Stop it, Dad. What do you mean? You're fine!" I smiled at him, willing it to be the truth.

Then, for the second time in my life, I saw my father cry. And I knew I was going to America.

Those years of relocation, disconnection, and illness changed all three of us forever. It took me two decades to understand why my mother had no choice but to restart her life in America. Eventually though, as I became a mother, wife, and ex-wife myself, I understood it all – and with that understanding came the relationship with her that I had for so long rejected and repressed. It took me longer to realise that no one, not even my father, could save me from inner demons – demons I insisted on feeding and keeping alive – the very same lesson my father learned when he lost his sixteen-year-old daughter to the other side of the world. He booked himself into hospital a week after my mother and I left for The States and dried out. He is still sober today.

We were, and are, three flawed people battling to stay alive. Between us we fought, we drank, we binged, we starved, we screamed, and we cried. But through it all, we loved.

Stolen Dreams
and
Lullabies

Jacinta McDevitt

Jacinta McDevitt

Jacinta McDevitt's latest book, *Write A Book In A Year, Writing Workshop & Workbook,* is a must for all budding authors. Jacinta is also the author of three bestselling novels, *Sign's On, Handle With Care* and *Excess Baggage.* She is one of the authors in Poolbeg's *Thirty and Fabulous* collection in support of Women's Aid and she is a contributor in the short story collection, *Mum's the Word,* a book in aid of Cystic Fibrosis research in the National Children's Hospital in Tallaght.

Jacinta has been short-listed for the Francis McManus Award and has won various awards and prizes for her short stories.

Stolen Dreams and Lullabies

It's there again this morning. The soft, puffed white veil on the
virgin mountain. She's waiting. Waiting for her lover to commit.
Waiting where the world ends and there is no space. No space
between us, God and me and mine.

My memories fog and fade. In light and dark the shadows
stretch and billow. So near and yet just out of reach. I try to catch
the essence of the mist, but can't. Not with open hand or broken
heart. I'm lost. Sealed in. Lost in the lacy haze of him and me.
Sealed in the toxic mix of youth and age and timing in the cycle
all gone wrong. There is a raw reversal of the chain. A ganging
up of circumstance and chance. It should be him to lay me down
to rest. Mourn a while. Cry few but bitter tears. Pray, then carry
on.

And today it is his birthday. His fifth. I want to cuddle him.
Caress him back to life. Feel little hands mould to mine. Watch
him try to keep in step. Pick up the pace, stumble, fall, bleed. I'd
kiss the pain away. Tickle tanned pod belly to hear him laugh. To
see him squirm and wriggle, toss and turn. His luscious halo

shine and bounce and curl. But not today. Today the sun has given up and so have I.

No party now. My party days are done. Long gone. No invite now for happy clowns or fools or joy. Just quiet. Silent days. Long lonely feasts of gluttonous memories of my boy. Starved of all the happy times. The yearly rites of lighting coloured candles in the dark. Now only I can close my eyes and make a wish and keep it to myself. Bright balloons. Prussian. Cobalt. Blue. All blue now for my boy who's lost the mix of youth and gentle man. Won't toil or sow or sweat out bloody tears. Won't know the touch of love from one he loves. Won't fall in love and watch her swell his seed and labour in the pouring out of life. Nor hear the first sharp cry, then cut and seal the cord. To hold that little life in palm and heart.

And me. Me left. Casting shadows from myself to feed some grand need in me. A need in me to mourn or grieve or cry. For all of it. The waste. I do whatever those who practise skills of life and death and passing on and staying still would do. Perfect the art of pouring forth while holding back. Add, subtract and multiply the length of time before I see him. Frustrated as these days tick on and on. Night slips into day and charms her with the stars. I wake, I sleep, I dream. I wake again to dream.

I am. I live. Not here. Not now. But somewhere. Somewhere in the magic of the light. I stand and watch. I see him daub the cracking rod that brings it all to life. Young flesh ripe for every parasite. Mine hard, worn out, not making any feast. Fat maggots on a hook and bones are left. To torture mine. In night and light I see it all again. Pulled out limp and damp. Unclean with bluish lips. Pruned. White. Vacant staring eyes. Dragged out asleep with no sweet goodnight kiss. Dimpled flesh. Wounded, sore and raw. Naked feet and tiny cherub toes tangled in a mess of reed and mud and gut.

Grown men dragging, keening, weeping out to sea. Faces damp

from rain and tide and the effort of this illegal haul. Actors in a tragic play. They stage the roles of sorrow and regret. Use crude props, forget their lines and fumble by my side. Bowing, begging my applause. All done frame by frame. Just so I can't forget.

I cry a hundred, million tears for him and me. Friends come to mop my brow and furrow deep behind their silent eyes. They think what's best for them is best for me. Some break the rules and smile and pass the time of day. Make cups of tea and bake.

They don't speak his name or talk of him to me. They wait and talk of me in huddles by the door. Then give advice to start again. To take another chance. "You should move on." They say. "A fluke." "A dreadful accident." "A tragedy." They prattle on and on. "Try to have another one." Breed? Have more? A family of tragedies, maybe. I nod. I hope.

I love and hate the loving. I'm pulled and torn, drawn in the courtship game of love and hate and need. While every month the cure flows out of me. Caught between this rock and hard place I stand and feel the empty shelves that lost their childish charms. The bedtime books all tucked up safe and sound. Bike, bat, ball, all neatly put away. Dragons gone to darker dungeons in the loft so now we can move on with clean and Spartan things. Lapse into a world of sparse, uncluttered minds. With fresh sky paint that drips and covers up the prints of grubby hands I want to trace along the stair. No touch of what he touched is left for me. I search and find, hide and seek, hunt and scour for hidden treasure in the dark. The worn-out teddy bear that hid beneath the bed in dust and fluff and waited there for me. Naked. Neglected. Unkempt. Unloved.

And so today. Today it is his birthday. His fifth. Today a gift. A gift to see a smile. Just that. A smile. Not costing much, the price I cannot pay. So, I borrow from my heart, my soul and there he is. Still. So still. I try as I have tried and tried before to make the rhythm of my breath be his. Trace crown and cradle in the cushion of this life where he belongs. With taste of salt and bitter baby smells. Broken dreams and shattered lullabies. Mute chuckled music for these deafened ears. "Love you, Mam." Words I'll never hear. I'm robbed again and no one to repay. Fuck God and every smiling cry of joy and pain in birth and life and every crawling thing that hacks away at me. To peel me layer by layer to face myself. To see it's only me. A silhouette of what I want to be. I'm finished waiting now for time to do the trick or fate to play his hand again.

Today I will go to that grave and rancid place. White box and forget-me-nots. Caught up with weeds and weighted down by sods who dig and curse and spit and dare to laugh. Don't cross, bend, bow or genuflect. Drills head to toe and side by bloody side. With 6ft plots now framing one so small. Lost where Pio smiles and does the father act and bleeds stigmata to my heart. Oh, that he might heal with laying on of hands in pure white cotton gloves. To call me to a place where Mother Mary stands between the peaks and valleys tossed with green. Cajoles with Mother Earth to join her in the coup. Employ their charms to do the job that I was meant to do. So, I'll retreat there for a while and kneel, give in, put on a party smile and visit for a while.

For today there is an air about the mountain. I feel her strain. The icy string of pearls about her neck break and roll away. Luscious, juicy tears, flow down her side. One by one. They pool. They pond around her feet. She blushes purple in between the gray. So, today. Today the chance to take the risk. To lift the veil and take the first sweet kiss.

The
School Reunion

Marisa Mackle

Marisa Mackle

Marisa Mackle is from Armagh and lives in Dublin. Her novels include *Mr Right for the Night, So Long, Mr Wrong, Mile High Guy, Chinese Whispers* and *Confessions of an Air Hostess*. Her books have been translated into eight different languages.

The
School Reunion

Dianne worried that there wouldn't be enough wine to go around. It was hard to know how much people would drink. Some might drive and not drink at all, while others would leave their cars at home and take a taxi instead. Those non-drivers might end up drinking a whole bottle of wine by themselves. It was hard to judge. You couldn't exactly phone your guests up in advance and ask them how much alcohol they planned on consuming now, could you?

In the end Dianne decided to order in more wine than she knew she would need. Better safe than sorry. After all, there was nothing quite as miserable as a party where the booze ran out early. They were the parties that people tended to remember for all the wrong reasons. Dianne's mother had always told her that the quality of food wasn't so important as long as people had a damn good glass of wine in their hands. Wine, or champagne, of course. Dianne's mother was a fan of both. She'd fancied herself as something of a connoisseur. Sadly she had died of liver failure a year ago and her dad had proposed within two months to a girl three years younger than Dianne.

Dianne wished her mother had taught her how to cook when she was still alive. Mrs Whyte had been an excellent cook and had gained a reputation around Dublin for being a wonderful hostess. Her parties had been legendary where people usually ended up dancing on the furniture. The rich and the famous used to turn up at the Whytes' South Dublin mansion to be entertained and they were never disappointed. A former beauty queen, Mrs Whyte rubbed shoulders with the cream of high society and many a secret affair started at these legendary parties too, apparently. Indeed, rumour had it that Mr and Mrs Whyte's marriage was of the open kind but of course this had never been confirmed outside the gossip circles and certainly the young Dianne had been blissfully unaware of any untoward shenanigans as she'd spent most of her childhood at a very small, exclusive boarding school just outside Dublin. On Sundays the teenagers were allowed buy a Sunday paper and more often than not the Whytes, all tans and perfect white teeth, would be smiling out of the back pages alongside some puff piece written about their latest charity venture. Her teenage friends thought it was very cool that Dianne's parents were almost celebrities and that they hung out with rock stars and politicians and got invited to all the best parties. Not Dianne however. Privately she wished her mother would write her a letter sometimes like the other girls' mothers did. Or visited the odd time with a tin of freshly baked scones. But that never happened. Mrs Whyte quite simply did not have the time to be writing letters, although she did often get her secretary to send Dianne a generous cheque.

Once, just once, did Mr and Mrs Whyte visit. They arrived in a helicopter in a flurry of designer gear and flash jewellery. They brought Dianne, all her friends and the headmaster to a very fancy restaurant and also gave everybody in Dianne's class the chance of a helicopter ride. Everybody agreed that it had been a wonderful day. Everybody except Dianne, who had quietly cried herself to sleep that night. She just wanted a normal family. Her parents had barely said two words to her during the entire visit, apart from her mother criticising her for being too skinny. She'd also smelled very strongly of alcohol, Dianne felt, and it embarrassed her. Kissing her was like kissing a wine bottle.

Dianne went down to the local library to use the Internet. She wanted to be sure that she had enough money in her bank account before she splashed out in the swish but very expensive Donnelly's Deli down the street for the occasion. She checked her balance online and decided that she'd just about have enough if she brought in her own lunch to work for the next fortnight instead of forking out a fortune for fresh rolls and take-out coffees every day like she usually did. Her job as an assistant at a friend's crèche four mornings a week was just really to keep her going until she decided what she was going to do with the rest of her life.

Mind you, looking after other people's children was an enormous amount of responsibility, not to mention the fact that Dianne had caught every bug going this winter and permanently seemed to be buying Panadol in an attempt to banish the constant headaches that just seemed to be part and parcel of the job. Why did little people make so much noise?

Thankfully the crèche was located across the river from where Dianne had grown up so that there was precious little chance of anybody from her past dropping in their kids to be minded. Over on the north side of town, on the street where she now lived, nobody knew anything about Dianne Whyte and that was preferable. She didn't know anything about the neighbours only that they had a constant stream of washing hanging on the line and they tended to leave the volume of their TV turned up a bit too loud for Dianne's liking. She'd nod to them going in and out of her drive as she went about her business and they always politely nodded back but that was about the height of it. It wasn't like the road where she grew up where everybody knew everybody else and regularly threw drinks parties at Christmas or during the summer to show off their magnificent lawns. People around here tended to drink straight from the can rather than use glasses and spent a lot of time outside the corner shop still dressed in their pyjamas gossiping. Dianne was sure they gossiped about her sometimes, the lady who wouldn't even pop out to the shop for a pint of milk without applying a faceful of make-up first, but she didn't really care. She'd learned from her mother to always take pride in her appearance, just in case.

She reckoned that the best option was to buy in a selection of meats and salads the morning of the party. That way everybody would be catered for and the vegetarians, if there were any, wouldn't be complaining that there wasn't anything to eat. She'd also buy two different types of bread loaves; tomato and fennel perhaps, as well as a nice lemon cheesecake for dessert. One cake would be enough, she reckoned, as women her age were usually watching their figures and would only take a sliver anyway. She'd serve the cake with coffee from the delicate china set she'd inherited from her mother. That was everything sorted.

She hadn't bought invitations to be posted out, as in this day and age nearly everybody was on email or at least had a mobile phone. Finding everybody's contact details hadn't been as difficult as she thought. First of all Dianne had phoned her old school and explained that she would be organising a twenty-year reunion for the Class of '67 and would they be able to help her out. There was a new headmaster there now but his secretary couldn't have been more helpful. Most of her class were back in Ireland now. Many had lived abroad shortly after leaving school or college but were back settled now with their young families. Dianne wondered if any of them were widowed like her, or would she be the only one.

Tears welled in Dianne's eyes now as she thought of Derek and what might have been if only for circumstances. She had met her handsome husband in UCD and had fallen head over heels with him. They'd had a lot in common, both driving their own cars while other students had to walk everywhere in the rain or take the bus. Dianne hadn't taken a public bus anywhere until she was in her thirties. People often found that hard to believe but there had never been any need. As a child, there had always been the chauffeur and then at seventeen she'd got her car, so why on earth would she have ever got the bus?

Both sets of parents had given the couple hefty deposits for their first house, as wedding presents. After a lavish reception party in The Shelbourne Hotel, they'd spent a fortnight in The Maldives before returning to move into their brand-new starter home in Ballsbridge at the joint age of twenty-four.

Life continued to be just one big party. Derek and Dianne knew everybody and everybody knew them. They were on the guest lists at all the right parties and were a constant fixture at the races where Derek's father usually had at least one horse running. Maybe that's when Derek had started his gambling. It only started out as a flutter here and there, of course, and he seemed to be extremely lucky, often coming home from a day at Leopardstown with pockets full of cash. But then it became more serious and he was soon putting crazy money on horses. Sometimes he would close his eyes and recklessly just pick a random horse from the programme and put money on it. He couldn't understand why

Dianne would get so annoyed. After all, if you couldn't have fun with your money, then what was the point?

She grimaced now when she thought of it; the fun had run out and so too had the money. Dianne's job in an art gallery had been entertaining to say the least, meeting lots of interesting people at the exhibitions, but it wasn't the kind of job that made you rich. Derek, on the other had, had always worked for his father in the stud farm, commuting to and from Kildare every day in his BMW. The youngest of seven, it should have been apparent that his eldest brother, James, who also worked in the stud farm, would eventually inherit everything, but that possibility never even occurred to Derek and Dianne. After Derek's father died of a sudden heart attack at the age of fifty-nine, the shock result of his will was that James had been left the lot. As the stud was losing money at this stage, James decided to sell up and move abroad. Derek and Dianne had been left several valuable paintings, but apart from that they were broke.

Dianne had made Derek sit down and face reality. He would have to get a real job. It wouldn't be too difficult, she reckoned. Derek had a natural boyish charm, was well educated and had good contacts. He soon found a position in a Dublin auctioneering firm, which kept him busy and Dianne had traded in part-time hours at the gallery for full-time hours. Derek had promised not to continue gambling but although he stayed away from the big race meetings, it wasn't long before Dianne caught him on the phone to the betting office when he thought she wasn't around.

They'd had the mother of all arguments and he had packed a little suitcase and stormed off down the road. But it wasn't long before he returned again just as Dianne expected he would. Where else would he have gone? Who would have taken him in? Once you were out of the social scene, it was very hard to get back in again. And nobody appreciated a former drinking buddy turning up on their doorstep on a Monday evening, no matter who he was.

Life went on with Derek swearing he wasn't betting and Dianne working long hours in the gallery trying to sell paintings to people with more money than taste and putting any commissions she made carefully into her bank account. Derek began to resent working for the auctioneering firm, showing people around houses that they had no intention of buying. He could tell by their cheap suits and their mediocre cars that they weren't here to buy, only to gawk. They were just there for a half hour's entertainment or so. It was cheaper than going to the zoo obviously, or the cinema. Eventually he handed in his notice. There had to be more to life than this.

Dianne couldn't remember when Derek went from having just a glass of wine or two at dinner to drinking a half bottle of wine, then a full bottle, and then more than that. She was working ridiculous hours in the gallery so there were so many exhibitions to attend, but after a couple of months, when she was searching in the garage for something and found two plastic bags full of empty beer cans, she knew the Derek was now battling something deadlier than gambling; he had a drink problem too.

The night Dianne left her husband, she left him lying on the couch in a stupor surrounded by empty beer cans, scattered among used scratch cards that hadn't led him to the small fortune he was looking for. She had tried everything. AA said they couldn't help him unless he was prepared to admit he had a problem. But Derek wouldn't have admitted anything of the sort. As far as he was concerned he just liked to have a few to relax and unwind. Dianne often pointed out that there was a big difference between unwinding and passing out.

The night she'd left and checked herself into a B&B wondering what the hell she was going to do with her life, Derek hadn't even noticed his wife was missing. The former cream couch in the middle of their living room was these days covered in beer stains and sometimes stank of vomit. It had been Derek's bed for some time now as he always seemed to forget to come upstairs after a hard night's drinking. The night Dianne left, he woke up to discover he was out of booze. He shouted for Dianne but there was no answer so he presumed she was upstairs asleep. He stumbled into the hall, reached for his coat, and walked out leaving the front door ajar. He made his way up to the traffic lights and, not realising that the little man was red, not green, he stepped out onto the road, only focussing on the lights of the off-licence across the way.

The police told Dianne that her husband wouldn't have felt a thing such was the impact of the knock. She'd nodded, shivering in her own home, deeply ashamed of the empty beer cans strewn across the room, as a female officer made her a cup of tea. They'd been able to reach her on her mobile phone just as she'd climbed into her bed in the B&B, having finally decided to formally separate from her husband. Now in a state of extreme shock, she wondered, if she hadn't left, would he still be lying in a mortuary, stone-cold dead?

The table was set for a prince, Dianne thought, strangely satisfied with herself. You wouldn't think by looking at this glorious spread of food that the hostess herself hardly had two cents to rub together. Nobody coming to the party would ever know that Dianne Whyte's husband had secretly cashed his life insurance before he died to gamble it on the dogs, and had lost it all. Nobody would suspect either that Dianne regularly scoured the charity shops in town to buy clothes. If anybody were to remark on how slim Diane had become, she simply intended to smile sweetly and let them think that she was a member of a fancy gym, and not that she went hungry in order to get her hair done professionally sometimes.

She had ordered in glasses and crockery and white linen cloths. She'd had to pay a deposit on the wine glasses so hopefully nobody would break any. Even if they did, she had to try and not to worry about it. Accidents happened. She'd borrowed the extra stools from Irene who ran the crèche because it just wouldn't do to have people standing. But even at this stage she knew she had too many. Four out of ten people had already cancelled. Mary was in Australia to visit her grandchild. Mary had got pregnant straight after leaving school, and now her own daughter had just given birth to a baby girl. She had written Dianne a cheery note wishing her luck with the party, adding that she was over the moon abut her own daughter. Dianne had shaken her head in wonder. It didn't seem right that somebody in their class was already a granny.

Geraldine had written to say that she couldn't come because of prior commitments. She didn't say what those commitments were, which Dianne thought was a bit rude. Then again, Geraldine had been the oddball of the class, so nothing much had changed there obviously. Poor Terry was in hospital in France after breaking a leg during a skiing accident. She told Dianne to be sure to send everyone her love. Colette's husband had phoned to say that Colette had died of breast cancer earlier that year. He spent an hour on the phone talking about his wife and she'd told him stories about Colette's schooldays and the adventures they had both shared. By the time she had put the phone down both Dianne and Danny were in floods of tears. The conversation had left her feeling shaken. Colette had been the healthy one in school. She'd always been very sporty and had never been tempted to smoke or drink, not even when she'd left school and gone to college. It was an absolute tragedy.

So that left five others plus herself. Dianne glanced at the table, all the dishes carefully covered with plates to make sure no flies got at the food. There would be more than enough to go around, and the white wine was chilling in the fridge.

She hoped everyone would be able to find the small terraced house without too much difficulty. It wasn't the easiest place to get to, and you had to pass by four blocks of council flats first. There was no number written on the door, but the number on the house next door was clearly painted on the gate so it didn't take a genius to work out which house was Dianne's. It wasn't much to look at from the outside but inside was a little treat. Dianne had lovingly painted the walls herself, bought beautiful material from an interior design shop's closing-down sale and made her own curtains. And the paintings that hung on the walls were only exquisite. No matter how bad things had got, she had refused to sell them. They were probably worth a small fortune now but Dianne would keep them. She'd sold both her wedding ring and engagement ring for cash but she wouldn't part with her watercolours for anything in the world.

At eleven o'clock in the morning, Deirde rang to say her twins were sick and that there was no way she could cross the city in case their condition worsened. She said she hoped to meet up with Dianne soon for coffee or something because she hadn't seen her in such a long time. Dianne sympathised with her and wished the twins a speedy recovery. Then, with a heavy heart, she put down the phone. It was now down to four guests.

By midday a further two had cancelled with not-very-believable excuses. And just before lunch-time, Dianne received a huge bouquet of flowers from Suzy, her best friend from school to say that something had come up suddenly but she hoped everything would go well and that everyone would have a great day. Dianne, with a shaking hand, signed for the flowers and once the delivery man had disappeared back into his van, she closed the door and sobbed until she thought her heart would break.

Nobody was coming. That was the truth. Dianne didn't matter to people any more. She was out of the loop, no longer one of the smart set, and no longer of any use socially to anybody. It had all been different when she'd been daddy's girl with her own pony and the family helicopter and the twice-yearly trips abroad to Florida and the South of France, not to mention the weekend shopping trips away to London and New York with her mother. All Dianne's so-called friends had turned up to her wedding reception to quaff champagne and mingle with the highest of society. There had been no cancellations back then, as far as Dianne could remember. Not even one.

She nibbled uninterestedly at the tomato, mozzarella and basil salad, drizzled in Extra Virgin oil. She had enough food now to keep her going for a week, but she wasn't even hungry. She decided she might as well put some of the plates into the fridge. Else they would go off and it would be such a waste of money. She opened the fridge door. There were too many wine bottles taking up room. She'd have to take some of them out. She removed two bottles and stood them up on the kitchen counter. They were nice and chilled at this stage. For the first time in ages, Dianne felt like a drink.

She poured herself a large glass. She normally didn't drink at all. People drank to celebrate things, or to relax, but Dianne associated alcohol with disease. It had killed both her mother and her husband. Alcohol was the enemy. Dianne sat back down at the table with the enemy in her hand. "Happy 20th anniversary," she said glumly to all the no-shows, before polishing off the glass in seconds. Dianne wasn't drinking to have a good time. No. She was drinking to forget. The bite of the alcohol numbed her pain. Somewhat. Halfway through the second glass, the doorbell rang loudly.

Damn. It must be one of the local kids, collecting for something. The kids around here were always running or fasting for charity or raising money for the local youth club. It was so different from when Dianne was at school and nobody did anything except write home looking for some more money for themselves.

Dianne fiddled in her purse for some coins before answering the door. But instead of some eager-faced, grubby-pawed youngsters at the door, stood a tall, elegant blonde, perfectly made-up, in an exquisite, cream trouser suit, and a designer handbag hanging gracefully from one arm. There was no car parked outside, only a taxi with its engine still running.

"Dianne?" The handsome woman's face broke into a smile as she hugged her.

As Dianne inhaled her expensive-smelling perfume, she struggled to figure out who on earth this stranger could be. But before she could ask, the woman had turned around and said to the taxi driver, "You can go on now. It's the right address after all."

Speechless, Dianne invited the well-spoken lady into her home. "Would you like a glass of wine? Red or white?" she mumbled feeling rather foolish. Her mind was racing. Surely, everybody had already cancelled? Who hadn't?

"A white wine would be lovely. Am I the first here? I thought I was late. I came straight from the airport. The taxi driver got a bit lost, I'm afraid . . ."

Dianne poured a generous glass of wine for the stranger. "I have to apologise," she said, "but I don't . . ."

"Oh, hang on," said the woman. "Before I forget, I brought you a little present."

She fished out a little parcel from her handbag, handed it over and watched as Dianne opened up.

But Dianne unwrapped the gift slowly, biding her time. Who was missing? Geraldine had said she wasn't coming, Terri had sent regrets as had Mary, as had . . .

"Sheila!"

"Yes?" the other woman raised an eyebrow.

"Oh Sheila, this watch is beautiful but I couldn't take it. It must have cost a fortune!"

"Honestly though, you must have it. I insist. My husband and I run an antiques shop in London so we have great finds coming in all the time. When this little gem arrived in last week, I immediately put it aside for you."

Tears welled up in Dianne's eyes as she slipped the dainty gold watch onto her left wrist. "I love it," she said quietly. "The others aren't coming by the way," she added in almost a whisper. "It's a sign of the time, I suppose. Everyone's busy."

"Well, that's a pity," said Sheila. "But not to worry, as long as there's more than one person here the party can still go ahead, don't you think? I know I'm famished. Do you mind if I dig in?"

Dianne watched in amazement as Sheila heaped her plate with various salads. Not in a million years had she expected her to show up. Sheila had not been a boarder in their old school, but as the head gardener's daughter she had been allowed attend classes as a day pupil. When Dianne had contacted the school, they'd said that the gardener had since retired and it was believed that his daughter now lived in England. Dianne had asked them to try and contact her anyway, care of her father. She probably wouldn't come, but it would still be nice to be asked. When she hadn't heard back, she'd just presumed that Sheila wasn't terribly interested. A tall, gawky child with national health glasses and prominent teeth, Sheila had always been very quiet and hadn't really mixed with the others. She'd seemed to spend her spare time wandering around the school gardens with her father and sometimes she would paint pictures of the various plants and flowers her father had planted. The reason Dianne remembered this was because she had loved painting herself.

"So you're based in England now?" Dianne asked as she topped up Sheila's glass.

"That's right. I went to England straight after school to work in an art gallery."

"That's funny," Dianne mused. "I worked in an art gallery here in Dublin myself but it eventually closed down. I now work in a kindergarten."

"Really? How do you stick it?"

"It pays the bills, I suppose . . ."

"Anyway," Sheila continued, "I met an army officer at an exhibition. He was twenty years my senior and everybody said it wouldn't last but it did, and we married. We're still together. He retired a while ago and we run both an antiques shop and an art gallery in London. It keeps us very busy."

"It's better to be busy though, than to have too much time on your hands," said Dianne thoughtfully, raising her glass to her lips.

"Well, the only thing we never have enough of, is time. We have plenty of money and no time."

"It's always the way."

"We'd love to set up a gallery here in Dublin too if we could."

"Well, why don't you?"

"London is where we live now – we can't be in two places at once . . . you have fabulous paintings here, Dianne."

"Thank you."

"You always had an eye for art. Do you remember when we went on that class trip to the National Art Gallery and you and I were so thrilled to be there and everybody else was so bored? They wanted to go to McDonalds to get chips and the teacher had a hard job trying to drag the two of us back to the bus!"

"I had forgotten," Dianne grinned.

"I hadn't. I don't forget anything. You said you worked in an art gallery? How did you find that?"

"I loved it. That was always the dream so I'm lucky to be able to say I lived my dream, if only for a few years. Some people never get to do that."

"You could live that dream again," said Sheila cryptically, dabbing her mouth with a serviette, and eyeing the cheesecake. "We're looking for somebody to run an art gallery here for us."

Dianne stared at her old school friend for a few moments. Who did she think she was? Her fairy godmother or something? You didn't just walk back into somebody's life after twenty years and offer to change their life around for them. That wasn't realistic. What on earth was going on?

"Sheila, why are you trying to help me out?" Dianne cut straight to the chase.

"How do you mean? I'm trying to suit myself. We need somebody and you seem perfect."

But Dianne wasn't buying that. "Come on though. You must know so many people in the art world . . ." she trailed off realising that she might insult Sheila by protesting too much.

"Do you remember your thirteenth birthday party? You invited me to stay with you and I rode your horse," Sheila said.

"I think I invited everybody. I don't really remember . . . there were so many parties."

"I never forgot. You invited me. So many of the others never invited me to their parties. They didn't think I was the same as them."

Dianne said nothing. She was beginning to know how that felt.

"And when your parents visited, I got to go on a helicopter ride. Do you know how much that meant to me? When I went to England, I went on the boat. Many people I met over there had been on a plane. I had never been on a plane, but I had flown in a private helicopter. That gave me confidence to be able to tell people that. I also knew how to ride a horse, thanks to you."

"But Sheila, all my friends who stayed got to ride Blackie."

"You used to lend me your paints so I could practise. If it wasn't for you I couldn't have painted because my father couldn't afford to go to Dublin shopping in arts and craft shops. Please work for us, Dianne. We know we could trust you. I also owe you one. You helped me years ago, without even realising. Whatever you're earning in the crèche, we'll pay five times more."

Dianne fought to hold back the tears. This was the best school reunion she could have possibly hoped for. After a moment's pause, she slowly she raised her glass and tipped it against Sheila's.

"Okay so, you have me sold," she said, her head swimming with excitement. "What can I say? To my new job and to the last twenty years . . ."

"And the next," Sheila smiled. "Most importantly. To the next twenty years, Dianne!"

A Recollection
of a
Love Lost

Anna McPartlin

Anna McPartlin

Anna McPartlin's first novel, the bestselling *Pack Up The Moon,* was published in January 2006. *Apart From The Crowd* was published in November of the same year and she is currently working on her third novel

A Recollection of a Love Lost

The year was 1979. In a dark room twin beds were separated by an old dressing-table with a scratched mirror. Under it rested a little stool that seemed too distressed to sit on, so instead it was shoved under the dresser and close to the wall. There were two old-fashioned wooden free-standing wardrobes at the end of each bed. At one time these wardrobes would have been considered quite expensive and possibly even chic but that time had long passed before woodworm had taken up residence. There was another dressing-table which sat under the window looking out onto the street and across to the green. That was the dresser that held personal items. It too had seen better days and seemed small; the items always seeming to be fighting for space or threatening to fall off its splintered edge.

"Mom?"

"What?"

"Do you need the loo?"

"No. You?"

"No."

Silence ensued but only for a minute or two.

"Mom?"

"Yeah?"

"Are you tired yet?"

"Yeah, I'm tired. Are you tired?"

"I think so but I can't sleep."

"Count sheep."

"I'll count dogs. I prefer dogs."

"Good idea. Dogs are brilliant."

"Yeah, they are. OK. Goodnight, Mom.

"Goodnight, Bunty."

"Don't call me Bunty."

"Sorry, Chickatee."

"Don't call me Chickatee."

"Righto, Bunty."

"Mom!"

Muffled laughter followed. I was seven. My mother was thirty-nine. We shared a bedroom in my grandmother's house. My mother had left her husband two years before and was slowly losing the power in her arms and legs to multiple sclerosis. She was alone and scared. She had a kid to take care of and a disease that she didn't understand eating away at her. And still she could laugh. When people ask me about my mom and what I remember most, I remember that.

Separating from your husband in the 1970's was not an easy option. She didn't embark on a new life in her mother's spare room without serious consideration and, to be fair to my father, neither her life nor mine depended on us fleeing a small town in South Kerry one Monday morning. My father wasn't a violent or dangerous man but he was a heavy drinker. Their marriage was loveless and consequently unhappy. My mom was unwilling to settle for unhappy. I remember the late seventies and early eighties background as being a little grey but against it she lit up. Mom hadn't got much, her family's fortunes having slipped, her husband's status and potential frittered away, but what she did have was all the more precious because she had sight. She could look above and beyond this place and time to another where she would glimpse a kind of inexplicable brilliance. Consequently Mom knew happiness had nothing to do with a decent house or a great car; she couldn't care less about money or status or what the neighbours were saying. She knew that happiness could be found in the here and now and in any moment. It didn't have to be gift-wrapped for her to spot and appreciate joy in a mere smile or a laugh or a good conversation or a visit with a loved one, a friend's kind word or deed, a neighbour's unsolicited help. A three-and-a-half-minute song could make her soul soar and inspired her to sing along which was unfortunate as her voice, once great, was shot to hell, leaving those close to cover their ears while she'd repeat the two sentences she knew over and over with a kind of gusto usually reserved for the Carnegie Hall.

Mom was popular, she had friends she could count on and was lucky in their unwavering support of her. She had met most of these friends while working as a secretary in Dublin and London. Her best friend only lived down the road from my grandmother's house which Mom always considered a bloody stroke of luck. Mom loved the word "bloody". It was most definitely one of her favourites: "bloody" and "gas". A lot of things were considered to be gas. He's gas, that's gas, I love a bit of gas and so on. And with respect to the proximity of her best friend's marital home, she was right: it was a bloody stroke of luck because mom's best friend would be the one she would turn to in her darkest hours and the one who made sure that the most mundane details of her life were handled until the day she would die. Her sister was another true friend and the matter-of-fact caretaker who handled the nasty business of ensuring that we weren't living in filth. My grandmother was nearing eighty, her sight was fading and yet it's likely she could see a little better than Mom because the disease affected her vision early on. I was the pair of eyes and because I was a kid I didn't really notice or care about things like dust or mess or grime. I was also the pair of legs and arms required to vacuum or clean. I was a kind of quick-rub-here-and-a-quick-rub-there sort of gal. I favoured the Freddie-Mercury-stand-in-one-position-and-stretch-in-different-directions mode of hoovering and, as for grime, well let's just say I cleaned around it. My aunt was the one who would leave her four boys and husband's business to drive across the city to clean out the house when we required saving from rampant germs. At the point when it became apparent that our collective endeavours were substandard, it was my aunt who would ensure that a cleaner was employed. The cleaner would appear once a week and handle the heavy stuff. For a long time Mom insisted that she could still manage the ironing. Every now and then her hand would tire of the heavy iron and she'd find a way to singe flesh.

"Blast!" she'd say. "Blast it anyway!" She'd curse the iron. She liked the word "blast". It wasn't uttered with the same kind of frequency as bloody or gas but it was another favourite. "Blast it again!"

She'd request a bowl full of cold water and plunge her hand into it. "Oh, that feels good!" She'd smile while wriggling her slim fingers. "It's almost worth the blasted burn."

Mom liked to do for herself and for me and for granny. She was afraid of help, afraid that if she admitted she needed help it would reveal desperation. More than that she was afraid that those helping would see that a single mother with an old woman couldn't take care of a little girl and that little girl couldn't take care of her single mother and an old woman despite all our best intentions. The Social Welfare was omnipresent and in the distance watching and waiting. In reality their *modus operandi* was purely to ensure each one of us was safe and properly cared for but at the time their silent surveillance seemed akin to that of vultures aligned on the branch of a tree waiting for a dying animal's last breath. Mom knew that time was tick-tocking by and with each tick-tock our little family unit was coming closer to its end.

Mom liked our cleaner because she was interesting and always had a story about something going on in the Ballymun flats. Tea and biscuits would be laid on and Mom would settle by the kitchen table while our cleaner would regale us with a recent dreadful event. We'd be riveted, Mom and I.

"Well, you're never going to believe it."

"Go on," my mother would urge.

"Only another young fella over the balcony."

"Jesus!" my mother would sigh shaking her head from side to side. "From what floor?"

"Oh, off the top."

"Jesus!" she'd repeat. "I presume he's a gonner?"

"Oh yeah, bleedin Batman wouldn't survive that fall."

"God help him."

"I know. Still, to be honest he was a bit of a scumbag." Our cleaner would nod to herself and my mother would push the biscuits under her nose. She'd take off a yellow glove and partake of a snack for a moment or two. "Drugs," she'd whisper, suddenly conscious of the presence of a child. It would appear the image of a dude diving off a fourteen-storey building and going splat was suitable but the word drugs was deemed too harsh for my little ears, despite the fact that I spent a good portion of my day divvying out my mother's drugs for her bladder, tremors, constipation and pain – to say nothing of the particular type of trial MS treatment that changed from month to month – before separating and allocating my grandmother's low blood pressure, arthritis and sleeping pills.

My mother would nod her head. "Desperate," she'd say, momentarily comforted that someone else had it worse off than her. "I'll say a little prayer for him and his poor family." My mother liked to pray, she got a real kick out of it and she would pray for the poor man and for his family and later when our cleaner had gone she might even shed a tear for them because she knew what it was like to lose.

"Mom, are you crying?"

"No."

"Are you sure."

"Positive."

"I love you."

"I love you too, Bunty."

"Don't call me Bunty."

I think our cleaner made a real effort to arrive at our humble abode armed with the most terrible tales just so the poor woman whose kid had to carry her from chair to chair could feel lucky, even if it was just for an hour or two a week.

Our neighbours were great characters. My favourite was a nice old lady five doors up who dressed impeccably and from a bygone era with lace-up black shoes with a tiny heel, various pencil skirts below the knee, thick tights, cardigans closed at the neck and sealed with an ornate broach. She wore her silver hair in a twist rather than a bun so that her look was elegant and not in the least bit severe. Our silver-haired friend would take on the weekly shopping and for three people it amounted to three or four bags. She'd return laden down and assign the various items to their place amongst good china on tired shelving. She and Mom would talk together before joining my gran who held court in the sitting-room. Mom would employ what my gran referred to as her newfangled walking frame to get from kitchen to hall and hall to sitting-room. It took her so long to journey from one place to another, she'd joke about requiring sandwiches and a flask.

Our neighbours to the right were a young couple with two kids. He was a karate instructor and I think he drove a van. She was a housewife and I'm not sure but I remember something about her and an ability to sew. Maybe she just sewed for us but mostly she was in charge of lighting and cleaning out the fire each day of winter. My mom would thank God for her because it was "bloody dirty work". She'd arrive every day with a bit of local news for which Mom would be ever grateful. She was a nice woman, small in stature with short brown hair. She favoured jeans, sweatshirts and sensible shoes. Given the chance, my mother liked to dress up; she liked her hair to be done and for as long as she could maintain her weekly visits to the salon she did so. She loved pretty dresses and high-heeled shoes. Unfortunately the shoes remained in the old free-standing wardrobe at the end of her bed. I pulled a pair of extra-high stilettos out once and tottered into the sitting room just as our fire-making friend had set some turf alight. So busy was I tottering that I nearly tottered into the fire. Our neighbour caught me before I landed in the grate head first while Mom could only watch with horror, her failing legs preventing her from being anything but an unwilling spectator. I remember she cried and our fire-starting neighbour made tea. I remember I was miffed because the shoes were confiscated. I also remember that when we sat on the sofa watching TV that night she kept her arm locked around mine the whole time.

The year I turned ten we endured an extremely cold winter. So cold that mice appeared to take refuge in every house on the street, like a plague belonging to another time. Every household was up in arms while knee-deep in mice droppings. Our neighbour from across the road, a giddy woman with lots of boys, took charge of us, ensuring her husband trapped our house. Mom, mortally frightened of mice, put on a great show of pretending she wasn't in the least bit perturbed by their unwelcome presence until one day she leaned over and put her hand in the bread-drawer, unaware that our overzealous neighbour had trapped it. Luckily for my mother's left hand the trap was already full – however, stroking a dead mouse did little for her mental health. There were screams and shaking and a lot of bloody hells and blast-its.

That year when the snow came every day we saw at least three neighbours, each one making sure we were warm and fed and cared for. They always had time to put on the kettle, chat or laugh about such and such in the newspaper or down the road or on the telly. My friends liked my house as it seemed to them that I had free rein and yet they weren't naive enough to think that my world was anything that approached their idea of normal.

"Mom?"

"What?"

"Can I play with your walking frame?"

"Use the one from upstairs."

I ran upstairs to acquire the now spare walking frame. By this point Mom could no longer make it upstairs. The heave-ho-push-on-three method had served us well but that time too had passed and now the dining-room was her bedroom.

"Got it!" I yelled to my pal.

"So?"

"Gymnastics."

She looked at me cautiously. "Gymnastics?"

It was then I began to swing out of the bars and I don't know how the thing didn't just topple over but it didn't. Of course I was too big for it but my half-cocked swinging and leg-twisting seemed to be stimulating enough to encourage my pal to have a go. She started off all smiles swinging away and then, slam, her head hit the wall and, wham, her back hit the floor. The walking frame was lying on top of her.

"What's happening?" Mom screamed from the sitting-room, betraying a mild form of hysteria.

"Nothing!" I lied.

My pal was now crying.

"I hear crying."

I was panicking. "Everything's fine."

"Oh God, what's happening?" There were tears in her voice. "Don't make me crawl up there!"

I was probably smart enough to know that by the time she did my pal would either be dead, in an ambulance or halfway home.

"Mom, it's fine!" I was holding my hand over my pal's mouth. She was wild-eyed and possibly wondering why in the hell I was suffocating as opposed to helping her. To be fair I knew she was fine – no blood and that fact that she was flaying around like a lunatic as I held her down using the walking frame as leverage meant no broken bones. After I made her swear she wouldn't shout, I let her mouth go.

"Are you all right?" I asked sheepishly.

She checked herself by feeling her head and then she stood and shook herself off.

"Fine," she said.

"Want a biscuit?" I asked.

"Anything but those rotten orange jelly ones your ma likes."

And that was it. She forgave me. I'm still not sure why I held my hand to her mouth. All I do know is that it had something to do with the fear in my mom's voice.

My gran used to fall a lot and unsettlingly these falls usually coincided with a visit to the bathroom. Mom and I would be watching TV. Gran would head off upstairs to the loo. Approximately three minutes later we'd hear a thud.

"Mother?" Mom would call up.

"I've fallen!" Gran would call down.

My mom would look towards me; I'd sigh as the fall never seemed to occur during an ad break.

"Anna's on her way up."

I'd make my way up to the bathroom and, two times out of five she'd be on the floor with her knickers and pants around her ankles.

"Knickers up or down, darling?" Mom would call up to me.

"Down!" I'd shout.

"Bloody bad luck, Bunty!"

"I'm not deaf, Patricia!" my gran would interject.

"And don't call me Bunty!" I'd add, then I'd whip up Gran's pants as fast as I could, eyes half closed and facing the wall. We'd spend another five to twenty minutes depending on her position working out the best way of getting her standing without either of us breaking our backs.

"On three, Gran."

"I'd prefer it on four."

"On four."

"Hold it."

"What?"

"You've got me now?" she'd ask for the one hundredth time.

"I've got you."

"OK, on five."

"I thought we said on four?"

"I heard four!" Mom once roared from the bottom of the stairs.

"None of your business, Patricia, and now we're going to have to start again!" Gran shouted while sitting on her own left leg.

Falling happened a lot in our house. Falling was a way of life.

The house to our left was interesting in that the rows would be loud enough to hear through the walls. She was a lovely woman who was extremely glam in a pre-drag-queen-Bet-Lynch way and often cared for me after school when early on Mom didn't know her husband was a maniac (my mother's phrasing, not mine) and while she was looking for work and before work was no longer an option. He was an angry sort. He arrived home once when I was there. He was shouting and shoved me out the door with such force I fell to the ground. At the time Mom still used a walking stick. I made the mistake of reporting the incident. She marched into the garden and banged on the door waving her stick and roaring through the letterbox that she'd bloody kill him. Later that evening her legs gave way, she fell onto the floor and I couldn't get her up for nearly an hour. While lying on the ground she mentioned the fact that it was probably a good thing the man hadn't answered the door as it was likely she wouldn't have been able to deliver upon her threat.

My grandmother stepped over her and sniffed. "That's what guns are for, Patricia." She then pottered on in search of a glass of whiskey while giggling to herself. My mother joined in as did I.

I often laughed when I wasn't sure of the joke, only because individually both women had infectious laughs but especially so in chorus.

Anyway, back to my neighbours to our left. Some time after

that, Pre-drag Bet did leave the angry man. Many years later, when I was visiting Mom in the Home, she told me that she'd heard a rumour that when Pre-drag Bet had sought separation it became apparent that the angry man was already married and as a result their marriage was deemed null and void.

"Lucky cow!" my mother had said, smiling.

I had just turned eleven when my grandmother took her last fall in our bathroom. It was the middle of the night. I slept heavily then and I didn't hear her scream. At the time I was living on a combination of Wham bars and macaroons which to me was the diet of the gods – however my mother and all those around us were troubled by my refusal to partake of the Meals on Wheels that were now being delivered to our door. I'm not sure if it was the lack of good food or merely sheer exhaustion that kept me in my stupor but my grandmother's continual cries, my mother's shouting, the sound of her crawling, the arrival of the fire-starter and the karate man, the ambulance men or even the fire-brigade men didn't wake me.

The next morning when I did wake I noticed the black rubber stretcher marks on our wallpaper from the top of the stairs to the bottom.

"What happened?" I asked.

Mom was crying. "Gran is in hospital but she'll be fine."

The game was up. It appeared to the outsider that the old woman had broken her hip, the young woman was helpless lying face down on the hall floor and the kid in the bedroom was in some sort of coma. All the while the old woman roared on, "Anna can do it!" The people who came to our house that night disagreed. That morning when Mom cried it was because she knew it signalled the end.

Gran never did come back. Instead she was moved from the hospital and, one unnecessary hip operation, later to a Home where she would live for a few years sharing with a woman who'd suffered a stroke and repeated the words "Ya pie" all day. The nurses were kind and they didn't mind when she called them Anna. When I visited I didn't mind when she called me by my male cousin's name and persisted in talking about rugby. My estranged father's sister took me to her home in Kerry where I would grow up with four foster sisters and a foster brother and live the life of a normal teenager. And Mom, well, she considered herself lucky enough to find her way into the Royal Hospital Donnybrook and there she was taken care of by staff as though she was family. She had friends her own age sharing her circumstances, she was a member of the drama club, she sang with the Christmas choir, again much to my embarrassment, she had an oratory where she'd disappear to pray for us all. It was shit, don't get me wrong, but I rarely saw her without a smile on her face. Her friends and the nurses were, as she'd put it, gas. On visits we talked a lot. We laughed a lot.

I was only seventeen when she died one summer afternoon in 1989. Today I'm thirty-four so my mom has been gone for exactly half of my life but I knew her and I still know her now. She said to me once that not all heroes wear costumes. She was referring to all those who helped us stay together for as long as we did. She was right; we had six extra years together because of those around us propping us up. I got to know my mom and she got to know me because of the matter-of-fact sister, the best friend, the cleaner, the fire-starter, Pre-drag Bet, the mouse-trapper, our silver-haired pal and so many more.

And so from both of us and people like us we'd like to say a big thank-you to all you heroes who don't wear costumes.

A Touch
of Magic

Mary Malone

Mary Malone

Mary Malone lives in Cork with her husband, Pat, and their teenage sons, David and Mark. As well as being a novelist and freelance journalist, Mary works in the Central Statistics Office.

Her first novel, *Love Match*, was published in July 2006 and her second, *All You Need Is Love*, will be published in September 2007.

For more information: www.marymalone.ie

A Touch
of Magic

I sit at a window-seat in Café Paradiso waiting for my lunch dates to arrive. Straightening my slate-grey pleated skirt and fiddling with the buttons on my lambswool cardigan, my gaze drifts to the street outside as I strain to catch a glimpse of Sara's copper mane or Lisa's blonde curls in the mêlée of passing pedestrians. I wish they'd get here. I can't wait to see them after all this time. I hope they haven't changed their minds about meeting me. I've been really looking forward to our reunion, even if I am trembling with a mixture of trepidation and giddiness.

Checking my watch, I see they're close to fifteen minutes late. It's one of those rare moments where I'd love to have a mobile phone. I assume the girls will have every convenience available when they arrive, but in my walk of life we're encouraged to be patient and wait for things to happen in their own time. Modern technology isn't forbidden as such, just gently discouraged.

Lifting the jug of iced water from the table and pouring some into my glass, I attempt to get a piece of lemon to drop from the spout but give up when it refuses to budge! For the umpteenth time since arranging this rendezvous, I try to visualise Sara and Lisa as adults instead of the teenagers I knew at school. Do they still wear their hair long, I wonder? Are they still fitting into Size 10? Or has middle-age spread caught up with them too, forcing them to shop for larger sizes?

I'll soon discover how the passing of time has treated them. My heart beats a little faster in anticipation, thumping loudly in my ear. I scan the menu as I try to choose what to have for lunch. For the first time in years my appetite has left me, neither savoury nor sweet options appealing to my senses. In all the challenges and achievements I've experienced throughout my life, nothing has made me feel quite so childishly giddy as the prospect of today's reunion.

Inhaling slowly, I struggle to keep my excitement in check. My face burns with embarrassment as I imagine us together again, hugging one another and squealing with excitement. Physical contact has been a rather scarce commodity for me since our heady school days and in a way today is somewhat of a personal milestone. Am I still the same old me underneath the restrictions of maturity?

It's not that I'm measuring my life against Sara's or Lisa's. This would be a waste of valuable time and energy under the circumstances, but I am curious to see whether we'll have anything at all in common other than polite small talk.

Surely it's too much to expect that any trace of the magical friendship we shared in school can still be alive? Are we kidding ourselves to think we can pick up on a relationship that's been neglected for decades? Or can it still be there, lurking underneath other passions, hidden in the years of events that have unfolded in our lives.

I rest against the soft brown leather-backed chair and fix the collar of my starched white shirt, ensuring both sides sit neatly on the revers of my cardigan while I allow my mind to wander as I continue to wait.

It's been more than a few years since the three of us shared a desk at the back of Sr Brigid's maths class. Three heads – one brunette, one redhead and one blonde – gathered together whispering silly secrets while others around us got on with their algebra and geometry! During class we'd discreetly catch each other's eye while Sr Bridget (or Budgie as she was commonly known) had her back to us, chalking her illegible loopy scrawls on the large blackboard. We'd scribble notes and quickly pass them across to each other underneath the desk. I'll never forget Sara's ability to make me laugh out loud at the most inappropriate moments. But the precious memory I cling to most is the way we came to each other's aid when one of us needed support; never judging, seldom critical and always there regardless. Unconditional friendship!

"Excuse me, can I take your order, please?"

A fidgety young waitress hovers close to my table, her brash tone interrupting my musing. She shifts impatiently from foot to foot, her eyes darting around the restaurant as she monitors what tables are ready for clearing and how many diners are still waiting to give their orders.

I reluctantly let go of my happy memories, temporarily returning my attention to the present and the gum-chewing waitress beside me.

"Not just yet, my dear," I reply, deliberately speaking in a slow steady tone, feeling a little mischievous as I know my delaying is annoying her. "I'm expecting two friends to join me. Can you call back to my table in a few minutes, please? They should be here any moment."

I'd hazard a guess at the silent expletives she's uttering. She probably thinks I'm sitting here out of loneliness. Huh! She wouldn't be the first to assume I don't have real friends to meet! Little does she know I've a black book filled with names and numbers of friends and acquaintances that I can call on day or night. Regardless of any progress society has made in accepting each other, some old-fashioned opinions will never change and ignorance will continue to prevail! While a woman in my position invariably attracts unnecessary curiosity, few people venture to invite conversation, instead treating us with aloof hostility.

My normality might surprise them, I think, suppressing an unexpected giggle as I sip my water and smirk cheekily at the waitress. If only she could read my mind . . .

The young girl stops chewing for a split second. She probably thinks I'm a little crazy. Staring quizzically at me for a moment, she shakes her head dramatically, throws her eyes towards the ceiling and turns to walk away. I glance over my shoulder and notice in surprise how the restaurant has filled up while I've been daydreaming. I watch my waitress strut to a nearby table, her confident swagger reminding me of Sara, Lisa and me as footloose Leaving Cert students.

The memory of our last day at school comes flooding back; how we excitedly tossed our textbooks and stripy uniform ties into the air, dancing with glee when they landed in rain puddles in the schoolyard. Teachers smiled with sympathetic understanding as we hugged and cried together, vowing solemnly that no matter what happened we'd never lose contact. As far as we were concerned, our friendship was invincible. We were thrilled to leave the classroom and its rules and regulations behind. Yet I still remember fearing that I'd miss the uniformity the school environment provided. In our bottle-green pinafores and white-and-mint-check nylon blouses, we were a united force, all but identical for the hours we spent in school. Other than the quality of our schoolbags and belongings, we all looked the same. I felt comfortable there amongst my fellow peers, enjoyed being part of our sisterhood.

Leaving the school firmly behind us, we strolled down the hill arm-in-arm for the last time, clutching the belief we'd step into the next chapter of our lives and nothing would change between us. Who were we trying to kid? All the intentions in the world couldn't save us from our futures and the choices we'd make which would directly result in our separation. Before long, Sara and Lisa had found their niche in the fashion world and, always being more adventurous than I, were venturing to pastures new to spread their wings and follow their dreams. They tried their best to drag me along with them, promising streets of gold at the other end and refusing to accept my string of excuses for remaining behind.

Banging at my mother's front door early one morning, they knocked until their knuckles were raw. Their insistent pounding woke me from a deep sleep, forcing me to jump out of my cosy single bed and scurry down the stairs without even pulling a hairbrush through my tangled knot of hair.

"It'll be fun!" they squealed, waving their airline tickets in the air, begging me to join them on their adventure. "There are still seats left. Please, please say you'll come!" Sara swung me around and around in Mammy's tiny kitchen until my head spun and dots danced in front of my eyes. I begged her to let my hands go and very nearly conceded to her pleas, if only to get my balance back.

"Please say yes! Imagine the three of us together having the time of our lives in America?" Sara wasn't one to give up easily. "Isn't it what we've always planned – to be together no matter what? We're not going without you and that's final!"

Lisa had nodded in firm agreement, her pale blue eyes pleading with me to agree to travel with them. I can't say I wasn't tempted and more than that, it was a scary prospect to be the one to break away from our tight group and be left behind alone. But standing barefoot on the icy slate floor in Mammy's cottage that morning, I knew in my heart I would have to let them fly without me. So I begged them to be patient with me and politely declined, suggesting instead that I might follow them when they were settled. At that moment in time, I really believed it could happen.

Looking back on that morning now, I realise with a start that my decision dictated the rest of my life. I could easily have taken the safe option and tagged along but I had my own dreams forming in my heart and knew I needed to take a stand and be an independent individual for the first time.

My eyes stung as I returned from the airport after seeing the girls off. Travelling to join them was never far from my mind in the weeks to follow, but for some reason I could never bring myself to make the commitment and book that flight ticket.

Months slipped into years and an endless stream of overseas phone calls and pages of gossipy letters gradually reduced to an exchange of Christmas cards. Needless to say, I've heard snippets through one avenue or another on their lively escapades and risqué adventures, as I'm sure they have about me and how my life has turned out. But the more I hear and the more time that passes, the less confident I've become about renewing contact and catching up once again. We're no longer protected by the familiarity of bottle-green pinafores and I'm terrified our differences will be too great to handle.

It's impossible to associate my memory of a shy Lisa, who invariably insisted on sitting in the middle chair at our desk so she'd be hidden from the teacher's view, with the image of a tough fashion critic I've created in my head. My goodness, if rumours are true, she even went as far as challenging *Vogue* magazine on its responsibility towards creating an illusion that Size Zero was the norm! Who is this new woman bearing my friend Lisa's name?

By all accounts, if the grapevine story can be believed, Sara has recently retired and sold all rights to the modelling agency she built from scratch to be able to spend more time with her husband and family.

I'm slightly envious that they've been a part of each other's lives, probably enjoying family barbeques and Sunday gatherings with their husbands and children. I've never been part of that and wonder if there's still room for me in the equation or how I can catch up.

What mystifies me most is that in comparison with the girls, I feel in some way inadequate and mentally require a seal of approval and affection from these two friends more than anybody else in my life. I haven't anything in particular to be ashamed or embarrassed about – quite the opposite in fact. In my own circle of friends and colleagues, I'm deemed a success story, someone who has made a difference to the lives of others.

The passing of time plays funny little tricks on the mechanics of our minds. It distorts memories and is capable of blowing the simplest of things out of all proportion. If you let it, of course! And I think that's my biggest problem; that's why I'm terrified to reunite with my old friends now that they've left the bright lights behind in favour of the green grass of home, for however long.

Part of me wants to hold onto the memory of the innocent fun I shared with Sara and Lisa just as it was. The other part of me is vulnerable, however, knowing as I do that these two old friends know the real me and at one time were almost capable of predicting my every move. What a disappointment it will be if today's meeting is a disaster, I think now, my heart sinking slightly. The memories I've treasured for years will be shattered forever.

Sitting straighter in my chair, I look at my watch once again. This is ridiculous. Another ten minutes have passed and I'm still here alone. I raise a hand to the waitress as she passes, not surprised when she ignores me, pretending not to notice my waving arm, and continues to the next table. My earlier anticipation is being replaced by irritation and I'm no longer that concerned about what Sara and Lisa will think of me. I just want this meeting to get underway and end my curiosity for once and for all. Noticing the waitress is finished at the next table, I lean across and tap her on the elbow, hard enough so she's forced to turn around.

"Can you bring me a nice frothy cappuccino please?" I demand sternly, putting on my special voice that I save for exerting a little authority. "Extra hot milk and four sugars," I add, forgetting any attempt at self-denial or calorie-counting.

From the corner of my eye, I notice two elderly ladies at a large corner table turning awkwardly around in their seats. I frown slightly, refusing to catch their eyes, the nosy old dears. Why are they looking at me like that? Don't they realise it's rude to stare? Surely they've heard someone order extra milk and sugar before?

The lady nearest to me swings right around in her chair so she can get a proper look at my face. I frown slightly and try to avert my eyes, but I can't help staring back as she analyses me from head to toe, at least the bits of me she can see! The insolence of her, I think, as her gaze travels from my short snow-white hair to my sedate blouse and cardigan, grey skirt, dark opaque stockings and flat leather moccasins. A cold shiver runs through my body and I turn my back to them and look to the street outside instead. As I watch mothers, children, workers and students walk along the busy street outside, I let out a heavy sigh of disappointment. I may as well accept that Sara and Lisa have forgotten about meeting me today.

I slip my hand into the pocket of my cardigan and take out a creased page of notepaper. Unfolding it gently and laying it flat on the table, I read the words through. If the truth is known, I could recite them aloud without looking at the page, I've read them over so many times. But it fills my heart with joy to look at Sara's handwriting, slightly shakier than I remember from before, but still familiar in its style and tone. I check the details to see if I can possibly have got the date or time wrong, but no, just as I thought, today is the right day and it's now well past the hour. I'm pulling back my sleeve to check my wristwatch once more when I feel a gentle tap on my shoulder.

Turning around quickly, expecting it to be the waitress with my cappuccino, I gasp when I see it's the gawping pensioner from the table further down. I'm more than surprised to notice how pleasant her expression is up close.

"Yes?" I say, my lips pinched. "Can I help you with something?"

"Kate? It's you, isn't it?" the expertly made-up lady says, her voice little more than a loud whisper.

To hear someone call me by my real name is something of a shock. I haven't been called *Kate* in such a long time. It feels as if she's talking to somebody else and not me, Eliza, as I think of myself now. As I stare into her face, taking in the intensity of her pale blue eyes, I want to pinch myself.

"Lisa? My Lisa?" I ask, my mouth falling open in amazement.

So much for thinking we'd be jumping around and hugging each other, I think now, as I remain firmly frozen in my chair, unable to move a muscle! I continue to stare.

This older Lisa is smaller in stature than I remember. Her once platinum-blonde curls fall in shoulder-length silver waves. Her upper body is slightly hunched in her short brocade jacket and age spots camouflage her once flawless skin. Though she's remained slim and, judging by appearances, life has treated her well, I'd imagine it's been quite a long time since she encased her arthritic body in a pair of Size 10 jeans.

But all these changes are merely cosmetic and when our eyes finally meet and connect, I'm instantly transported to the back row of my Leaving Certificate maths class.

As my eyes hold Lisa's, her face creases in deep-etched wrinkles and she breaks into a broad beaming smile, a smile that I'd recognise anywhere.

"Sara! I've found her!" she calls to her waiting companion, helping me to my feet and leading me to their table where Sara waits with a big grin on her face and outstretched arms.

And that's what breaks our reserve. Awkwardly we pull each other into one group-hug and instantly we're inconsolable, tears streaming down our faces and each of us blubbering as we try to talk.

"Have you really been sitting there waiting all along?" Sara scolds gently, flopping wearily into her seat once more. "We thought you'd chickened out and stood us up! But when we heard your request for four sugars in a cappuccino, we just knew!"

She grabs my hand as if to check I'm really here beside them. "It never dawned on us that we wouldn't recognise you! Though we've aged, we somehow thought you'd be just the same as you were."

The intermittent years instantly slip away and we huddle together once again, no longer a blonde, brunette and redhead but varying shades of grey instead.

"So, my good friend," Sara continues in a deep gravelly voice, getting straight to the point as usual, "were you trying to confuse us by dressing so sedately in your skirt and cardi? I thought nuns dressed in black and white? And wore a veil? Explain that one, Sister Eliza! Or," she adds in a tiny whisper, "can we still call you Kate?"

I throw my head back and laugh out loud, my earlier anxiousness slipping away. "You can call me anything you like, girls, and I'll have you know that nuns have changed a lot since the days of Sr Bridget," I tease, the knot of tension in my stomach being replaced by a nice warm glow.

"Thank God for that," Lisa says. "It took us years to believe you'd actually joined a religious Order."

"That's why I couldn't tell you at the time. I knew you'd find it difficult to understand. Now, enough about me for a moment – what I want to know is what happened to your copper hair? I've been staring at every redhead that passed by this window for the last half hour!"

Sara ran a finger through her hair and shook her head. "Oh God! If only I still had my crowning glory!" she sighs dramatically. "But I'm afraid nothing lasts forever."

"Some things do," Lisa interjects gently, looking from me to Sara and back again. "Here we are after all these years," she smiles, "and it's just like old times!"

"It is," I say, nodding my head, my voice catching in my throat. "Even though helping the poor and high couture are opposite ends of the spectrum, it seems the magic between us is still very much alive. I can feel it in here." I place my hand over my left breast and feel my steady heartbeat.

No words pass between us for a moment. We just hold hands and smile.

When the gum-chewing waitress stops at our table once again, I remind her about my cappuccino and introduce her to my companions. "We've been best friends since we were your age," I boast proudly, feeling a sudden urge to tell the world.

For the first time today she actually returns my smile and I can't help wondering if her teenage friendships will survive as ours did. Or am I just the luckiest woman alive?

Secrets and Lives

Anita Notaro

Anita Notaro

Anita Notaro is a journalist and TV producer. Her fourth novel *Take A Look At Me Now* will be published by Bantam Press in October.

She has also written stories for children for *Den TV* and works as a director on Ireland's top-rated soap, *Fair City*.

Secrets
and Lives

"So, how old are you then?" The guy flashed her a smile so bright she could have done with her shades as they walked off the handkerchief-sized dance floor.

"Eh, thirty-eight," Martha Rowley replied, giving him an encouraging look. He really was the cutest guy, lean with floppy hair and an energy about him that made her want to tag along.

"Gosh, really?"

She didn't like that gosh.

"I'm afraid you're just a bit too old for me in that case." He swallowed the last of his drink.

She tried to hide her dismay. They'd been getting on so well. He'd monopolised her ever since he'd joined their office party over an hour ago, flirting with her and asking friends for her phone number.

"I'm twenty-nine," he gave her an apologetic look, "and I like my chicks, well . . . fit," he grinned. "Thirty's my absolute max – not that you don't look great, mind," he added as an afterthought. "It's just – not my scene. Too many hormones and way too much angst. It wrecks my head. But hey, nice meeting you." He was gone.

"Well, look on the bright side," her friend Laura told her next evening as they chatted on the phone. "You actually got asked to dance."

"Is that so incredible?" Martha asked indignantly.

"Nobody except losers ask strangers to dance any more at our age. It went out with nylons," Laura laughed.

"Well, he was sort of in our group. At least he joined us shortly after we arrived at the club. Noeleen from reception knew him – he's a friend of her brother, apparently. And he was no loser, that's for sure. I fancied him actually. And that hasn't happened in ages."

"Fancying is good; you're making progress." Laura knew how badly her friend wanted a relationship. "And I'm not surprised he made a bee-line for you. You're looking great these days, better than any of us."

"Yes, but am I 'fit'?" Martha was still miffed.

"Don't ask me. I can barely run up the stairs without my knee giving in. Old age is not for the faint-hearted, isn't that what they say?" Laura sighed. "Anyway, gotta go. James is trying to sew a button on the dog."

Martha heard a yelp in the background followed by Laura's screams. She hung up, still thinking about what her friend had said.

You see, Martha was older than anyone knew. In fact she was forty, the most depressing number ever invented. It was her only real secret. No one knew – well, except her family, obviously. She'd burnt the "Fabulous at Forty" birthday cards seconds after they arrived. Even her best friend Laura thought she was thirty-eight, as did her doctor, bank manager and local garda station.

And compared with some of the secrets that others had kept from her over the years, this one was unlikely to feature on *Crime Call*.

From the time she was five and her best friend Eva Connors began sharing things with Lulu Barnes and excluding her, Martha always seemed to be on the wrong side of secrets.

At school she was the only one who didn't know that her nickname was "Miser" because she put half of her pocket money each week into a post-office account. In college two of her close friends went off on holiday together and didn't even tell her, let alone invite her along. She overheard someone saying it was because they thought her a bit of a "wet fish" around boys. There were countless others, but the final, fatal wound came when she discovered her boyfriend Andrew had been keeping the biggest secret of all: another woman. And not just any old girlfriend either. This one – safely tucked up in medical school in London – was actually a bona fide "fiancée".

Whether it was the conversation with Laura or the mortification of the previous night she wasn't sure, but as Martha climbed into bed that evening she found herself remembering that other, much more painful humiliation.

She could still clearly recall how excited she'd been when Andrew had told her he wanted to have a serious talk with her. She'd lit the fire, unwrapped some scented candles she'd been saving for a special occasion and opened a bottle of wine. As soon as he came in she realised that something was wrong.

They'd been together for over two years at that stage and he was her soul mate. She'd never been as close to anyone before in her life, so one look at his face had her heart hammering, and not with excitement any more.

"What is it?" she asked as soon as she'd poured him a drink. She was convinced he was ill or something awful like that.

"Martha, I'm not quite sure how to tell you this . . ." He took a gulp of wine followed by a deep breath. "The fact is I haven't been completely honest with you . . ."

"In what way? I don't understand." She was puzzled. They shared everything, told each other all about their insecurities, no matter how trivial.

"I really do care for you, you know that?"

"Yes." And she did know it. "Just tell me, please. We'll handle it together." She stroked his arm, still convinced it could be sorted out.

Andrew didn't look at her at first, then he shifted slightly on the sofa, so that he was a little further away. That was when she became really nervous.

"I don't know where to start. Christ, this is bloody difficult." He buried his face in his hands.

"Andrew, tell me. I'm frightened," she said in a quiet voice.

"I'm . . . when I moved back to Dublin that time, I left a girlfriend in London. Fiancée, actually, although we had decided to take a break. Things weren't going well. Neither of us was entirely sure what we . . ." his voice trailed off. "Then I met you and . . . it just took off. You were just what I needed." He smiled at her but his eyes were sad. "You were great," he said softly. "But . . . Helena and I, well, we never completely finished. We stayed in touch by text, a quick call, the odd lunch, stuff like that. I was back and forward on business as you know."

"Were you sleeping with her?" Martha couldn't figure out what she was hearing. This was Andrew. Her Andrew.

"No, no, of course not. I told her I was . . . seeing someone else. And she had a couple of guys in tow, or so she said. But then last year we sort of . . . got together again and now she wants us . . . to go ahead and get married." He bit his lip. "Martha, I'm so sorry . . . you don't deserve this." He tried to grab her hand.

"And what about you? Is that what you want?"

"I think . . . I'm not sure," he shrugged.

"Do you love her?"

He didn't answer immediately. "I don't know," he said softly. "I used to, she was my first love, we'd been together since we were kids. Our families were – are – very close. Then, when she decided to study medicine it totally absorbed her. She'd no time for me and I suppose my pride was hurt. So we agreed to separate, although we never made it official. Then I met you and . . ."

"And you let me fall in love with you. You even said you loved me back!" Martha was crying now even though she knew he hated it when she cried. Claimed he never knew what to do around tears.

"Please don't cry. I did. I do. Oh God, this is such a mess!" He bowed his head.

"Give her up," Martha knew she was begging. "Give her up and marry me. We've talked about it, we're good together, you're – you're my whole life." She'd never felt such raw pain before.

"I can't," he said quietly.

She looked at him and saw that he had tears too.

"I owe it to her. She's helped me all my life – we've always been there for each other." He looked grey and tired.

"But that was long before us." Martha despised herself for pleading with him. "I don't know what I'd do without you, please . . ."

"Stop!" He begged her with his eyes. "I can't, honestly I can't. Besides," he took another huge mouthful of wine, "she called me last week. Said she'd been keeping a secret from me."

That word again. "What was it?" She had to know.

"Martha, I never meant for this to happen." He looked far away. "Helena's pregnant."

And that was when Martha knew she'd lost him. It was the loneliest she'd ever been in her life.

That was months ago now and since the dreaded fortieth birthday her single state had haunted her even more. She'd crossed the line between "career girl" and "middle-aged woman" overnight, it seemed. And the world – her world anyway – was simply chock-a-block with couples. Everything, it seemed, came in twos.

So Martha eventually decided it was time to become part of a couple herself and a pet seemed the only way of having someone to come home to at night. She needed love and companionship and right now she'd settle for anything. A few visits to her local animal shelter convinced her she was right. There were so many unwanted animals, it was depressing. And lots of them were too old to be re-homed, she was told.

"And these are just the cute ones," Lisa, one of the assistants, told her. "We've twice as many again out the back. And I won't tell you how we came upon most of them," she shook her head. "There are a lot of heartless people out there."

"And I've met most of them." Martha was feeling sorry for herself all the time these days.

Finally, the day came for her to choose her new companion.

"Have a look around," said Lisa. "I'll be just over there in the office," she pointed to a cubby-hole in the corner. "Give me a shout if you want to take any of them for a play in the back garden."

There were mongrels of all shapes and sizes, some in excellent condition, some looking a bit neglected. But all were well cared for, she knew, and wished she could take every one of them home. That was when she spotted him. He was small – a little Jack Russell cross, she suspected. Sooty black with one white eye.

And it was his eyes that she noticed first. As well as his energy. He was the liveliest dog in the place and he bounded over to the front of the cage as soon as he spotted her, tail going furiously. Take me home, he seemed to be begging her and she was still there, down on her hunkers playing with him, when Lisa came past ten minutes later.

"Ah, I see Batman's found you," Lisa grinned.

"Batman?" Martha looked puzzled. "You're not seriously telling me someone called a dog Batman?"

"Yeah, and then abandoned him shortly after birth. The note just gave us his name and a few other details."

It was how she felt herself. Abandoned. They'd be good together, she decided.

"I'll take him." Martha knew she'd never escape those eyes. "He is free, isn't he? He's not reserved or anything?"

"No, no, he's free. They all are unless it says otherwise on the cage, but I'm afraid there's a catch."

"Don't tell me – he's got a girlfriend," Martha said sarcastically.

Lisa crouched down beside her and rattled the cage. "A boyfriend, actually," she grinned. "Where the hell is he?" She rattled the door. "Robin, come 'ere!"

"Batman and . . ."

Martha wanted to laugh until she saw him. He poked his head out from under a pile of newspaper, where he'd obviously been hiding. He was almost identical to the other little fellow, but much thinner and he was shaking like a leaf. And he had the saddest face she'd ever seen. Batman meanwhile was doing handstands trying to attract attention. When he saw that the girls were focussed on the other dog, he went over and growled, causing Robin to shake even more.

"Oh my God, he's terrified," Martha said. "Can I hold him?"

"Yes, but take Batman out first, give him a bit of attention, then pass him to me," Lisa told her.

Martha did as she was told and as soon as the little thug was happy she reached in and scooped out the other fellow. He was still whining and he looked so depressed it was comical.

"He's soooo cute," Martha said. "Now I'm torn between the two of them but I did see your fellow first." She laughed at Batman, who was trying to bite her handbag.

"I'm afraid that's not really an option," Lisa said gently. "You see, they come as a pair. We really don't want to separate them if at all possible." The younger woman was apologetic. "They're very cute, so I don't think we'll have any difficulty finding them a home together, to be honest. Not like some of the others . . ." She looked around. "I do have a lovely collie-type thing . . ."

"But I want these, I mean one of them!" Martha wailed. Either would do, she now realised. She was captivated by both of them.

"I'm sorry – if anything changes I'll let you know first, I promise."

Martha looked at them for a final time, one oozing with confidence about life and the other scared to death. She knew now that she wouldn't have been able to choose between them anyway. She took a deep breath and instead of saying goodbye she announced, "I'll take them both."

Lisa hugged her, delighted. "You won't regret it, I promise." They'd become friends over the last few months. "In fact, I think they're perfect for you." Lisa knew that Martha was lonely, despite her glamorous job in PR and huge circle of friends. She'd visited the shelter before, several times, and Lisa had gone to her home to check her suitability and had seen the spotless unused kitchen and gleaming floors and perfectly plumped cushions.

So now they arranged for a "getting-to know-you" visit the following day and Martha went home via her local vet.

She'd known Pete Winters since national school. They'd both grown up in a small fishing village in Connemara in the West of Ireland. He was tall and well built and as solid and dependable as his frame suggested. And very attractive to boot.

He looked up as she entered. "Martha, hi!" He was down on his knees, trying to comfort a little girl whose hamster had been kept in for observation. At the same time he was rubbing the belly of a very fat Westie who had rolled over and was demanding attention.

"What are you doing here? You've not become a pet owner, have you?" He led her to a quiet corner just as soon as the little girl had calmed down.

"Looking for a vet for the two mutts I've just acquired," she told him and wondered once again why they'd never got together.

He was the nicest man. It just always seemed to be the wrong time for one or other of them, she knew. He was a year older than her, so he already had a girlfriend by the time she developed her first crush on him. Then she'd only just moved to Paris for a year when she heard he was single again but by the time she got home he was engaged to Orla, whom he married two years later. Then three years ago his wife had been killed in a car crash and it was at the funeral that Martha met Andrew. Shortly after they'd broken up her mother told her that Pete was going out with another vet.

"Two dogs!" He whistled and winked. "That could spell trouble. Are they from the same litter?"

Martha nodded. "Either that, or they're gay," she joked. "They're called Batman and Robin."

"Ouch!" he grimaced. "What are people like? I had two cats

in this morning called Bart and Homer. Sorry, excuse me for a sec . . ." He smiled at the young woman who'd just appeared. They exchanged a few words while Martha tried to wrestle a shaggy heap away from the diamante strap on her shoe.

"Martha, have you met Jenny before?" Pete asked her then.

"No, I don't think so." She stood up. "Hi."

"Hi, Martha, Pete's mentioned you, I think. You grew up together, right?"

"Yes, he tried to paint out my freckles when I was six," Martha told her. "After that it was all downhill."

"Only because you were in floods of tears over someone calling you Carrot Top," Pete tweaked her ponytail. "You begged me to do it."

"I did," Martha laughed and the three of them chatted for ages and it was obvious Jenny was the new girlfriend.

"Shame she's such a nice girl." Martha was talking on her mobile to Laura as she walked back to her car twenty minutes later, having arranged an appointment with Pete for the following week. "He always meets lovely women. Why is it so easy for men?" she grumbled as she searched for her keys. "Anyway, I don't care, I have Batman and Robin." She brushed against someone crossing between her car and a lorry. "Oh, sorry, I wasn't —"

"Martha, hi, how are you?"

She didn't have to look up. As soon as she heard the voice her heart practically broke through her chest. "Call you back," she clicked off her phone and met his eyes slowly.

"Andrew!" it came out as a squeak.

"This is a surprise," he said quietly. Martha was staring, trying desperately to read his face, so it was a second or two before she noticed the woman beside him.

"Yes, I was eh, just coming out of the vet, chatting on the

242

phone, lost my keys," she was waffling. "Hi . . ." She smiled at the very pregnant woman who smiled back warmly.

"Oh, sorry, excuse me. Martha, this is Helena. My, eh . . ."

"Wife, he keeps forgetting," the young woman grinned and poked him in the ribs. "Nice to meet you, Martha." She had a firm handshake.

"You too," Martha swallowed hard, wishing her hair wasn't greasy and that she hadn't just spotted her shiny nose in the car mirror.

"Martha's an old friend," Andrew said quickly. Too quickly.

And getting older by the second, Martha thought, wishing the ground would open up. "So, how are things? It's been . . . a while."

"Good, yeah," this time his eyes were searching her face, "fine. Busy, you know." He looked at the woman beside him then back at her. "The baby's due any day now."

"We've just moved over here," Helena explained. "And so far you're the only one of his friends I've met. He's keeping them all a secret, I think."

"I know that feeling," Martha told her while staring straight at him. "Anyway, I'd better fly. Nice to meet you." She smiled at the radiant young woman. "And good luck with the happy event. Take care." She didn't meet Andrew's eyes.

"Yeah, you too." He watched her as she leapt into her car and drove off.

Martha could have done with ten puppies that night to lick away her salty tears.

The following week she was back to see Pete, this time with the two monsters in tow.

He roared laughing when he saw them. "Batman and Robin they ain't," he told her. "They're pathetic!"

"I know. Don't remind me," she grinned at him. "Anyway, they suit me. We're going to be pathetic together, all three of us."

"You look fine to me." Pete tickled Robin's chin and as usual Batman nudged his way in.

He spent ages with them giving each a thorough check-up. "They're perfectly healthy," he told her eventually, "although I'm sure the people at the shelter told you that."

"Yes, they were terrific. They've already been neutered and they're even micro-chipped," Martha explained.

Pete nodded in agreement. He'd been dealing with that shelter for years and they were first-class.

"I was really just looking for a chance to show them off, to be honest," Martha told him then. They'd saved her life this past week, and she was every inch the proud mother.

"Well, I'm finished for the evening, so I'll walk you to your car and you can show them off a bit more. Just give me a second to get changed." Pete disappeared and when he returned a minute or two later it was the first time she'd seen him in civvies in ages. He looked relaxed and healthy and very handsome.

"How much do I owe you?" she asked as they walked together to reception, Pete carrying Batman.

"Nothing, call it a christening present." He tickled the little dog who was trying to chew his keys.

"Are you sure?" Martha was touched.

"Certain, you'll be a good customer, I suspect," he winked at her.

"So, what are you up to for the evening," she asked as he held the door open for her. "Going anywhere nice with Jenny?"

"No, actually, Jenny and I – we're not together any more." He looked away.

"What, my mother said you were glued together in the pub at

home a few weeks ago!" She could have kicked herself for letting him know she'd been gossiping about him.

"Ah, it just wasn't working out." He looked embarrassed. "No one's fault, just —"

"So why did you split up then?" Martha had had it with men who just dumped nice women. "I take it *you* ended it? So go on, spill the beans. What happened?"

"It's a secret — for now, anyway." He grinned at her and pulled her hair.

"Well, well," she opened the hatchback and had to force Robin out from under her arm, "why am I not surprised? Men like you always have a few secrets up their sleeve."

Pete looked puzzled.

"I hope your secrets keep you warm at night!" She grabbed Batman from him and dumped him on the back seat. He yelped. "Sorry, sorry," she tickled his ear, "I didn't mean it. Let's get away from this nasty man, before I tell him exactly what he can do with his secrets."

"Martha, what's going on?"

"Nothing. Sorry," she said sheepishly, the fight going out of her all of a sudden. "It just seems like people have been keeping me out of the loop all my life." She made sure the puppies were secure and opened the passenger door. "But in this case you're entitled to. It's none of my business. Thanks for checking them out. I owe you." She sat in and closed the door. "Take care!" she called through the open window as she pulled out into the slow lane.

Martha bit her lip and stared straight ahead as she stopped at the traffic lights a few yards further on, wondering when she'd see him again. Suddenly, she heard the passenger door click open.

"I'll tell you my secret then, if it's that important." He slipped in beside her. "I finished with Jenny because when I saw you last week I realised I was in love with you and as you must be at least forty by now I thought it was about bloody time I did something about it."

Pete's frame filled the small space and as he leaned over to kiss her Martha realised that probably for the first time in her life she'd been told a secret she really wanted to hear.

Rónán's Arrival

Clíodhna O'Donoghue

Clíodhna O'Donoghue

Clíodhna O'Donoghue was appointed Property Editor of the *Irish Independent* newspaper in 1989 and has grown the Friday residential supplement and Wednesday Commercial Property supplement to the largest national property publications. She has also just completed a comprehensive step by step book on buying property and is a judge on the National Property Awards panel. Clíodhna also presents and produces *Property View*, a monthly programme for City Channel, and is a regular commentator on property issues for TV and radio. She lives with her son, Rónán, partner, Ciaran, and dog, Toffee, in Blackrock, Co Dublin.

Rónán's Arrival

It's funny how you gain confidence from people, not funny ha-ha, funny serious. It's not as though you would think I was lacking confidence. I had reached a wonderful stage in my career – appointed head of department at the tender age of twenty-nine, I was articulate, outgoing, self-sufficient, and had my own home. However everything changed just two years later. I was pregnant, it was unplanned and I was not married to the father.

The first person I told was my former school principal, Dympna, who had to put up with terrible trouble from me in secondary school, and is a great stalwart. About ten years after leaving school I had come across her while researching an article on how children with problems can articulate their distress or concerns through art, especially when they find it hard, or are too young to communicate through words.

When I realized I was pregnant some time later and told her, I expressed my belief that I would not be able to deal with a child. She would have none of it, stridently proclaiming "Of course you will be more than able!". She also reminded me that I had fought tough battles previously and came out relatively unscathed and often victorious. "You can do the same now," she said, adding that this was more important than anything else that previously took place in my life.

Of course she was right, but sometimes you just don't think that way. You become so flustered and concerned that you don't see the wood for the trees.

When I told my close friend Eileen in a restaurant off Grafton Street in the very early stages, she was literally unable to contain her excitement. Never once did something like financial stability cross her mind. It was all about having a baby to love and cherish and how she envied me, and how life was going to be wonderful. She inspired confidence, and also reminded me of how competent I was in handling other major issues that had arisen in my life.

My sister Maria, however, was my saving grace. She was, and still is, a legend and made the pregnancy "rock," as my now fifteen-year-old would say.

Maria was pregnant too and we were inseparable throughout our pregnancies. It was her second baby and my first, so she was the font of knowledge and wisdom, always had been, really. Anyhow we complained and compared daily over the months. I suffered morning, afternoon and evening sickness more or less throughout. She escaped that, though she did suffer a little initially.

We went for scanning, we measured our babies' heads, and the machine told us how many weeks and days they were alive, and exactly when they would be born. We marvelled over their shapes, heartbeats and movements. We also studied the ultrasound images intently for sexual organs. I was convinced mine was a girl; I saw no signs in the scans of anything to indicate otherwise. Maria was unsure of her baby's sex, but kind of hoped for a girl because she already had lovely Conor, her first-born.

It was not as though we were in any kind of a competition, or there was sibling rivalry between us, but daily we communicated on weight gain, nourishment, best treatments for stretch marks, good maternity wear, bras, and a big one was which name to choose. We even discussed schools and their future careers.

Maria was much braver than I about the whole pregnancy lark. No wonder, I reasoned, this would be her second baby. I also comforted myself with the knowledge that she was a trained army officer, one of the first commissioned by the Irish army in 1981. She was a woman afraid of no one.

She trained platoons of men, which included route marches in full army gear, was the first woman to lead the Army Number One Band as conductor, and had seen action in Lebanon while working for the United Nations.

How could an ordinary everyday journalist compare with that record of courage and strength? The most I ever lifted was a pen, and albeit it is potentially more mighty than the sword, I'd have opted for the sword any day in my condition then: heavy, nauseous, scared and excited all at once.

As the eldest of seven children, Maria was always a rock of sense. She never got caught sneaking out the window – I did. As a teenager she was always at home on time while I was always late and caught the ire of my dad who, being an army officer too, was a stickler for punctuality. She never was caught drinking under age – guess who was? – and she was a wonderful student in school and college – guess who was not?

Maria was also responsible enough to be godmother to our baby sister, Mairead, who was born when Maria was just sixteen. I was hardly allowed to hold the baby at that time despite there being only eighteen months between us. As kids we fought like cat and dog, shared a bed that was divided into two by a line made in the coverlet. She was tidy, I was messy; I used to drive her crazy when quite young because I would not go to bed without her and when you are seven years old being forced to bed at the five-year-old's bedtime it can be quite frustrating. Not so much battling took place during adolescence – we were often at the same discos and partied in the same group of youngsters.

In fact, we started the first mixed-sex "gang" in Athlone during our early teenage years and we were the only two girls in it. I should have seen Maria's suitability for the defence forces back then. She could out-run, out-climb and out-shout any of the lads and we set up temporary homes in a tree-house in Heaton's Wood and a stone single-storey hut made by us, constructed from pieces of materials from a nearby building site, just off what was known as "the mucky lane".

Maria was as masterful in her pregnancy as she was in her teenage or army years. But for me it was difficult enough, especially because of the daily nausea. I still thank my lucky stars for a contact in an airline who sent to my office several boxes of travel-sickness bags each month which I gratefully used throughout, because it meant I didn't have to rush from the desk to the ladies' if I could manage it quietly. In fact I often interrupted a phone call to be sick, only to return to it immediately afterwards without disconnecting the call. However, one memorable day, when I decided to treat myself to lunch in Clery's new restaurant, I did a projectile on some poor unsuspecting man sitting at another table.

It was not pleasant, particularly for my work colleagues who initially did not realise, that the daily nausea was pregnancy. They thought it was ulcers. I told them when I was more than four months down the line because I had to let them know in order to organise maternity leave and my replacement at the office. But there was another problem. What was I to tell my parents? My trio of special carers, Eileen, Dympna and Maria, knew my parents well; they understood my anxieties. You see, my marriage had split up after just a short while and I became involved with Rónán's father about a year later. I became pregnant pretty quickly and accidentally and it scared the life out of me, truth be known. Would I be able for this? How could I bring a child into the world without so much as a few bob in my bank account and no obvious route to accumulating money either? How would I be able to fund crèche, school, or horror of horrors, college fees? Dympna was a wonderful aide. She made me feel so capable and strong. She was a marvellous art teacher when I was in school, instilling a love of the medium in kids who generally would prefer to spend their Saturday morning having a lie-in, or down town with their pals. I happily did without these Saturday treats in order to take some extra classes with her. She left her principal post in Athlone, and moved into caring for troubled children through the medium of art.

It was a joy to see her again, even though I broke her heart in school. We met up regularly for a while, Dympna and I, and through our chats I felt counselled, and more in tune with why I am the way I am, and why sometimes "things just happen".

Much later, to celebrate the birth, Dympna painted a beautiful picture called "The Secret" which in abstract form shows two adults cradling what could be a baby in swaddling clothes. It has pride of place in my sitting room still, and is flanked by other paintings by the same artist, who has since made a big name for herself in the art world.

Eileen promised that if I got stuck financially she would help me out with work in her PR firm, and would also assist me in preparing a series of lectures on public relations for a course in which I had just undertaken to lecture. The course was starting about six weeks after my due date but I had decided to recuperate in my parents' home in Athlone and Eileen invited me to stay with her when I overnighted in Dublin on lecture nights. Maria helped me to prepare my speech and imagine my parents' reactions. Her advice was that instead of saying bluntly "I am pregnant" a much warmer way of expressing the impending addition to the family was to say "I am going to have a baby". So, with confidence sufficiently boosted, I made the move to tell Mam and Dad. Maria's impending baby's birth had already brought great excitement to the parental home – their second beloved grandchild was on the way – not realising that I was expecting around the same time.

So, one weekend about four and a half months into my pregnancy Maria and I drove to my parents' house in Athlone. Despite the fact that I was still not showing, I reckoned it was time to break the news.

We were sitting with Mam at the dining-table, chatting and having lunch, with me running off occasionally to the bathroom to be ill. Maria guessed exactly what I was up to and knowing that our mother has the keenest sense of smell, she took responsibility for the distasteful odour emanating from the toilet, and it was passed over as just another side effect of Maria's pregnancy.

"Oh! It will be worth it all in a few months' time!" my mother rattled off innocently.

Dad was away for the day so I got up sufficient courage to tell Mam, and her reaction was one of pure joy for me, mixed with a bit of anxiety about how I would cope as a single mother. But in

a way I think Mam was more excited than conce
me a great boost, so that when my father ʏ
evening I was better prepared to break the news ᴛᴏ

A very strict disciplinarian, I expected some backla
him. So imagine my surprise when I told him and he saiα,
"Wherever there is new life there is God. Congratulations!" and
gave me a warm hug. You could have knocked me down with a
feather.

The only negatives expressed by my family were in relation to
smoking. I know, it is a disgusting habit. Maria campaigned long
and hard to change this; even to the extent of visiting my
obstetrician, and demanding that she order me to stop
immediately. As an army officer, Maria was not someone easily
ignored.

Fortunately my obstetrician took my side of the argument. I
could have kissed her, she was so nice and kind. She understood
my addiction and dependency better than Maria, which is no
surprise, considering she herself drank pints of Guinness and
smoked pungent Gauloise cigarettes.

In fact she was wonderful. She told me that because of the
stress the pregnancy was creating and the sickness I suffered
several times daily, a few Silk Cut Blue (I cannot stand them now)
would not really do any harm. She also had a bundle of research
completed in an Edinburgh City hospital which proved what she
was saying to Maria's satisfaction – well, almost.

Even better, she insisted that a few times a week I drink a half
bottle of "very good" red wine with a steak meal as I could not
handle the iron injections and the tablets made me vomit. By good
wine she meant that I was to spend freely on Margaux or St.
Émilion. Apparently I was worth it. And that was long before the
cosmetic group, L'Oréal, came up with that logo for themselves.

Oh, the joys of pregnancy! People talk lovingly of feeling the baby growing inside you and the tiny kicks and movements that feel like butterflies in your tummy. My baby was more like David Beckham taking penalty shoot-outs, and I was convinced that if I could be turned inside out that I would emerge bruised and battered. Because I was so slim, and had no comfort-zone fat to protect me, you could actually see the baby's foot or elbow pushing out my tummy, as if something from *Alien* was trying to get out of me.

But you do forget these things within a few minutes of birth, I promise. Otherwise why would people have more than one child? They are completely infused with love for their offspring. However, if I could have any wish, it would be that all pregnant women share the same obstetrician as I did. She was just marvellous and made me feel that I was very important to her. And before you knew it, the time came. It was 3 a.m., the gnawing pain more than irritating, when for the first time it occurred to me that perhaps my baby intended to arrive early, at least a week ahead of schedule. Simultaneously I began to panic, heart thudding, tummy churning and fearful thoughts flitting through my brain.

What the hell was I doing? I was on my own, in Eileen's posh house in Sandymount while she was on a trip to Washington State. I had only decided to stay there at the last minute and had ordered and eaten a Chinese, which I thought was responsible for my "indigestion".

My first reaction was the horror of being on my own, and in someone else's home, and not among my own comforts and securities. Following in quick succession was the realisation that I needed to be beside a phone, and there was none in the bedroom I had chosen earlier. So, I moved to the main bedroom which had a phone connection. No sooner did I lie on the bed when I began thinking of "breaking waters" and the possibility of drenching her bed. Who was going to dry out the mattress while I was in hospital? Would Eileen arrive back to this mess? What kind of a pal would I be if I let that happen?

So I was afraid to relax in case I snoozed between spasms, and my waters broke before I had a chance to get out of the bed. At 6a.m. I phoned Maria, who just happened to be in Mount Carmel hospital, having given birth to a baby girl five days earlier. Maria had been overdue and I reckoned I would be too. Some mistake.

"Call your obstetrician *now!* Well, as soon as I get off the phone," Maria advised loudly, "and come straight in here to me afterwards." Before I could respond I was inundated with "Where are the pains? What are they like? How often do they come? Can you get a taxi? Have you got your long-prepared hospital case?"

I was worn out already trying to answer these but at least it took my mind off other things.

I felt I could not phone my obstetrician until after 6.30 a.m., a more decent hour, especially because I was not bent over in pain or anything like that then. So, on Maria's advice, I tried to relax, made a cup of tea and thought back over the eventful previous eight months

"Clíodhna, is that you?" were perhaps the most welcome words I could have heard the day my baby was born. My obstetrician recognised my voice on the phone at 6.30 a.m., an amazing feat for someone who must have had thousands of worried young mums expecting babies. And, given the ungodly hour, most people would require at least a few minutes to wake up properly, but she answered the phone as though she was expecting my call. "Come straight into the hospital," she advised.

"This is probably it."

The pains were getting worse, there was no doubt about that, and they doubled me over as I prepared to leave my friend's house with my little hospital bag. I was hugely anxious, but also very excited and didn't perhaps realise the ultimate pain involved till I tried to get out of the car in Mount Carmel Hospital. I discovered that it was impossible for me to stand up straight and instead hobbled like an eighty-year-old geriatric into the welcoming calm of the reception area. It was around 7 a.m.

I went straight up to Maria's room while I waited for the obstetrician to arrive and she promptly jumped out of her bed and said, "Take this bed. I'm leaving today!". We admired her new baby girl Orla for a while, fascinated that such a much-wanted and heralded human being was with us at last. And a girl too! Maria was ecstatic. It was all ahead of me. I was shitless, I don't mind admitting, but Maria comforted me by telling me she would stay with me throughout labour. And she did every step of the way, with the exception of an hour, when she brought her new baby home and returned to hospital to me.

Sixteen hours later, at five minutes to midnight on October 2, 1991, I was just as enthralled with my own bundle. A boy! And it's funny because I had thought it would be a girl, and was amazed when informed otherwise, but delighted too. The baby did not cry, instead he stared and stared and stared intently at me with big, huge dark eyes, trusting that I would care for him and love him till the day I died.

Unbelievably, he was also a good weight – seven pounds four ounces – given my illness throughout and his premature birth. Maria's baby, Orla, who was so reluctant to enter the world that she was over a week overdue, was only five ounces heavier or the equivalent of one baby's bottle. The smoking argument was won.

Slightly jaundiced, with a crushed expression, my baby was nonetheless wonderful in hospital – not so much so afterwards when he got colic, asthma and later whooping cough. But the hospital days were ideal. Nurses were kind, and you felt well protected there too. If you had queries or worries, they were all around you to answer immediately.

Mount Carmel also insists that new mothers go out for an evening while still in hospital, and it was Eileen, fresh from her visit to Washington State, who undertook this event. We had a bite to eat, and retired to Slatterys in Rathmines, where neither of us had been since we left the College of Commerce more than ten years earlier.

Because I had been expecting a girl, I had no chosen names for boys and it was in Slatterys that Eileen decided to do a vox pop on most popular boys' names. We had decided over dinner that the options were Shane, Rónán or Eoin. People we never met before, or ever would meet again, gave us their views on each, and Eileen did a poll. Rónán won.

The Shoppers

Geraldine O'Neill

Geraldine O'Neill

Geraldine O'Neill was born in Lanarkshire, Scotland, and has lived in County Offaly in Ireland since 1991. She is married to Michael Brosnahan and has two adult children, Christopher and Clare.

She has written *Tara Flynn*, *Aisling Gayle*, *Tara's Fortune*, *The Grace Girls*, *The Flowers of Ballygrace* and *Tara's Destiny*.

She is currently working on her seventh novel.

The Shoppers

Scotland
1967

A car horn outside wakened Lily with a start. She stared into the semi-darkness, gathering her thoughts together. It was *Saturday*, she suddenly realised – and no school. It was also her big Christmas shopping day. She sat upright and squinted at the crack in the curtains, trying to see if the snow that had started last night was falling again today.

A *bit* of snow would be just right. A regular swirl of white flakes falling from the solid grey Scottish sky, and coming to lie in a thin layer on the ground and hedges was enough to add a tinge of excitement to the day. Any more would be too much.

A thick layer could grind everything to a halt and spoil the day out.

This Saturday was thirteen-year-old Lily's shopping day for her neighbour, Kate, who wasn't able to go to the shops any more.

Kate spent most of her days in bed. Some people described her as an invalid, but Lily didn't think the word suited Kate at all. Invalids were quiet, faded kinds of people like Clara – the young girl in *Heidi* – and they were usually in wheelchairs.

Kate wasn't a bit like that. She was lively and funny, and she loved hearing all the news in the village. And she wasn't in bed *all* the time. On her good days, she was up and dressed, her black hair pinned in a fancy style. She would be waiting for the early morning baker's van and would walk out to pick her fresh bread and buns. Later, she would watch at the window for neighbours passing and go out have a chat at the gate. She would also catch up on her housework.

When her heart was bad – when she couldn't catch her breath and was very tired – she stayed in bed.

Kate would never be fit enough to walk up to the Main Street to get the bus into town, and then walk about the shops. But she still liked to keep up with everything, and that included doing all the usual stuff for Christmas. Since Kate couldn't do a lot of the things herself, she had to delegate the various jobs. Her husband, Stephen, would buy the real Christmas tree and bring it home in his work van, and her brother Patrick would fill a galvanised bucket with soil from the garden to hold it, and he would sort out the box with the decorations and the crib. Patrick would moan and curse about having to do the jobs for Kate, and she would shout and curse back at him until he gave in and did it.

That was just their way.

If it had been in her own house – if it had been her mother and father shouting at each other – Lily would have run a mile. But Kate and Patrick rowing never bothered her. Kate never shouted and swore at Stephen. But then, she never had to.

Patrick was a different kettle of fish.

He was Kate's older, bachelor brother and he had lived in the house all his life, and when their mother died, Kate and Stephen moved in with him. A fact he often threw up in arguments with his sister – that *they* had moved in with *him*. Patrick had no scruples when it came to telling people the truth.

Behind his back, people said he was simple or "not right in the head", but Lily thought that he just did things his own way.

Lily threw the covers back and padded barefoot across to the window to open the curtains. Disappointingly, it wasn't snowing, and most of the snow from the night before had melted. Bits were still gathered in greying drifts at the sides of the road and there was a white icing on top of the hedges – but it was definitely disappearing.

As she pulled her dressing-gown on, a broad smile crossed Lily's elfin face when she remembered her blue duffle-coat. It was an early Christmas present she'd got last week and she wasn't allowed to wear it to school until after the holidays, but her mother had said she could wear it to Mass this weekend and for going shopping. All the teenage girls in the area were clambering to get coloured duffle coats with leather toggles, and Lily was delighted to be ahead of a lot of them.

She could picture herself walking down the aisle tomorrow morning at Mass. It would be as good as a fashion show as everyone noticed what everyone else was wearing. And there would be a good chance of bumping into girls from school when she was in town wearing the coat this morning.

Since it was just after half past eight, and her younger sisters were still asleep, Lily was delighted to have the sitting-room and the crackling fire all to herself. Her mother was busily occupied hanging the morning's washing on the clothes-pulley, and she left Lily to her own devices at the cooker.

After her usual Saturday morning breakfast of scrambled eggs on a roll and a mug of milky coffee, Lily took up residence in the bathroom, and emerged some fifteen minutes later wearing her good brown polo-neck with matching corduroy jeans and heeled boots. Her long blonde curly hair was held in place by a wooden clasp at the back of her head. She halted at the mirror at the bottom of the hall to pose in the mirror – first with her blue duffle-coat hood up and then with it down – giving a self-knowing giggle at her own vanity.

Lily slipped and slid her way across the road to Kate's house. When she arrived at the door, she kicked her boots clean and then gave a quick ring on the bell before letting herself in. "It's only me!" she called as she stepped into the dark hallway.

"You nearly gave me a heart attack wi' that blidey bell!" Kate yelled from her bedroom. "I wasn't expectin' you until ten o'clock."

Lily poked head around the bedroom door. "Why, what time is it now?"

"It's not half past nine," Kate said, struggling from under the mound of covers to get into a sitting position. "Is it freezing outside?" Kate was obsessed with the weather because she felt the cold badly, even in the summer.

"I never noticed," Lily replied, "but most of the snow is gone."

"Thank Christ," Kate muttered. She reached over to the small table beside her bed and lifted the tablets her husband had left out before he went off to work, and then washed them down with the small glass of lemonade left beside them. She grimaced as she took the pills. "Right," she said, putting the glass down and lifting a sheet of writing paper. "You go and tell Patrick to get the kettle on, and I'll check over this list for the shops."

The sitting-room was empty. "Patrick?" Lily called.

The kitchen door opened and the small figure came towards

her, the greying ruffle of hair behind his ears all sticking up, and his face unshaven. He wore the old navy suit that he wore every weekday (he wore a brown one on Sundays) with a grubby striped shirt and a V-necked sweater underneath. The hems of his trousers were so long that he walked on the back of them, and the laces on his shoes were undone. "Well?" he said, raising his bushy eyebrows. "What does Hitler want now?"

"Tea," Lily told him. "She says will you put the kettle on?"

"It was done ten minutes ago," he said triumphantly. He turned back towards the kitchen.

A short while later Patrick appeared in the bedroom with two cups of tea on a tray and two slices of toast. "What I'd like to know," he said, plonking the tray down on the empty side of the bed, "is how everybody in this house would manage if I had to go and get myself a job?"

"Thanks for makin' the tea, son," Kate told him, not even registering his question. There was no fear of Patrick getting a job, and now, in his late forties, it was highly unlikely that anybody would come knocking on the door to offer him one.

They discussed the shopping list over the tea, and Kate gave instructions about certain Christmas gifts that had to be exactly right, and gave alternatives to others.

"Pick your mother a nice underskirt or a nightdress," Kate instructed. Then she dropped the bombshell. "I've told Patrick that he's to go into town with you to help carry all the bags and parcels . . ."

Lily's eyes widened. "But I don't need him – I can manage on my own," she said.

"No, you can't," Kate told her. "Apart from all the gift sets, you've got shoes and slippers to carry, and three or four games and selection boxes. You'll never manage that on your own."

267

"I could ask one of my friends to come with me," Lily suggested.

"It's too late." Kate's decision was final. "By the time you'd go around to their house and waited until they got dressed and had their breakfast, the shops would be packed." She took a sip of her tea. "Patrick's good at carrying bags, and I've given him money for your fares and a cake and a cup of tea, and a taxi home."

A short while later Lily and Patrick were heading up the street with only minutes to spare for the bus. She was grateful that he had at least shaved and laced his shoes, and a raincoat hid the worst of his well-worn suit.

Although his feet turned in towards each other, Patrick could move at a considerable speed when he needed to, and Lily found it hard keeping up with him in her heeled boots. There was little or no conversation as they both concentrated on saving their energy for catching the bus. As they rounded the corner at the top of the street they could see half a dozen people waiting for the bus, and Lily suddenly wondered if anyone would notice her new duffle coat.

"Look at this blidey crowd in front of us," Patrick moaned as they neared the stop. "And the bus will probably be packed, and we'll likely all have to stand when it comes."

Lily was delighted to spot a woman she knew and went over to chat with her. The woman had immediately deduced the situation.

"I suppose you and Patrick are doing Kate's shopping," she said. "And that's a lovely new coat you're wearing."

When the double-decker eventually arrived, Lily followed the woman onto the lower deck, intending to sit beside her. Then, she suddenly heard, "Hoy, Buggerlugs!"

Lily looked up – along with practically everyone else inside the bus – and saw Patrick signalling to her to come upstairs as he wanted a cigarette.

Lily was mortified but, since he had the fares, she had no option but to follow him.

Fifteen minutes later the bus stopped outside The Household department store. On the ground floor were the toy and sweet departments, alongside the china and fancy goods. Lily's annoyance at Patrick evaporated as she walked into the shop and saw the huge decorated Christmas tree in the centre of the floor.

"Will we start here first?" she asked, heading towards a large display of selection boxes and chocolates.

Patrick halted her in her tracks. "Are you daft? The blidey chocolate will be melted if we buy it now." He narrowed his eyes. "I thought you got a school prize for being brainy?"

Lily swallowed her annoyance and reached into her shopping bag to get the purse with Kate's list.

"And you'd be better putting your purse into yer pocket and holding onto it," he warned, "because this place will be full of thieving bastards at this time of the year."

They made their way upstairs and after a short discussion, Lily was relieved when they split up and she went to the Ladies' department and Patrick to the Gents'.

Lily stifled a sigh when she saw seven people ahead of her and she wondered if Patrick was facing the same queue. Then, it dawned on her that she had the credit book for the shop which she had to hand over in lieu of payment and then sign for the goods. Patrick would need it when he came to pay for things as well. Lily wondered what would happen if he finished first.

The queue moved slowly as each person who reached the desk took ages picking their items. At least they had a line of chairs out for the customers to sit on which helped matters. As she moved along the chairs to the front of the queue, a woman with a baby started chatting to Lily, and then she noticed two girls going by whom she recognised from a neighbouring school. They were both wearing duffle coats – one brown and one green. She was just comparing the coats with her own, when suddenly Patrick appeared in front of her.

"That oul' cow over in the Gents' department is goin' blidey daft at me because I didn't have the book to pay for the things," he told her. "Why did ye not give it to me first?" Patrick grabbed the book. "If she starts again, I'll tell her to shove her vests and slippers up her big backside!"

Lily couldn't believe her ears. And she deduced from the sudden deathly silence, neither could the other people in the queue. Patrick disappeared off as quickly as he'd come, leaving her red-faced with embarrassment.

The silence was suddenly broken when the sales lady called, "Next!"

The abrupt manner of the assistant told Lily that she had also heard Patrick's outburst and the description of her colleague in the Gents' department. When she reached the desk, Lily tried hard to make up for this, by being extra polite. She was trying so hard to be quiet and inconspicuous that the assistant had difficulty hearing what she was asking for, and several times she brought the wrong thing or the wrong size. The lady was huffing and puffing and looking heavenwards every time that Lily consulted her list to ask for something else.

Then, Lily felt a tap on her shoulder. It was the lady with the baby. "You left your bag behind, hen," she said, holding it out. "You'd better keep a good grip on it, or you'll be getting into more trouble with your daddy – he doesn't seem to be in a very good mood."

Lily's face was a picture. "*He's* not my daddy!" she gasped.

The baby suddenly started crying and completely distracted the mother, and Lily's explanation about helping a sick neighbour was drowned by the screeching.

Then, it dawned on her that the rest of the queue probably thought that Patrick was her daddy as well, and the thought horrified her. How could anyone think they were related? How could they? He didn't look a bit like her daddy, who wore a clean shirt to work and another clean one when he came home. He also wore lovely-smelling aftershave. Her thoughts were brought back to the more pressing situation of the sales lady who was now waiting for Lily to choose between two nightdresses. Thankfully, the woman's attitude had softened when she'd heard the girl's protests about Patrick not being her father.

"You're a good wee lassie, helpin' a sick neighbour," she said, as she put Lily's purchases in carrier bags. "And between you and me, that fella with you is more of a hindrance than a help."

Lily felt a sudden surge of guilt for having betrayed both Patrick and Kate, by explaining their situation in front of this condescending woman. "He's not that bad," she backtracked, "he's just not used to waiting in long queues . . ."

She was just leaving the desk when she saw Patrick coming towards her, his brow deep in concentration.

"I'm goin' outside for a fag," he told her. "You go on into the shoe department and I'll catch up with you."

Lily went across the store to join yet another queue. She asked the man in front of her the time, and after checking his watch he launched into a tirade about how long he had been waiting and how shopping was nothing short of pure torture. Then, in a loud voice he said that the shop was a disgrace and needed more staff. To Lily's surprise several other people chimed in with him,

271

and one of the sales assistants had nodded in agreement as well.

It was after twelve o'clock now, which meant they had been in the shop for over two hours. By the looks of things she could be in the shoe department for another two. Patrick came shuffling towards her and sat down, and Lily was grateful to turn away from the man who had been complaining.

"What are you gettin' for Christmas?" Patrick asked her.

Lily launched into all the things she and her sisters were hoping for.

"You'll be blidey lucky," Patrick laughed. "Bicycles and scooters? D'you think your mother and father are made of money?" He then went on to say that he wanted Lily to help him pick a present for Kate. "I'm gettin' Stephen a bottle of whisky but I want to get her somethin' nice."

"What about perfume?" Lily suggested. "They had some nice bottles downstairs."

Lily sprayed various perfumes on her wrist and eventually settled on one called *Evening in Paris*. "That is gorgeous," she said, closing her eyes to breathe in the scent, "but it's the most expensive."

"That'll do fine," Patrick decided. He handed the sales assistant the credit book. "Give me two bottles. I'll pay cash for one and you can charge the other one to the book."

Lily's brow furrowed. "Who's the second one for?"

Patrick tapped the side of his nose and winked. "Kate told me to look for something nice for you, but don't tell her I told you."

"But it's too dear . . ." Lily protested.

"It *is* blidey dear," Patrick stated, "but Kate thinks you deserve a decent present."

A little thrill ran through Lily. She'd never had her own bottle of perfume before.

It was going on for two o'clock when they finally picked up the selection boxes downstairs. Lily looked at Patrick – who had two or three bags in each hand plus parcels under his arm – and she realised that Kate had been right about her having help. It was just a pity it had to be Patrick.

"Are we going home now?" Lily asked.

"We're going for fish and chips," Patrick informed her. "Kate can pay for it." He gave her a sidelong smile. "She's the very one who would be treating herself if she was fit enough to be out shopping, and we deserve the same. There's a café around the corner that does lovely fish."

Lily was delighted. On a few special occasions her father had brought her and her sisters into the café and she really enjoyed it. The snow had started again, and they had to tread carefully. The café was busy but there were a few seats at the back, so they pushed their way through.

"Thank Christ we don't need to queue up in here," Patrick said as they slid into the vinyl seats.

They gave their orders and then Lily got up to go to the Ladies'. She was on her way back, when she felt someone tugging at her sleeve. It was a girl from school.

"Hi, Lily, I thought it was you." The girl turned to the woman beside her and started to giggle.

Lily waited, wondering what was so funny.

"My mother and me were just saying that you must be out shopping with your daddy . . ."

The penny suddenly dropped. Lily felt herself blush. She drew herself up to her full height, ready to explain about Kate being sick and then she suddenly stopped.

"If it's any of your business," she heard herself say in a quiet, dignified voice, "Patrick's not actually my daddy. He's a good

273

friend of our family and a very nice man." She looked the girl's mother straight in the eye. "He's also very well-mannered and never makes comments about other people."

Then, she turned on her heel and walked back to her table.

Patrick stared at her as she sat down.

"You were good today," he suddenly said. "I wouldn't like to have done all that queuing with some other people I know."

Lily felt a wave of guilt. She hadn't been good at all. She had been embarrassed and ashamed when people thought Patrick was her father, and she hadn't been able to stop herself from feeling it. Before she could ponder the situation any further, Patrick stood up and started lifting his bags.

"C'mon, Buggerlugs," he said, loud enough for all around them to hear, "we'll go and get the taxi home."

Lily stood up and they headed out into the busy, snowy street towards the taxi rank – their final queue of the day.

Liberty
&
Linda

Sharon Owens

Sharon Owens

Sharon Owens was born in Omagh in 1968 and moved to Belfast in 1988 to study illustration at the Art College. She married husband Dermot in 1992 and they have one daughter, Alice.

Liberty
&
Linda

February 2007

"It's at times like these, you really find out who your friends are. Isn't that right, sweetheart?" Linda sighed softly, gazing down at the impossibly soft and beautiful face of her one-year-old daughter, Liberty. The baby snuggled into the warmth of Linda's woolly sweater and sighed contentedly.

"Yes, indeed. With friends like mine, sure, who needs enemies? It'd be easier to get Johnny Depp round here for a visit, than those ones."

Liberty didn't answer. She just went on sleeping, her little eyelids flickering in a baby dream.

"I wonder what babies dream about," whispered Linda. "All they do is eat and sleep and have cuddles. Well, maybe that's enough material to be going on with."

And then she laughed at herself.

This is why I've lost all my high-flier friends, she thought. Because I go around saying soppy things like that to people! *What do babies dream about?* And where does all the love come from, that you suddenly find in your heart for a new baby? And why does everyone in the media conspire to make women think being a mother is dull as ditchwater and totally second-rate, when it *so* isn't? All the money in the world couldn't buy a mother's love. As if my old job selling time-shares was any more exciting than washing out feeding bottles! Mind you, it's lonely sometimes. There's no getting away from that uncomfortable truth.

"I mean, why would all my supposed best mates rather go to Ibiza than come to your lovely party, Libby? Huh?"

The room seemed to vibrate with silence.

"The eejits, they forgot all about your very first birthday when they booked that silly last-minute holiday," she whispered to Liberty. "Ibiza, at their age! Talk about having an extended adolescence. And I even bought giant metallic pink balloons and a cute teddy-bear cake and everything. And in the end, there was just you and me and your daddy, and my parents and his parents, and Granny Isobel. It was a total riot. Not!"

Liberty smiled in her sleep and Linda touched the baby's tiny foot and suppressed the knot of fear that was forming deep-down in her stomach. Over by the dining-table, the clutch of pink balloons swayed imperceptibly. Linda blew a sigh towards them and they moved suddenly and startled her.

"You see how boring I've become, Libby? A bunch of harmless balloons can rattle me! *Me*, that once went bungee-jumping in New Zealand. Me, that once went to New York on my own for a business conference on time-shares. Me, that once auditioned to go on Blind Date. What's happened to me?"

The small pottery clock ticked loudly on the mantelpiece. Linda wondered if she should give the clock a name and start talking to it. Ivy, maybe, since the base of the clock was painted with delicate fronds of trailing pale-green ivy. A wedding present from Mike's mother.

Blimey!

Talking to a clock! She really was getting lonely!

Won't it be great when Libby starts to talk in proper sentences, Linda thought wistfully.

"Oh, the fun we'll have then, my darling, when you say all the funny things that children are supposed to say. I'll start a big glossy diary and I'll stick loads of photos in it, to help us both remember all the good times."

The baby sighed and her miniature pouting lips blew a tiny bubble.

"I hope I haven't made a big fat mistake, calling you such a fancy name, my darling. But you were never going to be lumbered with Mary or Margaret or Anne or Bernadette, or any old-fashioned saint's name like that. This is a new start for the two of us. You're going to be whatever you like when you grow up, young lady. Not what I think you should be or what your daddy wants you to be, or what the teachers say is most suitable! You're going to be truly free and independent. You can be a human-rights lawyer or a mother-of-six, or both. And I'll be there to help you, every step of the way, if you want me to."

Outside the window, snow fell silently. As if it knew the baby was asleep and must not be disturbed. Giant flakes swirled right up to the glass, then spun away into the afternoon gloom. A chill wind came dropping down the chimney and the room was suddenly cold and cheerless.

"Come on, now, let's get a meal organised," Linda scolded herself.

She went over to Liberty's cradle and laid her daughter gently down in it. And then covered her little body with a peppermint-coloured blanket with adorable pink ducks on it. She pulled the curtains closed and switched on both table-lamps. She flicked on the imitation stove and immediately the room was cosier and more friendly. Mike had bought the stove a few weeks earlier and although Linda had said it was a bit tacky at the time, she loved it now. And she was glad she hadn't bought the space-age silver display of steel cones that she'd planned to set in the empty fireplace.

"I'll make hot-dogs. And an apple-pie," she said cheerfully. "Then, when Mike gets in from work, there'll be a lovely smell in the house. And he'll be all impressed with me because he's never seen me cook anything from scratch before."

Not that I'm turning into a 1950's housewife, she told herself sternly. I'm definitely not! I'm not wearing a floral apron and I'm not going to cook properly every day of the week. And I can go back to work the minute I want to, and enrol Liberty in a trendy nursery, and everything is going to be just fine.

Then she sat down on the nearest chair and cried her eyes out.

Liberty was never going to be enrolled in a trendy nursery, was she? Linda could never part with her precious child. She just couldn't bear it, not even for a few hours each day. And anyway, it was far too expensive. She'd be working round the clock to pay the fees. Mike and herself would have to borrow money from the bank to pay the fees . . .

"Those selfish bitches," Linda wept. "How *could they* forget about Libby's party? How could they just drop me like that? Like a hot brick? After four years of the great craic we had at university, and then four more living it up as outrageous singletons?"

But they had.

"The times I stood up for them at work when projects were

completed late! Honestly, it was an absolute joke! I picked up the pieces when their relationships collapsed, I helped them to move flats, I lent them my best clothes. Most of which I never got back, now I come to think of it. I got them taxis home when they were plastered drunk. I lent them money I could ill afford. I was a great friend to all of them. Nobody could say I wasn't a terrific friend."

Yet, one by one, they'd deserted her.

As Linda settled down with Mike, bought a tiny terraced house in the city centre and then a bigger house in the suburbs, and then discovered she was pregnant, the phone calls grew more and more infrequent. And the excuses they made not to see her when she rang them: they were only hilarious! Like when Harriet said she couldn't make it to Liberty's christening because her car had broken down on the way, and then Linda found out Harriet was actually having a naughty weekend with her oily old (married) boss. Or when Jane said she couldn't baby-sit to let Linda go to an urgent dental appointment because she'd fractured her ankle playing squash. Of course, Jane hadn't fractured her ankle at all. She'd been queueing up all night to buy concert tickets for U2, of all people, and she was just crawling into her bed to catch up on some beauty sleep! For heaven's sake, Jane had seen U2 in concert twenty-seven times already! Bono was never going to leave his beloved wife Ali and run away with Jane Snoddy from the Ardoyne Shops, was he? No matter how often she struggled to the front row and roared her head off.

Fan?

Fanatic, more like!

The list was endless.

None of Linda's single friends were the slightest bit interested in Liberty. It was so hurtful. And the baby was a pure poppet, too. Her fluffy blonde hair was tapered at the top like a coconut. Her enormous pale-blue eyes missed nothing, her rosy pink cheeks were divine and her perfect little hands could grip your finger so tightly it was amazing. What was it about the little angel that had repulsed an entire set of friends? Was it because Linda was boring? Because Liberty was boring?

"Stop it," Linda told herself. "Stop feeling sorry for yourself and get some food ready. I'm just the first one in the group to settle down, that's all. They'll be battering my door in when they start having babies of their own, asking me for breast-feeding advice and baby-sitting favours."

And I'll be far too busy swanning round the boutiques with my gorgeous daughter, Linda thought bravely. By the time those good-time girls manage to snare themselves a bunch of husbands, my daughter will be giving me fashion advice and we'll be sharing shoes and handbags and bottles of perfume.

Still, it *was* lonely sometimes, living in the suburbs as a new mother. Everybody else seemed to be out at work. Only a few retired couples seemed to be about on the estate during the day. And even *they* were busy doing the school run for their grandchildren, by the looks of it. There were a few melancholy widows and widowers pottering along the footpaths, forever picking dead leaves out of their immaculate shrubs and hedges. And waving in the window at her as they hobbled by on a walking stick.

"Oh jeepers," sobbed Linda, and the tears flowed again, "what have I done? What the heck have I landed myself in? How will I survive years and years of this carry-on? Nothing ever *happens!*"

She hurried into the kitchen and decided to get busy with baking the pie. Anything to keep her mind off brooding over lost friendships and not being invited on hedonistic trips abroad.

A loud knock at the front door made Linda jump into the air

and drop the bag of cooking apples she was holding. She reached for a clean tea-towel to dry her eyes. A quick check in the hall-mirror to make sure she didn't look too upset, and then Linda opened the door, expecting it to be a lemonade salesman or a double-glazing salesman or a plastic-guttering salesman or a clean-shaven religious crusader of some kind. But no, it was a fit-looking, thirty-ish woman with curly brown hair and a big bright smile. Linda glanced out towards the road, looking for some sign as to what this particular sales pitch would be about. Cleaning out drains, by the looks of it! A worn anorak and paint-spattered jeans on her visitor. Ancient wellingtons, and a smear of engine oil on her face.

"Hello, I'm Melanie McAleer from four doors down, number fifty with the blue door and the row of flowerpots by the wall?"

"Yes, I know the house you mean," said Linda. "Can I help you?"

"Well, I hope you don't think I'm a nosey parker but I've seen you out walking with the baby these last few months and I wondered if you were new to the area? Only, there's a mother-and-toddler thing we've set up and maybe you'd like to join us?"

"Oh, thanks very much but I don't know," Linda began, worried about committing to anything she might find it awkward to extricate herself from later on. Especially since Melanie looked like an out-of-work hippy or something.

"It's nothing formal," Melanie said quickly, sensing Linda's reluctance. "Just one day a week, we meet up at the café on the main road and have a chat. Mondays at eleven usually, it's quiet then and the staff don't mind the buggy invasion. And maybe if it's fine, we might go for a stroll together down the road, or as far as the park even, let the kids play with a ball. Like I said, it's nothing formal and if you can't make it sometimes, that's no problem. We just keep in touch with one another, you know? Swap phone numbers and useful information. It can be lonely with a new baby, believe you me."

"Um, yeah. How old is yours?" Linda said. More out of politeness than anything.

"I have five kids, ranging from ten years to eight months."

"Blimey! I mean, that's incredible. I mean, how lovely . . ."

Linda wondered how much Melanie's Child Benefit added up to, each month.

"Yes, so I've been a full-time Mum *forever*. I used to be a GP but of course, nobody could afford the childcare for five kids these days. So, I'm on a career-break. A twenty-year career-break. My husband is a doctor too, so we manage, just about. Do you drive at all? Only I didn't notice a car just now."

"Well, I've been meaning to take lessons," began Linda, mortified at having misjudged Melanie so completely. "My husband drives but I've not got round to it yet. I think I'd be hopeless, though. I've no hand-to-eye co-ordination."

"Oh, you must learn. It's so handy for when you have more than one child. I can give you the number of a great little chap; he has the patience of a saint. Honestly, he taught me to drive and I thought I'd never learn. My first lesson, I drove over a bollard and flattened two signs."

Melanie looked as if she could witter on all day, but Linda didn't want to give out too much information about herself in return. She was still smarting from being rejected by her old friends, she realised. And also, her old friends were cool and edgy and sexy and great fun. And here was poor old Melanie in her tattered anorak, offering the giddy excitement of a weekly stroll past the shops. Even if Melanie *was* a qualified GP, she could never be as much fun as Harriet and Jane and the others had been.

Oh Lord, this was going to tricky! Maybe she should stop answering the door altogether, Linda thought desperately. Creep about with the lights off and pretend to be out?

As if reading her thoughts, Melanie laughed and said, "I don't always look this shabby, only I was sorting out the shed, you see. I was looking for my puncture-kit and then I decided to tidy up the whole thing, and just when I had everything laid out on the grass, it starts to snow. And the whole sky darkens. So I had to fire all the junk back in and now it's worse than it ever was before. Wouldn't you know it!"

"Oh, indeed . . ." Linda trailed off.

"And I never found the puncture-kit. Oh well. Me and the girls are going on a sponsored bike-ride tomorrow to raise funds for a school we support in India. Well, we will do if the snow clears up, which I expect it will. It rarely lies along the coast. Twenty miles to the seaside and back, we're doing. It's great fun, we do it every year. We take a picnic. It's so refreshing to cycle in February. And there'll be a party the night after, to celebrate, at my house. Why don't you pop in and meet everyone?"

"Me?"

"About eight o'clock? Can your husband baby-sit? I'm sure he can. We were thinking of going out to India some day and seeing the school for ourselves, you know. Just a three-day trip, maybe next year if we can sort out some cheap accommodation. And cheap flights."

"Wow, that's really amazing. All the way to India? Oh, I'm Linda, by the way, and my daughter is called Liberty. Libby, for short. Would you like to see her?"

"I'd love to," said Melanie, who was shivering with cold. Immediately she nipped into the hall, stepped out of her muddy boots and tiptoed towards the cradle in the sitting-room.

"What a gorgeous, gorgeous little girl, and what a lovely name you've given her. I'm all for new-fangled names, me. Too many of us were stuck with some awful boring old name. I think you're absolutely right, and it suits her perfectly. Mine are called Sebastian, Toby, Oliver, Amy and Tabitha. Well, Libby's asleep now so I'll leave you in peace to enjoy a cuppa. And don't forget to call in to mine, and meet the gang. They're all super girls. Cheerio, I'll see myself out."

And as soon as Melanie had appeared, she vanished again. The front door clicking softly shut behind her and Linda noticed a little pool of snowflakes lying serenely on the rug. Linda did make a cuppa then and took the time to enjoy it and flick through the pages of a gossip magazine, pleased that Melanie had remembered to call the baby Libby.

There wasn't time to bake a pie though, as Mike came home, starving as usual, and devoured seven hot-dogs before he could even stop to chat. He made a big mug of tea and gazed down into Liberty's crib as he gulped it back.

"Watch that tea near the baby," Linda fretted. "You might spill it."

"How was my little princess today?" Mike said gently, stepping back with his dangerous mug of tea. "What did the two of you get up to while I was hanging round the station, waiting to put a fire out?"

Usually, Linda said, *nothing much*. But today she said, "Well, we had a visitor from down the street. A nice lady called Melanie McAleer. She's a GP on a career-break with five children of her own, and she's invited me to meet her friends the night after tomorrow. A mother-and-toddler thing, she said, although all the children won't be there this time. It's a party to celebrate a charity bike-ride."

"Cool, are you going? I can mind this one on my own for a couple of hours, I should think."

Just then, Libby woke up and Linda went to fetch her bottle from the kitchen. Mike sat down to give it to her, a little routine he'd started in order to spend bonding time with his new daughter.

"So, are you off gallivanting to this wild party, or what?" he asked again. "Leaving me behind to hold the baby?"

"I don't know, Mike. What if it's really boring and they all sit round a table sipping lukewarm tea and talking about stretch-marks and teething and the price of shoes?"

"Steady on, missus! Aren't you the one always giving out to me about how unfair it is, the way society stereotypes young mothers and married women in general? Now you're doing it yourself. They're still human beings, you know? Aren't they having a party? That's not boring."

"Well, I'm sure it won't be anything like the sort of parties they have in Ibiza: all half-naked studs and gallons of booze."

"I should hope not! Aren't I enough for you any more? Are you still raging about the girls going abroad without you?"

"No, of course not."

But she was.

"Look, why don't you call in for twenty minutes and if you don't like them, just say you've got to be somewhere, and leave again. Then we'll do a midnight flit and change our names and have plastic surgery and we'll emigrate to Siberia, and you'll never have to see them again? Even Interpol won't be able to find us. We'll live underground and survive on berries and worms."

Linda laughed her head off. Something she couldn't remember doing since being diagnosed with post-natal depression six months earlier. Mike was delighted to see his wife so amused.

"Hey, I didn't know I was this talented. I must hand in my notice at the station and take a roadshow round the country. Paddy McGuinness, eat your heart out!"

"I'm sorry, Mike. I don't know why I'm being such a chump. You know I love Libby more than life itself, and I love you and I love being married. It's just, I miss all the girly stuff . . ."

"Then go and meet this Melanie one properly and give her friends a chance. They might be great fun. You've got nothing to lose."

"Okay," said Linda.

And she did.

With her heart in her mouth and a bottle of pink champagne in her hand, left over from Libby's first birthday party.

Ten weeks later, Linda was tucking into a hefty wedge of carrot cake in the local café with all her new friends when Jane and Harriet came in and sat down near the door. They didn't see Linda, obviously blanking the gaggle of mothers and toddlers in the corner right out of their consciousness. Linda felt a jolt of sadness in her chest and then she smiled at her little girl laughing with the other toddlers, and she felt at peace. Her old friends didn't think she was boring. And she wasn't boring, and neither was Libby. Harriet and Jane had simply moved on. Or rather, Linda had moved on and left them behind.

On the way out of the café, Linda said hello to Jane and Harriet, and was secretly pleased to see them looking slightly sheepish.

"Sorry we've not been in touch," said Harriet. "Things have been hectic at work."

"Tell me about it," added Jane. "It's been non-stop, installing this complicated new computer-system, and then there was asbestos discovered in the ceiling, and we had to relocate. And then there was a flood in the new building and we had to move again."

"Oh, that's all right," said Linda. "I've been all-go myself with Libby. And these ones here have me run ragged!" She nodded out towards the street where Melanie and the other women were waiting for her.

"Really?" said Harriet in a disbelieving voice.

"Oh yes," said Linda, buttoning up Libby's new pink jacket. "You wouldn't credit it, honestly you wouldn't. Coffee on Mondays, swimming on Tuesdays, gym on Wednesdays. I'm having driving lessons every Thursday. And Fridays we all go to the cinema and then on to Mario's for a couple of drinks and a pizza. Saturdays, our hubby's get their night in the pub and we take turns to host a girls' night in. I'm telling you, the housework's gone to the dogs."

"Oh my God," said Jane. Clearly impressed.

"Yes, and next year, we're off to India!" said Linda. "Mike and Libby are going too. And two of the guys from the fire-station. We're raising money to re-build a school out there, and the lads will be pitching in. Do give my love to the rest of the girls, won't you? I should call them but I'll probably never get round to it. Cheerio!"

She manoeuvered the buggy expertly out the door of the café and waved goodbye to her old friends as the little procession of buggies made its way down the street. Melanie and Linda were at the back of the group.

"Who were they?" Melanie asked quietly. "Were they two of the girls you told me about?"

"Yeah, but somehow, seeing them today wasn't as painful as I thought it was going to be. I showed off a little bit, which was childish of me but I couldn't help it."

"They seemed very nice."

"Oh, they are very nice, and that's why it was so hard when we drifted apart. Still, that's life, I suppose?"

"That's the spirit," said Melanie gently.

"Yes," agreed Linda. "I was obsessed with the way they just seemed to forget about me when I had Libby, but all I needed was the courage to let them go and move on myself. Thanks for making the effort to say hello that day. I really appreciate it."

"Don't mention it. You're great craic. Now, let's catch up with everyone else."

"Okay," said Linda brightly, smiling down at her beautiful daughter, "let's do that. Wait for us, you lot!"

Rock

Martina Reilly

Martina Reilly

Martina Reilly (Tina) is the author of four teenage novels and eight women's novels. She has won a number of awards for her fiction and her next book, *The Summer of Secrets,* will be out in October.

Rock

You are the rock upon which I build my life.

The rock that holds fast to the ground

When wind strikes and blows all before it down.

The rock that stands and takes the cold and the
snow, the hail and the rain.

The rock that shelters and keeps me sane.

The rock upon which I lie, when the sun pours
down hot.

The rock that soaks up all that I cannot.

And because you're always there for me

I can wander, far and free.

Friends
Like These

Victoria Smurfit

Victoria Smurfit

Victoria Smurfit is an internationally acclaimed actress who lives in Dublin with her husband and children. She has appeared in numerous major television productions including *Ballykissangel, North Square, Cold Feet* and most recently ITV's *Trial and Retribution*. She also works as a stage actress, and her film credits include *Run Of The Country, About A Boy, Bulletproof Monk* and *The Beach,* which is the principal subject of her story.

Friends
Like These

December 1998, Battersea Rise, London.

Perching on a bar stool laughing with a Green-Eyed Honey whose chocolate Labrador is quietly snoozing beneath his feet, I tuck into my ciggie packet for my last one. Each cigarette a thought, each thought a cigarette. He's far too old for me and, regardless of that, he is Irish and a businessman. Two boxes I will go to hell not to tick. Am I not in London? Am I not a creative actress? I come from Irish-businessmen stock so at twenty-five years of age it's certainly not what I am after now. Am thinking boho, slightly greasy from lack of nutrition, with a vocal desire to play Jesus at the Edinburgh fringe. Much better.

Fancy a beer but he's just ordered tea. What is the protocol? Damn it. One Corona and a camomile it is. As I stuff the lime through the neck of the bottle I see him check his watch. It's 3 p.m., the lunch crowds have left and it's just us in here. At least that's how it seems. The brick in my pocket rings as The Honey joins me in beer finally. The canine sighs. Or farts, not sure which. I almost follow suit when I read the big type on the phone's face: AGENT.

Every young actor's gut acidifies with the possibilities and dreams that can be opened or shut down dead by your agent's number appearing on your cell phone. My brain ratchets through the four auditions I have had in the last month: BBC period drama, ITV comedy, a Hollywood film and a roller-skating "woman's" commercial. I breathe and press the green handset button.

"Darling . . . sweetie . . . BBC . . . Anna Friel . . . different direction . . . no . . . no, you were wonderful but . . . but . . . too tall . . . blah blah . . . "

My heart firmly attaches itself to my toes. The blood drains from my eyeballs with embarrassment as I am suddenly aware of The Honey's proximity to my rejection. Head down, phone pushed almost into my ear cavity so he cannot hear what is spewing down the line, through the noise of my ego shattering I hear the agent say: ". . . of course you'll be gone for three months and it's only a couple of lines . . . quiet time of year and it *is* Leonardo DiCaprio . . . any thoughts, darling? Leaving the day after New Year . . . glorified extra part really . . . Thailand . . . do you want to do it?"

Before I answer I turn to himself. I can see in his big greens that he can feel the world has become a bit shinier and he raises his hand to order another round of limes.

"I'll be there."

Three hours four beers later, man and dog head over the rise to the other side of the Thames. Two weeks later I am not just on a beach but am in *The Beach*.

It will be five months before I see him in person again.

Back when airports' greatest threat was the Irish amongst us, you could see from one side of the check-in to the next. Ropes weren't necessary to herd the herds.

From Gatwick's revolving door I could see huddles of fifteen or more twenty-somethings kissing bye-bye to their current lives. I knew the members of this clutter of elegant hippies were to become my friends, family and nemeses for the foreseeable future. Everything I knew and everyone I had relied on up until that day were already slipping to the back of my mind as the fear of the unknown persuaded me to press forward.

I am sweaty and determined to show no quiver.

"Victoria Smurfit, aisle seat, please," I shoot out to the Thai airways check-in girl.

We're travelling business class and I am salivating at the imagined luxury ahead of me.

I turn to survey the group and to start judging them. Well, it's natural, isn't it? There is nowhere quite like the confines of an aeroplane for ten hours to consolidate those first fearful opinions.

I am sitting next to a blonde with a six-pack, her heart-shaped face welcoming despite the intimidating Aerobic Barbie look to her. On the adjacent aisle are a Loud London Italian in an open shirt and a corkscrew-curled slip of a hippy whose perfect vowels speak of BBC and Berkshire schooling. As my eye cruises down the aisles I realise that I am filling the Ginger Paddy role as in every seat sits an archetype. The Swedish male models, skinny and almost see-through in the lack of pigment; tiny pert French dollies more feminine than a bucket of oestrogen; Amazonian German women, every one a Valkyrie.

Touching down in Bangkok for our three-hour turn-around, the unbreakable bonding begins with four of us getting our first "dose". Scrabbling for tissues, clean undies and Rennies is a great leveller and right there these people cease to be intimidating gods of beauty.

The heat is chewy. Night is low and we can see nothing yet of our new country. The soundtrack speaks of small animals and insects that will surely end up in our shoes, sucking our blood for sport. The hotel swallows us all into our rooms. It's only the next morning that I realise I have a balcony, bathed in light and surrounded by thick jungle foliage. I stroll onto it. To my immediate right is a Lithuanian gymnast with a leg above her head, stretching, and a Diet Coke miniature in her hand. To my left a girl so thin I can see her heart beat. I think of breakfast.

Schedules arrive and information is doled out by crew members who are guiding us all out of the hotel canteen, hungry. Walking to the end of a pier I can see trestle tables manned by men with spoons. The smell of chicken's feet collides with the aroma of the sea. This is to be our dining-room. Perched on an upturned crab-pot, a rice bowl in hand. I won't see a slice of bacon or a slab of toast for three months.

Five Thai fishing boats like scooped-out bananas glide in to the pier and we set sail to our rehearsal beach. An island pops into view, white of sand and swaying with palm trees. This is where we will be given our motivation, our characters and all the attention we will need for the coming months. As we wade in to shore the Director is beckoning us to sit. Groups are naturally beginning to form. The Scandinavians huddle in a blur of blond, the French giggle and the Londoners all look as if it doesn't matter to them where they sit. I'm petrified with the thrill of being here.

Our orders are to get thin and brown. This is before the raging double-zero debate and the request is simply based on the need that, if we are to appear to be real islanders who'd live by hunting the sea and land, then we should be skinny and leathery. Simple. Nothing to do with political correctness, just an acting truth to realise. We have a trainer to whoop us into shape. He is kind of face and tough of body and you do what he asks.

I find myself doing sit-ups on the scratchy sand next to the star of the show. As my competitive side steals a glance to see if I have better abs than him, my eyes redirect themselves to the lack of pants. A major star is commando in baggy shorts next to me. I do at least fifteen sit-ups before I can take my eyeballs off their prize. Only the high buzz of an approaching speedboat is capable of pulling focus. Still exercising, I twist to see a five-foot, leopard-print-clad blonde cruising towards the rehearsal beach. She is standing on the back of the boat, hair longer than she is tall billowing out over the Thai waves. She has a shit-eating grin below her pink shades and I know she is going to be fabulous. Our Antipodean has arrived.

A man, easily six foot of designer white shirt and flowing dark hair, is milling about. He is our Director of Photography (DOP). His job is to light the film. A position of great importance as not only can he evoke a touch, taste and smell of location with his 10K lamps but he can also make you look crap should he decide. Never cross a DOP. Everywhere you look, boobs abound as tan-lines are not encouraged. After the first horrifying moment of disrobing to just a triangle of costume, it all becomes deeply ordinary to see each other as God almost intended. As our glamorous director of photography wanders around absorbing our faces and skin tones, jobs are doled out. Cooks, fishermen, house-builders, hunters and gatherers. All roles essential to "really" living like these people we are to portray. I am on murder duty. The crabs netted and the fish caught are brought to me. I have two stones and a knife and my job is to gut and remove the innards of the fish and kill the crabs with one brutal smash. Their claws continue to move while in the throes of death. An odd sight watching two halves of a crab scuttling in opposite directions. They won't get far as our chef is the exuberant Italian and we decide we are to be a kitchen husband-and-wife team. I prep and he creates. Wrapping a random fish in banana leaves soaked in lime juice and burnt over a beach fire, he delights all our starving comrades as the DOP tells me to stop getting freckles. Hmm, not so easy that.

The Aussie "G'days" her way around the group and on some instinct sits next to me. We are the only two singles, nationally speaking, for every other nation appears to have a mate. Rapt, I listen to her outrageous tales of friends marrying their gay best pals for visas and late nights in clubs from Sydney to Sidcup, punctuated by Marlboro Reds. I decide she is my alter ego. The girl I would have loved to be had Sunday school not been such a lynchpin in my childhood. Damn those Fair Isle jumpers and name tags.

A rhythm begins. Slowly an awareness that our feet are tapping. Behind us, sheltering from the relentless freckle-maker, is a man whose pallor speaks of a life in theatre. He is the head honcho and creator of *Stomp*, a show that captured audiences around the world by making music from, well, anything really. A broom, a dustbin lid, your cheeks . . . he is beating out a simple tune with a stick and one of my discarded crab-shells. It is contagious and alluring and we all think we are natural musicians. That is until he calls us over and begins to teach us the basics in rhythm, asking us individually to beat out a tune. Idiots most of us, but we learn over the next weeks. Actually we obsess over our "paradiddles".

I am learning to read tarot cards and busy myself telling everyone's fortune. Quite mystical. Except I have to read the card's meaning from the manufacturer's leaflet. It is giving me an outlet for getting to know all the people involved. Building our characters over the two weeks on this island becomes our touchstone for alleviating the tedium that is an inevitable part of filmmaking.

Deciding who we are going to be and who i٠
whom determines a lot of the friendships, all
next three months.

It's 8 p.m. The night drops like a stone as the mosquitos g٠
a busy night. In the morning a vast catamaran is to collect us for th٠
first day's shoot. Even though we are only lowly background artists,
our director has chosen to use actors, models and dancers as we can
bring more to the table and feel comfy in direction. Our director
oozes such creativity and vulnerability that my core vows to be my
best. A lone light bulb is swinging from a corrugated tin roof,
illuminating green plastic tables. A restaurant. Excellent news.
Curly-haired Hippy, the Aussie and I head to it, baht in hand. While
we sit over the most incredible stir-fry and three magnums of local
beer, I find that Curly is less BBC and more PSF – a self-titled "Posh
Speaking Fraud" born not in Berkshire but the North of England.
She is a vegetarian, a humanist and has tightened vowels until drunk.
She makes me laugh until I pee a little. Already I love these girls.

Staggering to our respective rooms I battle with the key to
open my door. I bypass the bathroom and my nightly ablutions,
citing exhaustion to self, when I realise I am not alone. A
cockroach, chihuahua-size, perches by the light switch twitching
his antennae at me. I am giddy enough to simply bid him
goodnight and crumple onto my bed.

Morning crashes through my brain and I realise not only is the
catamaran leaving in twenty minutes but the roach was not part
of a twisted dream but a hungover reality. I shriek loud enough
for a tiny member of housekeeping to push open my door and
rescue my pathetic Western fears from this creature. She just picks
him up and takes him out. I feel really stupid.

As it turns out the boat, idyllic and floating through the sunset

Ko Pi Pi (the island of *The Beach*), is riddled with cockroaches. They are so commonplace that it is like asking a grand Georgian pile in Meath to not have spiders. Curly, Aussie, Italian Stallion and I "spot" each other for vermin. As one lies down on the floor of the vessel having tan make-up applied by a professional, the others coerce the roaches in the opposite direction with some leftover breakfast crumbs. Ingenious and above and beyond the call of friendship as the animals scuttle after us in packs.

Unbeknownst to us, hours of our lives are to be spent lying under a canopy squabbling and playing Jenga, waiting to be called to toss a volleyball in the background or swing from a tree in the searing heat. We all, at one time or another get our five minutes of fame by filming with Leo. His talent is tangible and I sit back with pride watching my friends one by one go head to head with him and hold their own. My Italian "husband" is sensational covered in fish-blood swinging his kitchen cleaver, Curly is ethereal and glowing and Aussie chews up the scenery with aplomb. Me? Well, I get to ask for tampons.

Our Scandinavian boys are preparing for the big shark attack and the catamaran is filled with body parts. Chewed-off legs and amputated arms swilling in fake blood dominate the top deck. On arrival the prosthetics team dig tunnels under the sand for rubber tubing to squirt the pumping blood, and holes to hide the actor's real leg. None of us are ready for Action to be called and watching our blond boys roaring in pain, dragging themselves from the sea in tears, makes me realise I care. About them all.

As filming comes to its last weeks, we relocate to a converted shoe factory that is to be our new base for the homeward stretch. This is where the production team have been for the duration. We arrive, stinky and hippie-like. The cultures clash as they pour out of conditioned rooms, Levi-clad, to check out the state of us.

"Toast!"

"There is goddamned toast!" I hear roared out from my delicate friend Curly.

She has found buckets of bread and Kerrygold, all shipped out to the production team for their use. Well, not any more. Like rabid dogs we descend upon this utopia of wheat. Nearly three months of rice has taken its toll and we are savages. Two weeks later we receive a memo stating we've all porked out and continuity has gone to hell. Oops.

But so worth it.

It's the end of the journey. The friends I have made are for life as is always the way with filming. It is like surviving a train crash and being bonded to each other forever in some form. You may not like all of them but you have shared experiences beyond the mundane. If Curly, Aussie or Italian Husband call upon me in twenty years' time, having not seen them in the meantime, I won't hesitate to be there for them. No time in my heart will have passed and no judgements made. Friendship is based on knowing the bad as well as the good in someone and yet still being there hoping your own faults don't grate too loudly on them.

Packing up my Thai fisherman pants and bikini bottoms my mind runs to the Green-Eyed Honey.

I wonder what he is doing.

If I had turned to my tarot cards I would have found the Honey was to become my husband, the father of my children and most importantly my very best friend.

Friendship

Kathryn Thomas

Kathryn Thomas

Kathryn Thomas is the lead presenter for *No Frontiers* on RTÉ, along with a host of celebrity appearances on Irish television, including *The Panel*, *The Special Olympics Live*, and the *St Patrick's Day* celebrations. She is set to present and appear on more RTÉ programmes in the coming year.

Friendship

A blank canvas is a daunting thing. She had heard the expression many times before but firmly believed she had only truly grasped its significance in the past thirty-seven minutes. Her fingers hung patiently over the smooth black keys, like figure skaters at a competition, eagerly waiting for their turn to take to the ice. The cursor on her empty laptop screen flashed impatiently, challenging her to feel inspired, witty, engaging. She stared back. The cursor seemed to take on a personality of its own, arms folded stamping its foot in utter frustration. "Come on, come on, come on, get a move on, brains!" he screamed silently at her, with an accent she imagined to be from the Bronx. "You came to write, so prove yourself. Enlighten all of us, schmuck!" A surge of panic rose in the lower part of her abdomen. She had travelled all this way across the globe to clear her head, to get some space and to feel inspired to write her book, which she had tinkered with for the last six months.

A mosquito passed close to her ear; close enough for her to hear that one second of terrifying high-pitched buzzing, which always reminded her of a Formula One Ferrari. Having been attacked earlier that day, the result a cluster of bites on her rear-end resembling a nuclear explosion, she swatted the empty space around her like a maniac. Covering all angles of her head, she didn't give the bugger any opportunity to land and possibly help himself to a pint of 'red neck' on her.

Having worked up a sweat, she looked back at the screen. During her attack she had managed to write her first words: *gnokjo-fwmm./..././/l/l*

"Fabulous, very insightful," she muttered to herself. She could see the strap line on the back cover already . . . *A real page-turner.*

Jen envisaged the scene: snared like a rabbit in RTÉ's Studio 4 headlights.

"Jen, I'm intrigued by the opening line of your book."

"Well, Pat, it's like this – something struck me and I moved, or I mean I was so moved I just started tapping away and that's how it all began."

With a deep resigned breath her yoga teacher, Mr Chamar, would have been proud of, she absent-mindedly slapped her arm down on the delicate bamboo writing table, her hand landing squarely on a packet of Marlboro Lights. Staring out the window of her hut, she saw another outpouring of monsoon rains fall from the heavens and hammer the red earth of Southern India, making small tributaries which wended their way past her hut and down to join a river the colour of melted Dairy Milk at the bottom of the hill. Almost unaware of her actions, she put the cigarette in the left-hand corner of her mouth and struck a match. Nothing happened. Returning her mind to the task in hand, she struck another match. Nothing. The Indian rains in July bring with them humidity, enveloping everything in a layer of dampness. The towels were damp, the sheets were damp, her clothes were damp, and her brain was damp. Again a rising feeling of panic in the lower part of her abdomen.

Then she noticed him, dancing in the lower left-hand corner of the screen, before settling, attracted she imagined to the bright light emanating into her otherwise darkened hut. She studied the mosquito for a few moments, unlit cigarette dangling from her top lip, glad of the distraction. She leant forward for a closer look and also to scratch her bum, giving temporary relief to the bites she'd received earlier while lying naked on the bed in the all-consuming hands of jet-lag.

On closer inspection Jen realised the immense pleasure the mosquito seemed to be receiving was not from the light but from the faint warm vibrations pulsating from inside her machine. She stifled an embarrassed laugh and almost looked over her shoulder in case anyone should see her peeking. She was reminded of those awkward moments when a sex scene would come on when watching TV with her parents. Her dad would suddenly blurt out loudly, "Which of you savages ate all the chocolate biscuits?" (or something equally insignificant). On cue, everyone turns from the TV and joins in the conversation with a sigh of relief. "Well, I only had one . . . Dave, you had at least four!" "I did not!" Round and round it goes, nobody looking at the television until the moaning and groaning has stopped. The lustful couple give their own sigh of relief and a new scene brings a new day. Everyone turns back to the TV and forgets about the chocolate biscuits.

In this huge world, Jen thought, what strange things bring us together. Staring defiantly back at the cursor, she could feel her fingers itching to move and soon they began to dance. "A horny mosquito finds himself inexplicably drawn to my laptop screen and I feel compelled to write about it . . ."

311

Reaching for another Marlborough Light, Jen stared out into the black night. The heavy rains had become a therapeutic soundtrack, which soothed her.

It seemed like weeks ago that the double doors had parted in Trivandrum airport and spat her out into the oppressive heat where instantly her linen shirt hugged her for protection. It was her first time in Kerala, India's most southern state. The "land of the coconuts" with its deserted golden beaches, beautiful backwater canals and ayurvedic retreats offering spiritual and emotional wellbeing seemed like the perfect place in which to disappear. But on her arrival, the haggling, shouting, beeping mania of the airport carpark felt like the last place on earth where she would want to relax.

It was Jen's first time leaving Ireland since the car accident almost a year ago and she felt a shiver as she climbed into the back of the big old black Ambassador taxi.

"Hello, miss. Very good day. I am Nanji. I bring you. You very nice hotel. Very nice."

They left the frantic crowd of travellers, hawkers and taxi drivers behind and sped out of the airport. Jen had been warned about the hazardous driving in India and quickly whipped out her bottle of Rescue Remedy from her bum-bag, spraying its contents generously onto her tongue.

This is so ironic, she thought. I have survived a two-week coma, healed a broken arm, collarbone and fractured pelvis and I am now in the back of a 1960s car that doesn't have a seat belt with a man who is more interested in smiling, wobbling his head and enthusing over me visiting his cousin's fabric shop than keeping his eye on the road.

In fact, driving seemed to consist of erratic sudden overtaking, limited use of an indicator and plenty of horn-blowing. But Jen had prepared herself for this and focused on trying to remain calm. Nanji was sweet but she explained she was tired and closed her eyes so she did not have to witness the oncoming traffic. This did not prevent Nanji from talking loudly on his mobile and shouting at every vehicle he passed for the entire thirty-minute journey until they swerved off the main road onto a dirt track. Jen opened her eyes, relieved to be travelling at ten miles an hour as they bumped their way up a mile of bamboo-lined track. The peace and solitude of the long lane seemed reflected in the fact that even Nanji had stopped talking.

The car eventually pulled up outside two wooden gates.

This is like *Jurassic Park*, Jen thought.

A man in a green uniform emerged from the trees and came to the car to greet them. "Yes. Hello, yes. You are welcome. Yes? I am Mr Puna. Very good. Welcome to God's own country. Beautiful Kerala!" He had a beaming smile that occupied three-quarters of his face and Jen liked him immediately.

She watched the porter and Nanji smile even more widely as they greeted each other, wobbling their heads constantly throughout the brief exchange.

Jen paid Nanji and thanked him.

"Very very nice. Very nice beach. Good sleeping. You want any taxi, call on my card. Yes?"

Puna lifted her rucksack onto his back and they both waved goodbye to the back of Nanji's wobbling head until he drove out of sight.

Jen followed Mr Puna to the open-air reception area, checked in and then followed him down a long series of paths through the trees. Her room was a bamboo hut with a thatched banana-leaf roof. It had two single beds, with mosquito nets hanging from the roof, a huge old antique wardrobe and a wooden writing desk at the window where she could see the waves crashing on the beach in the distance. There was a small bathroom that was clean and smelt of jasmine. It was basic but it was perfect.

Jen took off her damp clothes and lay down on the bed taking in her new surroundings, which would be home for the next three weeks. The ceiling fan above her was covered in rust and made little difference in its attempt to cool her down.

That was three days ago before the rains had arrived. She had settled in, met a couple of the other guests, walked the beach and most of all had caught up on some much-needed sleep.

Sitting at her desk she pulled hard on her Marlborough Light and looked out into the night. Her thoughts drifted to Michael as they nearly always did. He had been there when she woke up from her coma a year ago, sitting at her bedside, unshaven, dishevelled and tortured with worry and guilt. He had been driving that night their car smashed into a ditch outside Kenmare at sixty miles an hour. He walked away from the accident without as much as a broken finger and followed the ambulance as the medics tried to resuscitate Jen. He along with Jen's parents and friends kept a twenty-four-hour vigil by her bedside. He had cried for four hours when she woke up, tears of joy, tears of relief, tears of fear but mostly tears of guilt, which is what eventually drove them apart. For six weeks when Jen was recovering in hospital, he visited every day but even her progress couldn't lift his morose mood. She thought this might change once she came home but it didn't. He found it too difficult to watch her in pain is what he had said and he walked out of her life. The man she thought was her rock had crumbled and left her to rebuild her life on her own. She didn't cry the day he left because she hated him then. She hadn't cried since. The shock and confusion left her numb and the same question haunted her a year later: "How could he claim to be wracked with guilt, yet walk out of my life when I needed him most?"

She crawled under her mosquito net and felt safe. Again she listened to the heavy rains ricocheting off the banana-leaf roof creating at the same time the most deafening soundtrack and the sweetest lullaby. Like the three nights before she felt lonely.

There was no mobile-phone coverage and the Internet cafe was two miles away. She had explained to her friends and parents that being incommunicado was not her going crazy but rather a way of being able to focus on this book; demolishing her writer's block and kick-starting her creative juices. She had been there three days and still she felt compelled to write nothing. She could not focus and any time she attempted an opening paragraph, she felt pressure descend like a grey cloud, fogging her thoughts. She sighed loudly into the darkness. Was she really here to write or was she here, alone, to wallow in self-pity? Was it to prove to herself that she was still independent despite everything or was she running away from reality? She wasn't sure. And right now, she thought, I'm so tired that I don't care. She closed her eyes and drifted off.

The following morning, Jen went down to breakfast on the open-air terrace. She had got used to wandering around like everyone else in her green robe although her initial perception of *Jurassic Park* had been replaced with *One Flew Over the Cuckoo's Nest*. She had learnt over the last three days that while some people like herself came to the Sivananda Retreat to relax and unwind using ayurvedic massage, yoga and meditation, others were there for medical reasons: depression, obesity, stress. Some people wanted to engage in chat while others were happy in their own company. There were people there from all walks of life. A stockbroker from Wall Street, the chairwoman of Sotheby's in Geneva, a gay opera singer from Wales, an obese family from London and numerous backpackers. But Jen didn't feel the need to make polite chitchat and pretty much kept herself to herself.

Everyone had his or her own routine. Meditation at 6 a.m., breakfast, yoga, ayurvedic treatments, consultations and massages. While Jen felt herself restless for the first couple of days, she took comfort in her routine and began to feel herself unwind. In the evenings she would sit on the long stretch of beach in front of the retreat and watch the local fishermen pull in their catch. Even with the monsoon rains they skilfully worked together, sometimes in groups of more than thirty, to pull in their nets and control their boats.

She didn't notice him approaching her until he was about a metre away and plonked himself down beside her in the sand. "Hello. I am Ashraf. That is my village behind you. I see you each evening. You are staying in amongst the trees. Always alone."

Jen smiled at his perceived view of her. "My name is Jen and, yes, I am living on my own in the trees and I am actually quite enjoying it."

Ashraf smiled and stared out to sea. "I also like to be alone. It is good for the soul. I think of my family. When I am not with them I think about them. Then I go home and I want to be alone again!" he laughed.

Jen studied his face and got a strange sensation down the back of her neck. Even with his dark Indian skin, jet-black hair and black eyes, he reminded her of someone. It had happened to her many times before on her travels in Africa or Asia, where she would see someone, a face in a crowd, on a street corner in a market who was the image of somebody back home but with a different skin colour. It had always intrigued her. She stole another sideways glance. He was young, maybe twenty-one. The sarong wrapped around his waist was damp and filthy from hauling in a catch. His bare feet and chest were wet and his hair like hers lay flat against his head in the rain. He was speaking to her about the tides, and how the rains made it much more difficult to fish successfully. He looked at her and in that moment he reminded her of a young Michael.

He stood up to go.

"So. I will leave you to be alone. I am sorry if I talk too much."

Jen realised she had probably made him uncomfortable. "No. Don't be sorry. I am sorry. You surprised me, I think, because you remind me of somebody I know at home. Well, somebody I used to know."

Ashraf thought for a moment. "You don't know this person any more?"

"No," Jen answered honestly. "I don't think I ever knew him".

Every evening after that for the next week Jen would go to the same spot on the beach and Ashraf with his baskets of fish would sit with her until it was dark. They talked for hours. He told her about life in the village and how he wanted to study hotel management in Cochin but his father needed him to stay and help look after his mother and his three younger brothers. He was twenty-four but like most Indian men looked younger than his age. "My mother tells me it's the salt in the sea keeps me looking like a boy!"

Jen told him she was alone because she was trying to write a book.

"Are you not married?" Ashraf eventually enquired. "In my village girls get married very young."

"Thanks a lot!" Jen laughed. "Well, where I live, believe it or not, thirty is still considered relatively young."

His direct questioning did not bother her because his tone was genuine and she found herself telling him about living in Dublin, her family and friends. As she spoke about them all in detail, she realised how much she actually missed them. She had sent one group email to everyone telling them that she had arrived safely and hadn't been in touch since.

"Good friends are precious, more than gold," he said to her, filleting some of the day's catch with a huge sharp knife.

"You're right and I am very lucky that I have great friends." She told him about the accident, and how everyone close to her helped her through her recovery for most of the year.

"God gave you another chance to live. You should be smiling more but I think you have a lot of sadness in your eyes."

Jen felt uncomfortable, almost as if she had said too much and she searched her pockets looking for her cigarettes. She lit one, knowing that Ashraf would probably not approve. He said nothing and they sat in silence for a few moments.

"This person, that I look like, he must be very handsome." Ashraf smiled. "But he must also not understand true friendship. You died in his heart when you were sleeping in the hospital. I think true friendship never dies." He stood up and walked to the edge of the ocean to wash his bloody hands and his bloody basket of fish.

When he had finished, he strolled back and reached down his hand to her. "Come and meet my family. I will make you tea. You will meet my mother and father and then you will want to be alone again. But I make very good tea. Very good."

Jen looked up at him and smiled. "You don't have to do that."

"I know this but I want to."

318

They turned toward the small clearing of trees at the edge of the beach. Jen could see a cluster of shacks as they walked up the beach, away from the ocean.

Ashraf was keen to point out as much as possible. "That is my cousin's house and the two boys playing football, they are his children. He has six children. There are about three thousand people in the village. That is where I went to school to learn my English. We have a market here every Saturday where people from outside the village come and buy our fish."

Unlike some other places in India that Jen had been to where even the poorest women were immaculate in their bright saris, this small windswept fishing village on the edge of the ocean meant that everyone's clothes were faded and weathered. There was no doubt that this was a poor village without electricity or running water. Children in rags ran along beside them, smiling curiously at Jen, chattering among themselves and giggling uncontrollably. Two little girls fought to hold Ashraf's hand.

Their merry little band, led by Ashraf, finally stopped.

"This is my house," he beamed. "It is very small but we are all there. I built it with my father. Come inside."

Jen bent her head and entered through the small doorway behind him. It was dark and eventually her eyes adjusted to the flickering candles. The house was one large room, divided into sleeping sections at the far end by three pieces of material hanging from the roof. Ashraf had spoken to Jen about his mother and it was clear she was the love of his life. She was lying on a mat on her back. Arthritis had ravaged her body and crippled her, yet she smiled brightly at Jen and motioned for her to sit near her. She did not speak English but Ashraf translated her Malayalam. His father sat in the corner with his two young sons on his lap. He was a strong powerful man who had spent all his life fishing.

Slowly neighbours and friends drifted into the room, unannounced and uninvited but heartily welcomed. Most of the younger people were keen to practise their English with Jen. Plates of food were passed around: pulicherry, pachadi, cabbage thoran and fish mollee. The smell of spices, naan bread, candles, damp and the low chatter and laughing that filled the darkened hut was intoxicating and Jen felt at peace, as if a huge weight had been lifted off her shoulders.

The next morning Jen woke up excited and with a longing to reconnect with home and Dublin and Ireland and the people she loved. As she walked the two miles to the Internet café she realised in losing Michael she had lost her way and did not *really* see and appreciate every other special person in her life, who had been there and who she had leaned on and whom she had taken for granted. She lost herself for an hour in emails and news and stories from home. Tanya had a little baby girl, Antonia was engaged, and Ruth had handed in her notice. Her sister Rebecca had decided she was moving to Australia for a year. Her mum and even her dad had typed a short email on their new computer, all in capital letters, which had taken two hours. And in all the news, they wanted to know how she was, where she was, was she okay? She cried, realising how much the people around her meant to her and that they had helped her more than she had ever realised. They had been there, her friends, more precious than gold.

Her last week in India, the clouds lifted and the rains ceased. Jen began to write the first chapter of her novel, set in a small fishing village in India. In the evenings she would go down and sit with Ashraf's family and neighbours and listen to their songs. She learnt some Malayalam and the young girls sat in a queue so she could brush and braid their long hair. Ashraf's father always made sure his wife and Jen were served their meal first without creating any sort of fuss. She had a wonderful time. Her last days in Kerala, Ashraf taught her to fish standing in the shallows using only a spear and a net.

One evening standing in the sea, water up to his knees, he turned to her. "Just because friends leave your life for a time does not mean that they leave your heart or you theirs." He looked at her and smiled.

Jen felt a lump in the back of her throat. She wanted to hug him and tell him that he had helped her in ways that he could never know. This young stranger whom she now loved as a brother had freed her from tormenting herself with self-doubt. That just being with his family and his friends had made her remember the true value of friendship.

He speared a fish and whooped with glee, holding it up triumphantly to the sky.

Jen smiled at his dark silhouette. "Ashraf, I am so happy to have you as a friend."

She couldn't see him smile but she could hear it in his voice.

"Jen, I am the richest poor man in the world, having you as my friend."

Giraffes
in the
Garden

Kate Thompson

Kate Thompson

Kate Thompson is the author of eight bestselling novels. Her number one bestseller – *The Blue Hour* – was shortlisted for the Parker award. Kate has also been published under the pen name Pixie Pirelli, and is a company director of Mischief Publishing. Her latest novel – *Love Lies Bleeding* – is an infinitely collectable www first. You can check it out on **www.loveliesbleedingthebook.com** and you can find out more about Kate by going to **www.kate-thompson.com**

Giraffes in the Garden

Somebody is living in my house. Moving around in the corridor outside my bedroom door, going in and out of the bathroom, cleaning their teeth, flushing the lavatory. Who is it? Do they have my permission to be here? They're not creeping around in a skulduggery fashion: from the confident way they're walking you can tell that they assume they have a right to be here. I can't call out to ask them who they are. If I do, I might give the impression that I am gaga. One would have to be gaga, wouldn't one, not to know who is living in one's own house? This is *my* house. Isn't it?

The someone has come into my room, and is pulling back the curtains. I can tell by the shape that it is a woman.

"Good morning!" she says.

"Good morning." Mustn't let her think that I don't know who she is. Don't want her to –

"It's Tessa, Eleanor."

"Oh – Tessa. Yes – of course I know who you are." I know Tessa. Know her voice: her voice is light and friendly. Think I can trust her.

"It's a beautiful day," the girl called Tessa says.

"Jolly good."

"I've some Crunchy-Nut Cornflakes here for you, the way you like them, with a little cream and some strawberries."

"Thank you. I . . ." Realise that I need the loo. "I need to spend a penny," I tell her.

"All right. Let me help you up out of bed."

She takes my hands and pulls. I stand up.

"I'll go and put the kettle on, shall I, for tea?" she says.

"Yes." *Tea for two, and two for tea* . . . I clutch the chest of drawers. "Which way is the bathroom?"

"Out the door, to the left. I'll show you." I follow her shadowy shape, and she opens a door. "Now. I'll shut the door and leave you to it."

She's off.

I pull up my nightdress, sit down and look at my legs. Don't like to look at my legs. They are hideous – like old sticks. Used to be very proud of them. They were my best feature once – apart from my face, of course, which was quite extraordinarily pretty. Could have been a film star when I was a girl – everybody said so. Looked a lot like Kay Francis. She was the living end: not a terribly good actress, but wonderfully stylish. I wonder what happened to her? They're all dead now, probably, all those old film stars. Norma Shearer, Constance Bennett, Claudette Colbert, Katharine Hepburn. All so glamorous, all so beautiful, all so young, once-upon-a-time. Like me. I suppose when one is young and beautiful and is surrounded by beaux it seems impossible that one should ever get old. Wonder how old I am? There's great longevity in my family. Mother lived well into her eighties.

Spent my penny. Where now? Bedroom. It's out there, isn't it? To the right. I'm hobbling. That's the very word to describe what

I'm doing. Hobbling. I, who was once lady captain of the golf club, am now officially hobbling! What a joke. Oh – better hold on here, to the chest of drawers. In case I fall. That happened once. Fell down on the bedroom floor. That's when the baby's face came out of the wall. While I was lying there on the floor, I heard the baby calling to me. I knew it was living in another place, inside the wall. Told some people about it, in case it was a matter for the authorities, but I don't think they believed me. Neither do they believe that I saw a couple of giraffes in the garden; but I did, with my own two eyes. I'm not so blind that I don't recognise a giraffe when I see one.

Nearly there now. Sit down on the side of the bed and lie back, drawing up my poor old stick legs with an effort. Can hear someone down the corridor: in the kitchen, possibly. Is that where the kitchen is? They're banging around, putting dishes away, by the sound of it. And there's a radio playing. Now someone's saying something. What? What are they saying? It sounds like –

"I've brought you some tea."

"Who is it?"

"It's Tessa, Eleanor."

"Tessa? Oh." *Tessa?* Tessa is – who is she? "Did you marry someone I know?"

"Yes, Eleanor. I married James."

"You married James? My son, James?"

"Yes."

"You don't mean to tell me that you two are married?"

"We are."

"Why did nobody ever tell me? That's great news! I'm so happy to hear that!" I remember now that I like this girl with the kind voice, even though sometimes she speaks a little too quietly.

Never been able to abide mumblers. I myself am very well-spoken – I even studied elocution once. "Well, welcome to our family, Tessa!"

"Thank you. Now, there's your tea, on the table by your bed. And a pancake. But have your cornflakes first."

She moves around to the other side of the bed.

"I need another pillow," I say.

"Yes. Here's one. Shall I help hoosh you up?"

"I can hoosh myself up."

But she does it anyway, and plops another pillow behind my back. "Would you like me to put on the radio?"

"No."

She's gone.

She always asks me if I want the radio. Can't abide the blasted thing. There's never anything on apart from bad news, and people shouting at you, hectoring you to buy things you don't want.

I dip a spoon into the cornflakes. I like cornflakes. And that other thing she brought me – I like that too. What is it? A pancake. I eat very simply now. Small appetite. Used to adore seafood. Lobsters and oysters, particularly. My beaux used to tease me about the way I could put back a dozen oysters. They have aphrodisiac qualities, apparently. Wasted on me, now!

Finish my breakfast, lie back against the pillows. I like my bed. It is a sizable single bed. Always slept in single beds, even when I was married. Richard snored so loudly we had to have separate bedrooms. My bed is just the right size, and is piled with lots of soft, furry toy animals. There's a lamb, and a dog, and a cat, and a tiger and a lion. Because I'm a Leo. The king of the beasts. Regal by name and regal by nature – that's me.

There's a kind of a fence thing on one side: suppose it's in case I fall out. If that happened, I wonder would the baby in the wall come out again. Maybe it's worried about me, the baby – the way I worry about my mother. She's getting on, now. Rather think I may have to put her in a Home.

The other thing I like about my bed is that it acts as a time machine. Transports me back to the days when I was young and beautiful, and could dance and play tennis and golf. I was the lady captain of the golf club, you know. And I was an actress, too. Was cast as Jane opposite Mícheál Mac Liammóir, in a Gate Theatre production of *Jane Eyre*.

That photograph they took for publicity purposes! It was in all the papers. Mícheál, with his handsome, patrician profile, clutching me to his chest, my lovely eyes gazing into the middle distance. Mícheál always made sure that he presented his left profile to the camera. So good-looking was he that people always used to ask me if I had a thing for him! I'd laugh and say: "Not at all!" And then they'd tell me that it was very odd that I *didn't* have a thing for him, and I'd tell them that *he* was the "odd" one out! I was very fond of Mícheál, but fonder still of Hilton Edwards, his "friend". Such fun, those days! But hard, hard work – such long hours, and for so little money! When we had to rehearse late, I'd stay in the spare room in the big house in Ranelagh. Belonged to my fiancé's parents, that house.

My fiancé was very chuffed that I was an actress. Quite a famous one at that, in Dublin. It was he who had the photograph of me and Mícheál framed. Wonder where it is now, that photograph – and all the press cuttings? Used to feature a lot in the Society pages, I did: *Miss Eleanor Beaufoy was seen taking tea in the foyer of the Shelbourne Hotel, wearing a meticulously tailored dove grey jersey costume . . .* That sort of thing.

The men from Pinewood saw my performance in *Jane Eyre*. They wanted to put me in the motion pictures. Suggested that I sign a contract, agreeing to make two motion pictures for them in England. Suppose I could have been another Maureen O'Hara or Vivien Leigh or June Duprez. But my parents didn't want me to leave – war was looming. I *might* have made more of a fuss and insisted on going, if it had been Denham Studios and Mr Alexander Korda who had come calling instead of the men from Pinewood. But then, Alexander Korda was responsible for master-minding June Duprez's career, and look what happened to *her*. Her career went on the skids after she went to Hollywood. I read somewhere that it was because she got too big for her boots. *These boots are made for walking . . .* Love that song!

I used to love reading the fan magazines. I had quite a collection of *Film Pictorial* annuals, all full of interviews with the stars, and pictures of them in their homes. Kay Francis was my favourite, because everyone said I looked like her. She was the most glamorous of them all – she was once voted the best-dressed star in America. And she was the highest-paid female star on the Warner Brothers lot. I wonder – had I signed that contract – would I have become a big star, too? Or would I have wound up subsisting on a diet of dog biscuits, the way June Duprez did? I read somewhere that she dipped them in marmalade.

Funny the way one's life goes. Ups and downs, downs and ups. I don't really do much any more, or go anywhere – unless it's to my son's house in England, in Leicestershire. I used to be able to get into my car and drive off to the West of Ireland any time the fancy took me. I had a place there, I seem to remember, overlooking Clew Bay. Yes, that's right – I did! I remember how I came across it – quite by accident one day, when I was on a jaunt around County Mayo with my sister, Sarah. We rounded a bend on a narrow road and climbed a lane, and suddenly found ourselves looking at the most breathtaking view either of us had ever seen. The crest of a hill, and below us Clew Bay with its three hundred and sixty-five islands – one for every day of the year. On the horizon, a perfect purple pyramid of a mountain: Croagh Patrick. A lark singing a mile high in the sky, and sun-diamonds ablaze on the water, and I fell in love at first sight.

Sarah and I got out of the car and sat on a wall to admire the vista, and a man came by and said good day and what did we think of the view? Because if I liked, he could let me buy an acre or two from him. We shook hands there and then – I always was impulsive! He was an artist, the man – I don't recall his name – and I soon learned that, like Mícheál, he was a nancy-boy, and great fun. I used to buy his paintings. They weren't very good paintings, but I bought them as a favour to him.

I've always surrounded myself with artistic people. When I was a very young woman, Sir William Russell Flint painted a portrait of me: *Gitana in the Vineyard* it was called. Would have liked my parents to buy it, but they declined. The subject matter was considered rather risqué in those days: the painting showed me barelegged, pretending to tread grapes. What a fuss over nothing! It was just a bit of fun. I studied under Mainie Jellett then. I understand her paintings are worth a lot of money now. And so are Sir Russell's. I owned one of Miss Jellet's later abstracts. It used to hang above the fireplace in my sitting room. It's gone now: I'm not sure where. I think I may have lent it to the National Gallery.

No wonder – growing up surrounded by all those artistic people – that I should produce artistic children. All grown now. A writer, a photographer, and an architect. I have photographs of them in frames all over my house. And photographs of my grandchildren, and – I'm told – my great-grandchildren. And photographs of that fantastic view from my place in the west. How I'd love to hop into my car, and drive there now! I'm a very good driver, you know. The only thing is, I'm not sure that the car that's parked outside my house belongs to me. I wonder who could possibly own it, if it isn't mine?

People come sometimes, take me out for jaunts in their cars. They're probably family, or friends. They dress me up and put a little powder on my face – but I do my own lipstick! Been able to do my own lipstick without the aid of a mirror for as long as I can remember. A perfect Cupid's bow. Anyway, these people bundle me in a car and take me to the Garden Centre in Wicklow, or to Powerscourt. We have lunch, and maybe a spin around the gardens. At Powerscourt they put me in what they call a "chariot". I ask you! They're humouring me. I know perfectly well that the "chariot" is a wheelchair. I can't walk far, you see. But I do like to feel the sun on my face, and see the colours of the gardens. Simple pleasures.

What other simple pleasures do I enjoy? The swing seat on my terrace: the motion is so soothing. And David Attenborough on the television. I can't see the pictures – I really should get glasses – but I simply adore his voice. I could listen to David Attenborough forever. And I love to listen to stories on my cassette player. Agatha Christie, and PD James, and Sir Arthur Conan Doyle. They're the best. Music? I've never really had much interest in music. But I do like that man – what's his name? Bob Marley. He makes me happy. He's coloured, you know.

My family has never had a problem with racism. I know they say that Ireland is a racist country, but some of my best friends were coloured. Kingsley and Miriam in New York, and dear, dear Winston in Jamaica, and – oh – lots of others whose names I don't remember now. I'll never forget the time my best friend's mother phoned me after I'd sent out invitations to a party, instructing me not to allow her daughter to dance with Winston.

Honestly! I've never understood what all that nonsense is about. After all, we're all the same under our skin. Just as I've never understood all the fuss about pansies. I think they call them "gay" now. Some of the most amusing people I ever knew were so-called "gays".

In the corridor outside my door, someone is moving around. I open my eyes. She's inside the room, now, taking something out of my wardrobe.

"Who is it?"

"It's Tessa, Eleanor."

"Oh, yes."

"It's a beautiful day out there."

"Good." *The sun has got his hat on, hip hip hip hooray!* "Have the giraffes come back?"

"Giraffes?"

"Yes. Remember? I saw two of them in the garden the other day. They belong to one of my neighbours."

"Oh – you mean the peacocks, Eleanor."

"Oh, yes. I suppose I do."

"No, they haven't come back. Now. I thought you might like a wash? And then you can go into the sitting-room and I'll bring lunch in to you."

"Oh."

The washing is a bane. A *bane*! It was a long time before I could submit with good grace. It seemed like the ultimate indignity to stand stark naked in front of another person while they sponge bits of you that haven't been exposed to the eyes of any human being for more years than I care to remember! Tch. I know, I *know* – it has to be done. As a treat, this person always sprinkles a little Chanel No 5 talcum powder on me after she's dried under my arms. Dabs my wrists with a little of the same perfume, once I'm dressed.

Except I don't get dressed now – unless I'm going out somewhere. Getting dressed is too exhausting. So every day I put on a fresh nightgown, with a long, ribbed cardigan over it. The cardigan is more elegant by far than a dressing-gown. Wouldn't be caught dead wearing a dressing-gown during the day! Remember the film about the woman who'd let herself go so much that she ended up slopping around in her dressing-gown morning, noon and night? No wonder her husband lost interest. To my mind, it is a wife's duty to keep herself looking good for her husband. I imagine I am a positive fright to behold nowadays, but at least my cardigan and velvet slippers are fairly stylish. *And* I smell of Chanel No 5!

Submit to the washing. The least said about it the better.

"Now, Eleanor," says the girl, all business-like, "shall we go into the sitting-room?"

"Yes. Where is it?"

"Follow me."

I follow her shape along an L-shaped corridor, turn the corner, and – there are no stairs! *No stairs!*

"Where are the stairs?" I ask.

"There are no stairs in this house, Eleanor."

"Oh, yes. I forgot. There were stairs in my old house, weren't there?"

"Yes."

Light is flooding through a door at the end of the corridor. I move towards it. Know where I'm going now. Left through the door, then across the room to where my armchair is, by the fireplace. Lower myself into it with an effort. I know that the walk was not a long one, but I tire so easily now. What age am I?

A bunch of flowers – tulips, I think – on the side table by my armchair. "Where did those come from?" I ask.

"I got them for you yesterday, in Tesco's."

"Oh – thank you! They're lovely."

"Yes, aren't they? I chose yellow and red because they were the brightest."

"That's very kind of you."

"You're welcome. I'll bring lunch in, in a minute. Are you comfortable?"

"Yes. Perfectly, thanks."

She's off again. I hear noises though the hatch that leads to the kitchen. It's comforting, sometimes, to hear these noises. It means that there is someone in the house with me. At night I often wake, and struggle out of bed to check that there is someone sleeping in one of the spare rooms. I do not know why I feel the need to do this. It's silly. After all, I'm perfectly able to look after myself.

More lunch-making sounds from behind the hatch. Lunch most days is soup, or chicken salad with a glass of milk. Ice cream to follow. Then television, or one of my cassettes until it's time for supper. Sometimes we watch the news before supper, but I don't like to, much. Agitates me, all that ugliness. Murders, rape, abused children, wars, pollution, corruption. Seems to me that the world is a far, far uglier place than when I was young. Wonder what age I am, now? Getting on, I know. But I get by, somehow.

Breakfast, wash, lunch, television, supper. That's how I get by. After supper we sometimes do the Simplex crossword in the *Irish Times*. I used to do it every day. Was very good at it. Nearly always got it out. But it frustrates me these days. Sometimes I can't hear the girl when she runs clues by me, and I tell her to stop mumbling, even though I know it's probably not her fault. It's probably *my* fault because I am old and could well be half-deaf, for all I know. So I don't mind if we don't do the crossword any more. It's not good for me to get upset before bedtime. Means I may not sleep well. And I do love my sleep, and my bed. Bedtime is precious. I may have told you that already?

Sometimes the girl reads me a story after I've got into bed. I love that – the stories are beautifully written – by Oscar Wilde, I think. But sometimes they can be very, very sad. The one about the giant who wouldn't let the children play in his garden is especially sad . . .

Oh! How did I get here? Did I nod off? Where am I? In my sitting-room? There's a vase of what I think are tulips on the table beside my chair. *Tulips, tulips – tulips from Amsterdam . . .*

Someone has come into the room.

"Where did those come from?" I ask.

"I got them for you yesterday, in Tesco's."

"Thank you! They're lovely."

"Yes. I chose yellow and red because they were the brightest."

"That's very kind of you."

"You're welcome. Lunch is ready."

The girl is holding out her hands to me. I take them and she pulls me to my feet. I follow her across to the table. She has to help me to sit down – these old dining chairs really are fearfully heavy.

We're both sitting now.

She raises her glass. "Cheers," she says.

"Cheers, back." I raise my glass of milk, and smile.

She's smiling, too, I think.

"I'll eat this, now," I say, looking at my plate. "What is it?"

"There's chicken, cheese, tomatoes, brown bread and a little potato salad."

"Oh, good. I love potato salad."

"I know. I'll prong some for you, shall I? It's a bit difficult to see, because it's the same colour as the plate."

She takes my fork, aims it at the plate, then hands it back to me.

I chew on the potato. *One potato, two potato, three potato, four . . .* It's funny, I muse. Don't know how one gets by, really: one just does. Sam used to say it much better than I ever could. Samuel Beckett, that is. He used to play cricket with my brother, in Trinity. The characters he wrote about all got by, didn't they? Molloy, Malone, those two tramps, that old girl in the rubbish heap. What was the name of that play? *Happy Days* – something like that.

Me, I get by, too. But I wouldn't go so far as to call these days *happy*. That would be as ridiculous as making believe that a wheelchair is a chariot. Or believing that I'm still as beautiful as I was in the portrait Sir Russell made of me. How – exactly – *do* I get by? I suppose you could say that I get by with a little help from my friends. Yes. That's it. I get by with a little help from my friends. Someone sang a song about that, once.

I get by with a little help from my friends . . . It sounds rather tuneless, when I sing. I never was able to hold much of a tune.

The girl sitting opposite me takes my fork, aims it at something on my plate, then hands it back to me.

"Thank you," I say. "What is it?"

337

How to
Marry a Sailor

Sarah Webb

Sarah Webb

Sarah Webb lives in Dun Laoghaire, Co Dublin, with her partner Ben, an aspiring Olympic sailor, son Sam, an aspiring teenager, mad toddler Amy-Rose, and sweet baby Jago. She writes when none of the above are a) hanging out of her arms b) crawling up her legs or c) playing loud, jittery music. Her books use biographical elements, which is why her friends and family are so nice to her. The latest, *When the Boys are Away*, is based on her vast experience as a sports widow. For more information check out her website:

www.sarahwebb.info

How to
Marry a Sailor

May 2007

Once a book is finally finished it's hard to let go of the characters that have lived in my head and kept me company for so long. Often they linger, asserting their independence, whispering in my ear, "I'm still here, you know. I haven't gone away". In *When the Boys are Away*, my favourite character is the rather naughty but fun Hattie. And she refuses to go away. She'll be whispering in my ear for the rest of my life, I reckon. So this one's for you, Hattie.

I'm not a natural short story writer; I always have far too much to say. So think of this as a self-contained chapter.

Hattie's Story

"A baby costume?" I stare at the balding fifty-year-old Kiwi. His head reminds me of a greasy bowling ball. I wonder if he's the kind of man my boss has warned me about. If he is, he's chosen the wrong girl to mess with.

"Is it for yourself?" I ask him, thrusting my hands onto my hips.

He nods mutely, his watery eyes glistening.

I square my shoulders and stand on my tippy-toes behind the desk. That way I'm taller than he is. "Dry all-night nappy or flexi-fit nappy?" I ask him in a sing-song voice.

He blinks several times, his nose twitching like a rabbit's. "What's the difference?"

I sigh, as if I spend my life answering the question, which I don't – actually it's my first time. "Flexi are less absorbent but more flexible. If you want to dance in your nappy I'd suggest flexi-fit."

His eyes narrow. "Dance?"

"At a party. I presume you're going to a fancy dress party."

He shakes his head. "Not exactly." He moistens his lips with a pointy pink tongue.

I shudder. Christ. I really don't want to know. "The baby costumes are non-returnable," I say quickly. "Three hundred euros."

"Euros?"

Jeepers, I keep forgetting I'm in New Zealand now. "Dollars, I mean dollars."

"Three hundred?" He narrowed his already piggy little eyes. "That's a bit steep."

"It includes bootees, a bonnet, a giant soother, a top-of-the-range bottle and, of course, the adult-sized nappies. Three of them. Take it or leave it. It makes no difference to me."

He sniffs. "S'all right. I'll take it I suppose."

"Good. I'll throw in an extra flexi-fit for free."

After the man leaves, I slip three crisp hundred-dollar bills into the till. Mordie, the owner, has promised me twenty per cent commission on sales of any of the "adult" costumes. He'd want to

– some of them are well dodgy. There's the Crotchless Pirate Costume, Hef's Favourite Little Bo-Peep Costume (although I doubt if Hugh Heffner would honestly be all that impressed with that cheap little nylon number), the Mummy I Don't Want to Grow Up Costume, which Mordie says is one of the bestsellers, which tells more than I really want to know about New Zealand men. It's a baby riding on an old woman's back. The top of the woman's body is inflatable as well as the baby's legs which dangle down her back, and the man wearing the costume (and oh, yes, it's always a man apparently) uses his own head as the baby's head and upper body. It's kind of hard to explain. You'd have to see it to believe it. Your man who bought the baby costume probably has it in his dressing-up box. What else? Ah yes, the usual sexy nurses, French maids, and sexy nuns. How original, yawn. Miss Minky is a bit more original, but please don't ask. And the Sexy Sailor Girl goes down very well here in Auckland, home of the New Zealand America's Cup Team. It's one of the few cute ones too. In fact – I'll stop right there.

As I work out my commission – which if my maths is right (and I'm surprisingly good at maths, not that my bank manager would agree) works out at about 60 dollars. Money for old rope. Ha! Maybe working at Costumes R Us isn't going to be so bad after all. Roll on the weirdoes.

"Shouldn't you be at work?" Megs asks. She's upside down so her voice is a bit wobbly. She's hanging over the metal banisters of her hotel duplex, her feet tucked under the railing at the bottom, her hair falling around her face like a wig on a washing line.

I twist my head to look at her. "What are you doing? You look like a bat."

"Filling my head with blood. It's good for your wrinkles."

"Says who?"

"Says the magazine I was reading."

"For feck's sake, Meg, get down before you do yourself an injury."

She swings her body up, clutches at the railings and then gives a squeal. "My foot's stuck. Help!"

"You big eejit!" I bound up the stairs, kick at Meg's runner until it comes unstuck and then pull her over the balustrade.

"Thanks." Meg slips her foot back into her runner. Her face is bright red. She bends down to rub her ankle and then follows me down the stairs. "Fancy some lunch? I wasn't going to bother; I've been snacking all morning. But now that you're here . . ."

"If you don't stop eating you'll turn into a blimp." I flop down on the small sofa and stretch my legs out in front of me.

"I know, I know, but I'm so bloody bored."

"I keep telling you, get a job."

"That's easy for you to say, but I can only work in the mornings because of the kids. And I don't have a work permit."

"And I *do*?" I grin at her. I *so* don't have a work permit. And to be honest I can't be bothered to get one. Far too much red tape for only six months. You see, Meg's hunky sailor boyfriend is over here doing the America's Cup. He's a Brit, so he's sailing for the British team. The Irish are far too poor to have a team, according to his mate, Slipper. Cheeky git! But there are a load of Irish lads over here, sailing on various teams, from the Italian stallion team to the Aussie one. Hey, did I mention it's hunk heaven? I bet you're jealous! I'm working my way around the continents, it's only fair. Meg says I'm spreading myself a bit too thinly sometimes and that kissing an American and an Australian on the same night isn't very politically correct, sailing-wise. I think she's afraid one of them might divulge a big America's Cup secret, like that winged keel thingy that there was a big hoo-ha about a few years ago. But really, even if they did shout out something secret in the throes of passion (highly unlikely), I wouldn't tell anyone. Unless they paid me large wedges of cash. Ah, no, I'm only joking.

As you may have found out if you read Meg's story in *When the Boys are Away* (which isn't a bad old story but it's a bit light on the old sex scenes for my taste), I recently broke up with He Who Shall Not Be Named. OK, OK, Ryan. He was engaged to a nurse in Dublin all along, bastard! So I'm just trying to cheer myself up a bit. I'm sure you understand. With all the talent around, it would be rude not to. I have to fly the Irish flag somehow.

Meg smiles at me. "You're different." (We're back talking about her job-hunt here, by the way.)

"Why?"

"I'd never just walk into a shop and ask for a job like you did."

"Why?"

"Will you stop with the whys? You're as bad as Lily. I just wouldn't, OK?"

Lily is her four-year-old. Cute but a bit hormonal. Like a mini-teenager. And "why" is her favourite word at the moment.

"OK, OK, keep your knickers on!" I stare out the window. The swimming pool below the balcony is hopping, and thick with screeches and shouts of young children. I try not to wince. Children are so bloody noisy. "Why don't you join the other sailing mums?"

I should explain. Some of the sailors' wives and girlfriends are living in Auckland with them, all in the same hotel, like one big happy family. More the Adams Family than the Waltons I'm afraid. It's quite a menagerie. Most of them are dead on, but one or two are a bit scary. Bossy types with teeth the size of piano keys. The type of women who were Head Girl at school and have never quite got over it. The type of women who run the PTA, plus all the school reunions and drive sensible estate cars that smell of wet gun dogs. You get the picture.

Meg shrugs. "I still don't feel all that comfortable with them. They all know each other. Maybe I'll go down later. I have to fix Dan's school trousers first. He keeps ripping the crotch playing soccer." Dan's thirteen. Nice lad, but a bit smelly and grunty.

"I didn't know you could sew," I say, genuinely impressed.

"Anyone can sew."

"I can't. My stitches look like they belong on Frankenstein's face. Not pretty." I stop for a moment. "Hang on, Mordie was complaining about the state of some of the costumes. Maybe he'd pay you to fix them. What do you think?"

Meg shrugs. "I'm not sure, Hattie. I'm not really qualified –"

"Can you use a sewing machine?"

"Yes."

"Well, there you go then. How hard can it be?"

Meg isn't convinced but I manage to persuade her. I'm good that way.

The following day she drops Lily into playschool and comes into Costumes R Us with me. I rang Mordie last night and he thought it was a "fucking excellent" idea.

"Do we 'ave to pay 'er?" he asked.

"'Course we do. But she'll be useless at selling the adult costumes, so it'll be just the crappy hourly rate."

He'd laughed heartily at this. "Bugger me, I do like ya, Hartie. You're a tonic."

"Hattie."

"Ya, ya, Hartie."

Mordie set Meg to work on a Commando Girl costume that had a ripped side seam and she flies through it with gusto.

"Anything else?" she asks when she's finished. She seems to be really getting into the swing of things.

"Can you hold the fort for a sec?" I ask. "I'm dying for a ciggy. I'm just going to pop out the back for a minute. And if any weirdoes come in, charge them triple for the costumes. Get it?"

"Is that ethical?"

"'Course not. But we get commission on any of the dodgy costumes."

"Really? Cool." She holds up the Commando Costume. "Like this one? The shorts are tiny. The seam at the crotch had split by the way, so I stitched that up too."

I smile at her and shake my head. My big sis really is quite sweet. Naive but sweet. "You'd better unstitch it. Mordie will kill you; it's a Crotchless Commando costume."

"Oh," she says, deflated. "I'm sorry."

"No harm done." I grab my ciggies from under the counter. "Back in a mo."

Ten minutes later (I couldn't just stop at one ciggy!) I go back in. Meg is grinning from ear to ear.

"Look!" she says, opening her hand. It's full of notes. "Five hundred dollars. We're rich."

I'm genuinely surprised. "Good on you, Sis. What did you sell?"

"The Sexy Firefighter costume. It's really authentic."

I look at her, baffled.

"It was hanging over there." She points at the rail. "On the end."

"Meg! You didn't?" I'm too shocked to laugh.

"What?"

"You just sold Mordie's dry cleaning. He's a volunteer firefighter in his spare time."

"Oops. Is he going to kill me?"

Just then the bell rings and a tall, dark-haired man who reminds me of John Cusack but with bigger muscles walks in. He hands Meg the plastic-covered firefighter's outfit. "I'm sorry, but I just rang my mate, and he nicked my idea. He's only going as a bloody firefighter too."

Meg grabs the "costume" back. "That's absolutely no problem at all," she gushes.

"What did you have in mind instead?" I ask him, stepping in quickly. He really is rather delicious, rough and ready, and after all, Meg's practically married.

"Something kinda sexy," he suggests. "To impress the ladies." He gives me a wink.

He's a bit obvious, but those pecs!

"Back in a mo," I mouth at Meg. "You owe me, big time."

"I have just the thing," I say smoothly, my hand resting on his naked and delightfully muscular shoulder. I sniff in his sweaty scent and almost pass out. It's gloriously fresh and salty. "Cowboys, cops, sailors, and my own personal favourite, the gladiator. Step this way."

"You're made for this," Meg calls after me. "I always said she'd end up in a sex shop," I hear her add under her breath.

"It's not a sex shop!" I shout back at her.

"John Cusack" looks at me with renewed interest.

I shake my head at him. "It's not a sex shop."

Extracts from

Total High, My Everest Challenge

Grania Willis

Grania Willis

Grania Willis became the first Irishwoman to climb Mount Everest's north-east ridge in June 2005. A former international three-day event rider, she has been *The Irish Times* equestrian correspondent since 1980. Two serious riding accidents brought her competition career to a premature end and mountains have now replaced horses in her life.

Extracts from
Total High, My Everest Challenge

The Willis Christmas dinner 2004 was at my elder sister Sarah's house in London. All the immediate family were there and, as everyone squeezed into their seats round the long dining-table, the usual Christmas Day reminiscences started. Always favourite was one about how, several years earlier, I had bought a fart cushion for my only nephew Joe and the mayhem and mirth it had caused when he'd put it under Grandpa's bottom just as he lowered himself onto his seat.

Joe was now nineteen. He'd just finished his first term studying geography at Leeds University and he'd grown up. But the playful, life-loving character was still there, inside a now tall and lanky frame. Joe's bright blue eyes would sparkle with merriment at the slightest provocation, his mop of flaming red hair joining the rest of his body in shaking with laughter. Joe and I had very similar senses of humour. The fart cushion was just one of the ridiculous presents in a long line of ridiculous presents. He was always easy to buy for.

I had got him a book this time: *1000 Places To See Before You*

Die. When we all met again at my aunt Jackie's the next day for further feasting I didn't know that that was the last time I'd see him. I went home to Dublin. He went back to college.

Nine weeks later, just as I was leaving the gym after an early Saturday morning workout, I got a phone call from my twin sister Megan. She was crying so hard I could barely understand her.

"It's Joe," she said, sobbing.

"What? What's happened?" I pleaded, knowing it was something catastrophic.

"He's had a heart attack. He's dead."

I felt as though I'd been punched in the solar plexus. I couldn't breathe. I couldn't comprehend what I'd just been told. Joe wasn't even twenty. How could he possibly have had a heart attack? How could he possibly be dead?

"Get over quickly," my sister was saying. "We need you here."

In response to a desperate phone call from me, my friend and neighbour, Carmel McShea, drove into town, scooped me up and took me back to her house. Jenny, the friend who'd bought me the Bear Grylls book that had re-ignited the Everest plan less than two years earlier, came as soon as Carmel told her the news. And then Yasmin Lowe, a wonderfully warm friend of Carmel's whom I'd met only a couple of times, rushed over too. I sat on the sofa and wept until I thought there were no tears left. The girls sat and wept with me.

My cousin Chris, in Dublin for the Ireland-England rugby match at Lansdowne Road, was in a pub when he got the news. He abandoned his pint and the rugby match and came straight to Carmel's house. And there were more tears.

I flew to London that night. Meg and my younger sister Kate met me at the airport and we drove to my parents' house. The three of us could barely speak, but they managed, between bouts of sobbing, to tell me that Joe had been out running that morning with one of his housemates, Stu. They'd sprinted the last couple of hundred metres back to the carpark in front of their apartment block.

"I feel really tired," Joe said as they pulled up.

And then crumpled and fell, face first onto the pavement. He was dead before he hit the ground. Mouth-to-mouth and heart massage from his frantic flatmates could do nothing. The ambulance was there inside two minutes. But it was too late.

My sister Sarah got the terrible phone call from Leeds Infirmary shortly afterwards to say that her son had been brought in and was in a bad way. The nurse didn't tell her immediately. She said she'd phone back. She gently told Sarah later that day that she couldn't bring herself to break the news all in one go. She'd rung back twenty minutes after the first call to tell Sarah that her son, her only son, was dead.

Sarah's husband, Fred, was away at a conference in Boston. Sarah rang him in the middle of the night to tell him the worst possible news. Their oldest daughter, Harriet, had just embarked on a post-university round-the-world tour. It was two days before they managed to get in touch with her in Vietnam, shattering her young life with those dreadful words.

Sarah and her youngest daughter, Eleanor, went straight up to Leeds on the first train they could catch. My mother went with them. They were too devastated to drive. Fred was with them by shortly after midnight in a hotel booked for them by the university. They went back to the hospital so that Fred could kiss Joe goodbye, stroking his poor battered face where it had hit the pavement, chipping a front tooth.

Sixteen-year-old Eleanor refused to be parted from her parents for a moment. Nobody slept for those first dreadful forty-eight hours while they were waiting to hear from Harriet. The second night, Sarah sat up in bed and saw Eleanor, cross-legged on the floor and rocking gently as she brushed her long hair, the same glorious red as Joe's. She was eating digestive biscuits, her first meal since her brother's death.

My poor father was distraught. He sobbed on my shoulder, inconsolable in his grief. "My lovely grandson, my lovely grandson," he kept repeating. He was heartbroken. Joe had been the light of his life. His only grandson in a family that had produced no boys since his own birth seventy-six years earlier. A boy with four sisters, a man with four daughters. And now his only grandson, a grandson who shared his love of cricket and rugby, had been so cruelly snatched away from him.

The initial post-mortem was inconclusive. The coroner wouldn't release Joe's body and the family had to wait almost a fortnight before the funeral arrangements could be made. Totally non-religious, Sarah and Fred wanted a humanist service. Joe, in a hideously prescient conversation about burial with his parents several months before, had said he wanted a green woodland funeral. Joe was an eco-warrior to beat all eco-warriors and a staunch supporter of the charity Make Poverty History.

I flew back to Dublin briefly to do a lecture at the Outdoor Adventure Show in the RDS, but returned to London the following week to help organise Joe's memorial. Sarah and Fred had asked me to be – for want of a better expression – master of ceremonies. I was deeply touched but also dreading it.

We spent hours in front of the PC putting together the programme, crying and laughing in equal measures. We knew the memorial was going to be tough on everyone, but especially for Sarah and Harriet, who were both going to be speaking. My father had said to Sarah that if she felt herself overcome with emotion, she should take a deep breath and exhale slowly before continuing. Both our opera-singing aunt and uncle were singing at the memorial and it was Nuala who gave us the real clue to preventing emotional outbursts. A singing teacher in New York had told Nuala during a lesson that she wasn't breathing properly.

"I want you to breathe more deeply," the teacher had said to her, "right down to your pubic bone. Think hairline to hairline."

It cracked us up and we used it on more than one occasion, both during the service and in the build-up to it. But, incredibly, I don't think Sarah needed it when she delivered her wonderfully touching and brilliantly funny eulogy of her only son to a packed assembly hall in Joe's old school. Her resilience and dignity were truly amazing and, actor's daughter to the last, even her timing was perfect. It was an astounding performance.

Leeds University had organised a coach for the huge number of students who wanted to say their final farewells to Joe. It was heartbreaking to see small clusters of them weeping quietly, their arms around each other as they looked at the pictures of Joe as a child and a young adult.

We gave Joe a more private send-off two days later. Honouring his request, he was given a truly green burial in a quiet corner of a vast multi-denominational cemetery in Surrey. The hearse had arrived on time, but then went to the opposite end of the cemetery. It turned out there were two green burial sites and the funeral directors had chosen the wrong one. When he realised his mistake, the driver reversed the vehicle onto the grass to turn round and the hearse got stuck in the rain-sodden ground.

The first we knew about it was when we saw the owner of the cemetery, an eccentric Turkish Cypriot, rushing off with his Jeep and two burly assistants. The hearse appeared shortly afterwards, decorated with thick spatters of mud above the wheel arches. A joker to the last, Joe was – quite literally – late for his own funeral.

After arriving in Tibet, we decided to save the Potala for our second day in Lhasa, opting instead to spend the morning wandering around the fifteenth century Drepung monastery up in the hills overlooking the city. After lunch a group of us joined the Barkhor kora, the pilgrimage circuit round the Jokhang, the most sacred and one of the oldest monasteries in Tibet.

As we waited for a bus to go to the Potala the next morning, I was talking to one of the Kiwis, Mary Hobbs. A fellow journalist also masquerading as a "housewife" on the permit, Mary was on the expedition as support for her husband Charlie, a mountain guide who runs a restaurant at the foot of Mount Cook in the New Zealand Alps. The pair are Scientologists and rumours circulated amongst the group that the Hobbs had come to Everest to do a recce for fellow Scientologist Tom Cruise.

Without intending to confide in anyone, I found myself telling Mary about Joe's death and could feel my heart being wrung out as I spoke. Mary could see the hurt in my face. "He's with you, Grania," she said quietly, her hand on my arm. The sceptic in me wanted to dismiss it as whimsy but, as she uttered the words, a slender pale brown bird alighted on a windowsill opposite.

"Do you think that's Joe?" I asked Mary and, as I pointed to the bird, it lifted its crest in a flash of brilliant ginger feathers, the colour of Joe's hair. From then on, Joe was with me always, in the wind scudding over rippled sand at a river's edge, in the swirl of dust from the vehicle ahead, in a wisp of cloud in an otherwise cloudless sky high up on the mountain. He was a constant and reassuring presence. And I was comforted.

―◁○▷―

I dragged my exhausted body up the final rocky outcrop to join my Sherpa, Karsang, who had his back to me and was leaning against a massive boulder. He turned as he heard me approach and watched as I heaved myself up the last step. "Summit," he said, pointing to the right. I turned and there, not much more than 200 metres away, was the highest point on earth, a snow dome draped with Tibetan prayer flags, which dripped down its side like a multi-coloured version of the drizzle icing my grandmother used to put on her lemon cakes. It was magical. I was totally stunned by the sheer beauty of the mountain and the unexpected proximity of my goal.

As I set off up the final summit ridge behind Karsang, I remembered Russ's warning to be careful here. Dean's words also echoed in my head. "If you trip on the summit ridge, you're gone." Without the comfort of the fixed lines I felt vulnerable and exposed. Beautiful scalloped cornices marked the edge of the ridge, but there was no temptation to inch closer and peer over. The cornice could break away at any moment and send me hurtling down the Kangshung Face. There was a well-trodden track going straight for the summit and I made sure not to stray from it.

As I inched my way towards the grail, I realised with surprise that there were two climbers on the summit itself. Even though I remembered Russ asking me earlier if I'd seen Paul, it hadn't crossed my mind that he was ahead of me. It wasn't until I got closer to the pair that I recognised the familiar outline of one of them. Unless there was another one-armed climber that I didn't know about, it had to be Paul Hockey and his Sherpa Nima.

I dragged myself up the final few steps and suddenly, dramatically, I was there. Paul and I were hugging and kissing, but

I was almost in a trance. I couldn't quite believe that this was it. After the weeks of waiting, I was finally standing on the summit of Mount Everest. I radioed through to Russ, but discovered later that the waning batteries meant I could only receive not transmit. My Himex team-mates waiting for news further down the mountain were becoming increasingly anxious about my welfare.

The fifteen minutes I spent on the highest point on earth were both the shortest and the longest minutes of my life. Like a drowning man, life flashed before me. But it was my nephew Joe's life that I saw, not my own. The fog cocooned me from the world outside. If there had been any sounds up there they would have been muffled. Despite the wind, the place seemed hauntingly still. And hauntingly spiritual.

And I cried. Big fat tears welled up in my eyes and spilled down into my goggles as I remembered why I had done this, why I had gone through the months of exhaustive training and why I had pushed myself to my physical and emotional limits and beyond. It was for my nephew, Joe. And although I felt his loss even more keenly in this beautiful but lonely place, I could sense his presence. He was with me on that summit, just as he had been with me every step of the way on the ascent. And I was comforted. Again.

—<o>—

Hours later and with the most dangerous part of the descent behind me, I stopped to reflect on the extraordinary events of the past hours, worried that Paul was in serious trouble and praying that Nima would manage to nurse him back down to safety.

I turned to look back at the summit behind me. It already seemed extraordinarily distant and I could scarcely believe that I had stood on that tiny triangle silhouetted against the blue of the sky, free, for once, of the familiar plume.

The wind had died down completely and I was surrounded by silence. I could have sat there for hours, relishing the peace and beauty of the mountain environment, but I knew that I needed to get a lot lower before I was out of danger.

I replaced my oxygen mask and checked the valve on the tube to see I was still getting air. The small clear section of tubing reminded me of a spirit level. The valve was where I expected it to be, right in the centre, showing that there was still a strong flow of oxygen.

I wasn't in any rush and, although I felt much stronger than I had on the descent to high camp, I knew my legs weren't capable of carrying me much faster than I was going. But it was some time before I heard Karsang's crampons scraping on the rock behind me. I stopped to let him go past, but he gestured for me to stay in front.

"No, I'm fine. You go on without me," I said, and I meant it.

I was quite happy to be alone and at one with my surroundings. Without saying a word, Karsang passed me and headed on down the rocky trail. He was no sooner out of sight than my oxygen ran out.

Supplemental oxygen is a boon to high-altitude climbers. A tiny minority are strong enough to climb without it, but for the rest oxygen has made the biggest and most challenging mountains accessible. Its use is almost as controversial as the birth of the commercial expeditions, with the purists scorning both. But, without supplemental oxygen, many of the world's greatest peaks would remain out of reach to all but a tiny handful of elite climbers.

The one major drawback is that, when it runs out, the contrast is huge. A climber on an oxygen-free ascent has gradually acclimatised his or her body to the thin air, but the climber who runs out of supplemental oxygen suddenly finds what is effectively their life-support system cut off. They have acclimatised themselves to the lower altitudes, but their bodies are not accustomed to the higher elevations.

I re-checked the valve and it confirmed what I feared. There was no sign of the valve in the clear section of tubing, meaning that there was no oxygen getting through. I took off my mask and breathed the fresh – but thin – mountain air.

I wasn't left gasping like a goldfish. I knew I could survive for a limited time without supplemental oxygen, but it was going to slow my descent drastically and I certainly didn't want to spend too long on the mountain without it. It was even more important now that I got down to Camp III without delay.

I was determined not to let the lack of oxygen affect me psychologically. I knew that I could get down to camp without it, but I was going to have to use all my powers of concentration to get my wasted body to respond. There was one bright spot, however. Without the oxygen mask blocking my view, I could now see my feet.

The deterioration came so slowly that I didn't even notice it creeping up on me until, suddenly, my legs just wouldn't obey any commands. Even the simplest step down was a huge task and all too frequently would result in my falling as my limbs buckled underneath me.

I took one tumble that would have looked spectacular if there had been anyone around to see it. I was attempting to climb down between two large boulders when, without warning, one of my crampons skidded off the rocks. Before I had time to try and save myself, I found myself plunging headlong between the two slabs of rock, landing awkwardly on my side with my right arm pinned underneath me.

I lay there winded, aware that my arm was hurting. I sat up gingerly. My elbow had taken the full brunt of the fall, but a speedy check with my left hand revealed that there was no serious damage done, except to my down suit. Every time I moved a cloud of soft white feathers puffed out of two huge gashes in the sleeve.

I was lucky. I could easily have broken my arm or, much worse, my leg. Without radio contact, I would have had no means of raising the alarm. How long, I wondered, would it have been before anyone noticed I was missing and sent out a search party? And would the rescuers have arrived before exhaustion and oxygen deprivation added me to the grim statistics and allowed the mountain to claim me for her own?

I only discovered later that my metal water bottle had saved me from more serious injury. When I was filling it in camp that evening, I noticed a huge dent in the side. Obviously it had struck a prominent rock in the fall. If the bottle hadn't been inside my down suit, my ribs or breastbone would have taken the full impact.

At least the boulders that had caused my fall provided the leverage to get me back onto my feet again. Heaving myself upright, I stood for a while trying to get my breath back and waiting for my heart to stop hammering in my chest. Expedition doctor Terry O'Connor had told us before we left ABC that the prolonged exposure to altitude resulted in a thickening of the blood, meaning that the heart had to work doubly hard to pump it round the body. I resolved to take more care for the rest of the descent. Having successfully reached the summit, I didn't want to injure or even kill myself with a fall on terrain that wouldn't normally cost me a thought at a lower altitude.

My elbow was sore, but my confidence was more severely bruised. The solitude that I had been so enjoying now hung over me like a threat. And every rock seemed to be lying in wait, its polished surface refusing to offer any purchase to my crampons and threatening to send me skidding off my feet again.

My wariness slowed my pace even more, but I was still endlessly stumbling and half-falling, making ever more demands on my body as I attempted to right myself. My lungs were screaming out for oxygen but there would be no respite until I got to camp.

I had thought I was tired coming back down from the summit, but that was nothing compared to this. I was literally having to will my legs and feet into making the next move, coercing them into taking the next step that would bring me closer to my goal.

My down gear was making me desperately hot and I was also parched with thirst. Whenever I came across a clean patch of snow I sank down into it, scrabbling at it with my fingers and shovelling it into my mouth. It was like the best ice cream I'd ever tasted.

Finally I could make out splashes of colour that marked the tents down at Camp III. But the surge of energy I thought this welcome sight would elicit just never came. My body and my mind were simply too drained to respond. The last vital reserves of energy had gone.

I must have been literally within 100 metres of camp when I fell again. It was more of a slide than a fall, but I hadn't got the energy to save myself and I found myself sitting on the scree when, a split second before, I had been walking. From this angle I could no longer see camp, which also meant that no one in camp could see me.

I had finally, genuinely hit the wall I had heard marathon

runners talk about and, as I looked round at the mountains, I realised that I didn't care any more. I was simply too tired to worry whether I lived or died. My body had had enough. I closed my eyes.

I don't know how long I sat there, but when I opened my eyes again I saw Karsang climbing up towards me, carrying a bottle of oxygen. I feebly waved a hand in his direction.

"I've run out of oxygen," I whispered, as soon as he was by my side.

He said nothing, but immediately unscrewed the regulator from the empty cylinder and attached it to the new one. I heard the rush of air as the oxygen hissed out from the top of the bottle, feeling an almost Pavlovian response to the noise.

I pulled the mask up to my face and sucked in as much air as I could in one breath. I felt the oxygen flood into my lungs, but it was a while before its restorative qualities took effect. I leant against Karsang's shoulder for support, half-expecting him to pull away at the unusual physical contact, but he remained still and I felt soothed by his presence. We sat there without speaking for what must have been at least ten minutes before Karsang shifted himself, getting ready to move.

I had felt so weak before his arrival that I hadn't expected to be able to get to my feet unassisted. But the oxygen had given me renewed strength and, when Karsang got up, I stood too and followed him – pitifully slowly – down the last few metres into camp.

◄○►

As I started on the final part of the descent to advanced base camp the following morning, I could see two yellow-suited climbers a good way ahead. They seemed to be spending more time sitting down than descending. They were too far away for me to see whether they were sitting talking or taking a silent break after the strain of the past few days.

I decided to take a break too and, just above a join in the rope where I knew my safety line would prevent me executing an unplanned glissade, I sank down onto the snow. As I looked over at Changtse on the far side of the North Col, I saw a single gorak soaring high above me, silhouetted against the bluest of skies. It flew in decreasing circles as if it was homing in on me, but then flew off downhill towards the North Col.

But as I watched the bird, it doubled back and flew in a straight line up from the Col towards me. When it was directly overhead, it stopped, hovering above me, its vast ragged black wings fully extended to catch the breeze. It seemed to hang there for an eternity, but then, uttering one harsh caw, it dipped its wings and flew off.

I knew beyond all doubt that it was Joe. But I couldn't decide whether the raucous croak was one of triumph at my success on the mountain or if it was a call of farewell from a spirit that had done its work. I never saw another solitary gorak for the rest of the expedition.

I sat in silence for a while, watching as the bird got smaller until it was only a black speck and then, suddenly, was gone. But there was no pang of loss. I felt a deep sense of calm.

It was more than a little help from a very special friend.

(Extracts taken from *Total High, My Everest Challenge,* by Grania Willis. Published by Red Rock Press)